Wicked Witch

Wicked Ties Book 1

E.A. Shanniak

Eagle Creek Books LLC

Wicked Witch: Wicked Ties Book 1 by E.A. Shanniak

Cover Design: Harvest Moon Cover Designs

Proofreading: J Bruckner, M Fritz

Published by Eagle Creek Books LLC of Coldwater, Kansas

https://www.eashanniak.com/

Dedication

To Jenni Bruckner,

Thank you for always encouraging me, for being an amazing friend and being the first person to want to read anything I write. I adore and cherish your friendship, honesty and kindness. I'm so incredibly grateful to have a friend like you. This book is for you. I love you sweet lady!

Love,
Ericka

Author's Discretion

Wicked Witch is an enemy to lovers slow burn paranormal romance where sex is guaranteed in book 2.

*** WARNING ***

This book contains scenes of abuse, attempted suicide, and peril, along with strong language that some readers may find disturbing and or triggering.

World of Quivleren

Contents

1. One   1

2. Two   8

3. Three   14

4. Four   19

5. Five   28

6. Six   34

7. Seven   41

8. Eight   48

9. Nine   56

10. Ten   65

11. Eleven   73

12. Twelve   81

13. Thirteen   88

14. Fourteen   97

15. Fifteen   103

16. Sixteen   113

17. Seventeen   119

18. Eighteen   127

19. Nineteen   134

20. Twenty   142

21. Twenty-One   150

22. Twenty-Two   158

23. Twenty-Three   165

24. Twenty-Four   176

25. Twenty-Five   188

26. Twenty-Six   199

27. Twenty-Seven   211

28. Twenty-Eight   222

29. Twenty-Nine   233

30. Thirty   241

31. Thirty-One   249

32. Thirty-Two   258

33. Thirty-Three   267

About E.A. Shanniak   275

Also by: E.A. Shanniak   277

One

Hadley

I couldn't remove the stench from my nose. The corpse was pungent, potently so, being left to rot in the sweltering summer sun for a couple of days. But this particular corpse would have to do. It was all I had.

Kneeling beside her prone form, I held my breath. I quickly rubber banded off a section of the corpse's hair. Putting my face into my left shoulder, I inhaled the scent from my shirt before I retrieved scissors from my pocket. I tried not to make eye contact with the woman's dead glassy brown eyes, but it was hard not to notice the vacant upward and horrified stare. I cut the lock of her copper hair and shoved the strands into the pouch around my waist. Taking my butcher knife, I cleanly chopped off her left hand, sticking it in the burlap sack at my side.

I darted to the right, sucking in a lungful of air once I was far enough away from the corpse. My body trembled, and I shook out the jeepers climbing up my back. The hairs on the back of my neck prickled. Taking a last look at the dead woman, I noted the jagged claw marks down her chest. *Werewolves.*

My eyes carefully peered into the dense forest, scanning for any sign of those bothersome lurking dogs. They didn't like my kind. I didn't particularly care for them either with the way they sniffed to deduce strong emotions. The entirety of it sounded ludicrous to me. I just wanted what this dead body could provide for my spells.

Creeping out of the area and back the way I came, I paused once I was far enough away. Summoning the swirling orange magic to my hands, I released it behind me to cover my scent and footsteps from the body.

We need to hide, my familiar screeched in my head.

Immediately, I darted to the left, going straight into the underbrush of the forest and toward a fallen tree with the base hollowed out. I scooted inside, feet first. My familiar scurried out of the leather pouch I carried her in and nestled into my messy red hair.

It's all right, Aysel, I telepathically crooned.

The whiskers on the tip of her nose tickled my neck. *Not in this territory,* she griped. *We need to get home.*

We will, I promised. Aysel's soft brown fur cuddled deeper into my hair. Her little mouse paws clung to me, shaking at the boot steps approaching. I wasn't far off the beaten path, maybe a few yards inside the forest. From my angle, I saw pairs of dark denim jeans through the foliage. One man sniffed the air. I quieted my breathing, slapping a hand over my mouth and nose, and waited anxiously for them to move on. The men just lingered, sniffing the air, and walking in circles.

"I smell the witch," one man practically growled. "Her magic is prominent."

Instantly, my body became ice, and I rolled my eyes at myself. In masking my scent, I hadn't thought to mask my magic. The need to summon magic to my hands surged within me, yet if I did, the orange flames would give me away. There was no way I could use my magic and have those wolves *not* notice. Or be able to get away in time with the spell I wanted to use. Their quickness and agility would have me pinned to the ground before I ever got the incantation finished.

"She's here somewhere," one said.

"I'm guessing she's by that corpse," the first male answered.

The men turned on their heels and continued where I just came from. I let out a deep breath.

Go dammit, Aysel yelled.

I scooted out of the log hesitantly, looking both ways before I summoned my fiery magic. The power surged, immediately swirling in a vortex to create an orb. The magic vibrated in my shaking hands. I needed to teleport back home. It was the quickest, safest way, but I hesitated.

Teleportation magic was hard. I wasn't the best at it, and never had been. I had to form my magic into a perfect triangle then, in the middle of the triangle, summon an image of my house before I cast it. So, I spoke the incantation rather than struggle to form the magic, but even speaking the spell was hard.

I licked my chapped lips, muttering underneath my breath. Aysel nuzzled my neck. *Keep going! Come on Hadley!* She cried, encouragingly.

"Well," a man spoke from behind me, "here's something you don't see every day. A cute little witch who struggles with magic."

Come on! Come on, my familiar urged. *We need to go!*

I'm trying, I'm trying, I cried back.

The man maliciously grabbed my shoulders, giving me a hard yank backward. I scrunched my shoulders inward to brace the fall my body was doing involuntarily. Aysel peeped, burrowing further into my messy bun. Landing on my ass, I somehow kept the magic swirling in my hands. Since my incantation was broken, I was forced to spell from memory. I stared blankly at the man, getting the magic to form into a triangle then pictured my house.

"Tootles," I quipped and cast the magic.

Well, Aysel said dryly, *we're back...*

"And in one piece," I replied.

Darkness surrounded me. I felt around with my hands, noting the cold stone, the feel of soot, and the scent of coal.

"Dammit! I'm in the chimney," I said dryly.

Aysel tittered. *But we're home*, she said, sighing happily. *Go down the chute*, she directed, her nose twitching on the back of my neck. *You're close to the bottom.*

"Okay," I softly replied, feeling a bit defeated.

Her keen sense was better than mine. I wriggled my body down the chimney flue until my feet struck the bottom grate. Giving it a hard kick, it gave way, and I plunked out, falling on my ass as soot dribbled on top of my head. I sighed contentedly, so relieved to be back in the safety of my home. I leaned against the firewall and soaked in the calming aura of my house and the scent of my freshly baked bread from earlier.

"At least I had the good sense to make the chimney as wide as myself," I told Aysel.

No shit. Could you imagine if you didn't?

Aysel jumped out of my hair and crawled down my body until she was on the floor. Knowing her, she was scurrying to her house to groom herself in private. One thing that mouse disliked most was being dirty.

What happened, Mahak murmured; concern lacing his droll voice.

I whipped my head in the direction of my ash barn owl. Mahak was a beautiful bird. His black face boasted speckles of brown around his mouth and the top of his head. He flapped his silky black wings flecked with a rainbow of brown and splattering of white.

"We ran into wolves," I said, picking myself off the floor and dusting myself off.

Mahak screeched, hopping along his perch by the fireplace to the end of it. *I should have gone with you,* he fumed.

"It's all right, Mahak," I crooned. "I got what I needed and got out quickly. They can't follow me here."

Candles softly glowed from their glass sconces along the walls, giving me soft light. The plants I had hanging from the ceiling and on shelves moved tranquilly in the gentle summer breeze from my open kitchen window. I went over to the window and shut it for the evening. Being on the outskirts of the Utah Mountains, I didn't want my scent escaping and having something break through my wards to get to me. I left my coven for a reason and cared not to be found.

Taking the hand out of the burlap sack, I set it in a protective rune bowl on the kitchen counter to await saging. Not truly knowing what transpired that led to the woman dying and if her soul remained attached, I didn't want potential evil in the presence of my spells. I also didn't want her spirit in my house.

Mahak fluttered over, his talons tapping on the counter as he circled the bowl. His head bobbed. Finally, he gave me a happy screech of approval.

It's a virgin's hand, he said jovially. *You did excellent.*

"Thank you," I replied, stroking the top of his head.

Mahak clacked his beak approvingly. He waddled over to his nearby perch and fluttered onto it. I waited until he was secure before I moved away to grab the sage I kept in a glass jar on my buffet table. My beloved Mahak was old and nearly blind. Anytime I had left with him was precious.

I went to the buffet table and opened the jar containing my bundle of white sage. I stared at the severed hand, biting my lip, and worrying it between my teeth. Rapping my fingernails on the counter, I debated upon my next move.

Removing body parts from dead people wasn't a particular habit of mine. I mainly dealt with potions and healing tinctures I sold to the humans in the town of Nukpana to the southwest. It was simple magic, hedge witch magic even though I had more power than I let on. I kept my powers and abilities hidden to keep myself safe from those who hunted me.

Sighing heavily, I brought magic to my fingertips and pushed it outward, opening the front door. I had to make this quick before the dead woman's spirit stayed. Lighting the white sage, I carefully blessed the ancestors and spirits assisting me in cleansing the hand while asking any negativity to peacefully leave.

The doors in my kitchen rumbled, shaking the contents to clatter boisterously inside. The items on my walls rattled. A picture crashed to the ground. *Good thing I decided to cleanse*, I thought. I kept repeating the same mantra until the drawers ceased clattering and the items on my walls quit moving. Walking with the smudge stick out the front door, I released the spirit of the woman's hand out of my house and ended the incantation by blowing out the sage.

Mahak hooted, flapping his wings. *She was a little pissed!*

"Yeah... Poor thing," I replied, coming back inside.

With a flick of my wrist, the door closed behind me. I stared at the hand in the bowl, the color of skin slightly darker now that part of the woman's spirit left.

Are you going to do it, Mahak asked.

I think she should, Aysel added, bounding up onto the counter. *Another layer of protection is a must. Especially with the way Quivleren is right now.*

I nodded. "I'm going to," I appeased, still staring at the hand.

Rumbling settled in my gut, and it wasn't from hunger. Somehow, I got the vibe I would never be truly safe no matter how many layers of protection I added.

Two

Hadley

I jolted awake. The glaring morning light streamed through the skylight in my house and bounced off the shining trinkets to make me finally stir. Last night, it took me an hour to search for the right spell to use and another couple of hours to use the virgin woman's left hand to make a protective ward on my house from vampires and wolves. It was exhausting, but hopefully now the added layer of protection might help.

I side-eyed the front door and sank back in my chair relieved no human was there waiting for a spell this early in the morning. I needed to recharge after last night's tediousness. A day of cleaning and listening to my favorite bands would do just the trick.

Rubbing my eyes, I broke free of my comfy soft blue recliner and shuffled my way toward the bathroom. The skylight in the bathroom hit the shiny gray marble and illuminated the room without the use of a light. Besides my spell room, the bathroom was my other favorite room in my small cottage. My beautiful purple clematis sat in a giant terracotta pot in full sun from the skylight and climbed all over the bathroom walls toward the open window to escape. The rich oxygen coupled with the aroma of the clematis, fern and jasmine was soothing to my soul.

Are you going to town today, Aysel asked from the bathroom floor mat.

I nodded, shucking my clothes, and turning on the water to warm. "Yeah, after a shower and perhaps a quick cleaning. I need to get some supplies to last us a while. I might go to town after my shower just to get it over with."

Aysel tilted her cute brown head. I swear her face scrunched as she looked at me yet said nothing.

"I'm just gonna head there and come right back. I have enough money for important groceries and Mahak's dinner choices."

Movement out of the bathroom window caught my attention. I slid closer to peek. My small cottage was warded, protected to a degree from outsiders who wanted me dead. Mainly, my old coven. Most anyone would see a dilapidated cottage in the middle of a meadow. However, those I needed protection from just saw a meadow. Humans could come see me at will. They were harmless, yet on edge from coming to see a witch. Mostly, they wanted "love" potions. The laws of magic wouldn't ever bend for love. So, I gave them an herbal remedy for blood detoxification and sent them on their happy way to shit their brains out. *Gotta keep that heart pumpin' good,*

I mused. I wasn't too mean, though. I gave them their desired potion, along with an herbal cupcake infused to help boost their mood and open their heart to hear their inner self. So, while they shat themselves to pieces, they would be joyous about it.

It's a human, Aysel said, sniffing the air.

Being my familiar, her keen senses were superior to those of other animals. Aysel or Mahak sensed beings long before I could and were able to tell whatever the being happened to be. I let out a long breath, stepping into the shower. Relief coursed through me. I had been in hiding for years since I left the Black Ash Coven. I refused to go back, yet I was being hunted like an animal for the blood coursing through my veins.

I wiped the water over my face, trying to calm my jittering nerves. I couldn't. Until I had the Mother's Amulet, I wouldn't ever stop being worrisome. Even after searching for almost three years, I haven't been able to find it. The amulet's powers could protect me from being hunted, but now, I was beginning to believe it didn't exist.

Pass me the lavender soap please, Aysel requested.

Taking the bar of soap from the tray, I set it down on the floor for her to use.

Thanks Hadley, her melodic voice said.

"You're welcome," I replied, washing my hair.

Even the water couldn't quench my nerves. The air, electrified with urgency, made the little hairs on my arm stand on end. I second guessed the vibes I was getting with being hungry and the fact a human was spotted walking near my home. I peeked over my shoulder. Nothing but the shower wall met my gaze.

When you go to town, can you pick me up some bananas, Aysel requested.

"Absolutely."

I finished and stepped out of the shower. I left the water on for Aysel until she told me she was done. It took her a while to get the soap out of her fur. Even with her grooming last night, she disliked smelling dirty, being dirty and overall uncleanliness.

I walked naked to my small bedroom, getting dressed in an all-black outfit with a cinched corset waist. My plan was to look like a menacing witch, even though I wasn't. I wasn't even confrontational. My lips pursed. *I was confrontational when it mattered*, I decided.

I sighed, whipping my long, fire red hair into a tall ponytail on top of my head. I put dark gray eyeshadow make-up on my eyelids, adding to the *don't-fuck-with-me* look. Looking like a hot goth woman, I could easily pass as a witch from Black Ash. Being across Quivleren, far away from OKimma, I didn't dare take chances and let my guard down. I was still being hunted for leaving.

Almost three years ago I fled the coven. Before me, no one left the coven alive. I didn't want to have my soul bound to them, forever bonded to the coven, and for reasons I was against. I wasn't a black witch, but I wasn't a saint either. However, with the direction they were headed, I wanted no fucking part in it. They wanted vengeance, death, and ruin at whatever cost. I wanted amicable relations.

I shook my hands out at my sides and got out my scrying mirror from the top dresser drawer, setting it on my bedroom dresser. Taking out a glass bottle of moon water, I put a splash on the mirror to scry my surroundings prior to leaving the safety of my home. With wolves occupying most of the forested areas, I really didn't care to run into them.

The mirror showed me the forest I had to cross to get to town. Wolves patrolled the lingering edges, searching... I had masked my scent when I went to take the dead woman's hand, and even though I didn't mask my magic, they couldn't smell it unless I used it; so, there was no way they would know my scent. Even when the one wolf found me, he wouldn't be able to discern what he smelled from me. Still... it had me on edge. They were looking for something, or someone. And Black Ash wasn't above involving other paranormals to get what they wanted.

I pushed forward, peeking at the old historic town with brick buildings and cobblestone walkways. It showed the typical humans outside along with the assortment of beings from ogres, cyclops, vampires, and centaurs. Even a dryad. My forehead lifted. For a dryad to come out of the Utah Mountains, it must have been important.

I flexed my hands, popping the knuckles simultaneously. "If I didn't need supplies to last us, I wouldn't be going," I mumbled. "But it doesn't look too bad."

I'll be with you, Aysel reassured. *I'm out of the shower.*

"Thank you," I replied, letting out a soft sigh. "I really don't care to be found, and I plan to keep it this way. It's been three years since it happened." I went back to the bathroom and shut off the water. I handed Aysel a small towel before going back to my bedroom to put the mirror away.

I know, Aysel shrugged. *What the Supreme did after your mother died is unforgivable.*

I nodded, thanking her with a warm smile. I glanced over my shoulder at my mother's framed portrait on the wall. She was glorious, with long red hair and vibrant green eyes. She was gorgeous, beloved, and I was just the meek daughter of her noble figure. I didn't like the violence Black Ash wanted to get into with the dragons or the dark magic. I didn't want the fight, the innocent blood on my hands. My mother, though, was diplomatic and reasonable, being the former Supreme. In the end, that's what got her killed. And part of the reason I fled.

"Ready to go?" I asked Aysel. "I want to get there and back before dark."

I turned around, watching Aysel climb the quilt of my patchwork bedspread. The little mouse nodded, cleaning her whiskers once she got to the top. *Yes*, she said softly, *could you take your big purse? I wanna ride in comfort.*

I grinned. "Yeah." I grabbed my purse from the end of the bedpost. "This one?" I asked.

Every purse I had had a lining and a little soft bed inside for Aysel. I used to carry around a different purse for Mahak until he got older and preferred to stay inside on his perch.

Aysel shrugged. *I'll ride in the other one by the front door. That one clashes with your outfit.*

I shook my head and laughed. "Only you would want me to match."

Aysel stared at me, appalled. *You might be hunted, but Goddess above, I won't let you die or be taken by anyone looking like a rat*, she said disgustedly, sticking out her tongue.

"I appreciate that," I replied, scooping her into my palm.

I left my bedroom, heading down the small hall and to the front. Mahak was fast asleep on his perch. I gave him a kiss on the top of his downy head. Mahak didn't even stir. Smiling wanly, I grabbed my purse by the front door, gently putting Aysel inside.

"Alrighty," I said, heaving a deep breath. "There and back."

Yup, Aysel agreed.

Three

Brooks

I cleared my throat and leaned back in my office chair. The witch across from me wouldn't leave. Since we had a treaty with those vile bitches, it prevented me from eating them. For now. My lip curled as I waited for her to get to the fucking reason she wanted to meet with me. I had a feeling I already knew, but wanted a direct answer instead of her petulant whining or remarks about us being together. The latter was never going to fucking happen.

The woman in front of me heaved a bereft sigh. "Come on, Brooks," she pleaded, leaning forward to flaunt her chest.

I nearly puked, clapping a hand over my mouth. The witch was tenacious.

"Brooks," she sighed. "I need you to track her down. You're the only one who can do it."

I blew my lips, chuckling. There were others who could do what she wanted. Hell, a damn dog would be better at it. She was just wanting a tie to my coven she's always coveted. Leaning forward in my seat, my countenance darkened. This dumb broad had no idea whom she was messing with. It was the treaty and the treaty alone that kept her alive.

"Keres," I spat. Even the taste of her name on my tongue was as bitter and vile as she. "I think you misunderstand me when I say I will *not* be tracking or finding anyone for you. That's why Elohi made dogs. Use one."

Keres leaned back in her seat, staring at her fingernails. I arched an expectant brow, waiting for more. I might be two hundred years old, but I was far from a dumbass. I sat back in my seat, strumming my fingers on the arm of the chair. This witchy bitchy knew something I couldn't refuse. I swore witches were more cunning than dragons.

"Oh darling," her smooth voice drolled. "*You* misunderstand *me*."

"How so Keres? Because from what you tell me, your little missing witch Hadley or whatever the fuck isn't my damn problem."

She smugly laughed. "The witch I need you to find is one I want you to eat. Bring me her soul trapped in this jar, and I will give you what you and your coven desires most," Keres said smugly, batting her long make-up globbed eyelashes.

I snorted derisively. "And what the fuck would that be?"

"Toan Castle and power."

My countenance must have changed as Keres looked at me knowingly. "Do we have an accord?"

I flicked my wrist, dismissing her. The action pissed Keres off as she scowled vehemently at me. I cared not for her coven, nor for her at all, but Toan Castle, the place my family called home for generations prior to its takeover by rabid dogs, was something I was *definitely* interested in. *Fucking witches*, I cursed, rubbing my chin. And whatever "*power*" Keres claimed she could give me was probably just some faulty spell derived from a weed and blessed with frog skin or some stupid shit. However, the castle she mentioned, I was *very* interested in.

The Moon Walkers, a repulsive bunch of wolves forced my father out of Toan. During the time of wolves' attack, our coven was quaint. We were easily overpowered, outnumbered, and decimated by the war between us. Only in the past several hundred years have we been able to grow our numbers.

Then Alpha Evander Akselsen combined numerous packs in Quivleren after the Hell War and lived there; only having recently left Toan for some other place. Of fucking course, in their leaving they left the castle in care to filthy dragons and guarded by witches. Our species weren't necessarily friends.

So, I was extremely curious how we would get Toan Castle in completing this task. However, getting back to ancestral ground was important. Items were hidden at Toan that had been lost for centuries. Having them back in our coven would be essential, pivotal even, especially for what I had planned.

"And where could I go about finding her?" I finally replied, taking her bait.

Keres's small body wiggled giddily in her seat. The old crone grinned, revealing black teeth and a severe lack of flossing. I refrained from cringing as I wondered if the person who procreated with her was blind. I knew Keres had several daughters as she once tried to throw them in my path along with herself. Goosebumps prickled the bare skin on my arm from the memory of that hellish event.

"Here's her scent," Keres said, leaning forward and offering a small lock of red hair tied with twine. She plopped it on my desk, scooting it forward with a flick of a black painted fingernail.

"How'd you get this?" I asked astounded, knowing witches never cut their hair and if they did, they burned the cut ends so it couldn't be used against them.

Keres smiled. "Track her. Do as I request... Then Toan will be yours, *Lord* Zygrath."

My eyes narrowed on the lock of hair sitting on my desk. The slight scent coming off her hair smelled of wheat fields and sunshine. The vibrancy and different hues of red was alluring. It made me curious who this witch was that the head Supreme would seek me out when a wolf was more suited to the task.

I grumbled under my breath. "We have an accord," I bit out, leaning forward to shake her clammy hand.

Keres shook my hand loftily before setting it back in her lap. I refrained from glaring at her simpering triumphant grin. May the almighty God Elohi claim my damned dead soul, I had a feeling this was going to bite me in the ass.

"Have a good day, *Lord Zygrath*," Keres crooned, rising from her chair. "May virgin blood forever fill your cup."

I gave a tight-lipped smile and thanked her for her visit. It took everything in me not to snort. *Virgin blood my ass*, I thought. Blood was blood. The only difference was what the being ate or used like drugs, that made the blood tasty or trash.

Rising from my seat, I ushered her to the door of my office. I was over her and our visit. I wanted a moment alone to plan and prepare not only to find this witch but to backstab the entire Black Ash coven before they could do so to me and mine.

Keres paused by the large wooden doors; her petite form barely came up to my chest. "I need her soul. Be sure *not* to lose it," she reminded, handing me the glass jar in her hands. "Instructions are on the outside," she finished, tapping a long black nail on the glass.

I nodded. "It shall be yours."

Keres finally left my presence, going out the doors and down the hallway. My butler ushered her out. With her finally out of my sight, my upper lip curled. I detested witches. They never gave the truth about anything. And hell forbid, I pay for a spell and expect it to work.

I cracked my knuckles, waiting for the front door to shut before going back to my study. I wanted to ensure Keres left.

"What did she want?" my brother growled.

I crossed my arms over my chest and leaned against the door frame. "We have a hunt, Lydon."

"Do we get to eat the hunt?" He asked eagerly, pushing his shaggy brown hair off his face.

I handed the jar over to my brother. "So long as we get her soul."

"When do we start?"

"Tomorrow," I replied, looking at the stock of red hair on my desk. "She'll be easy enough to find."

Four

Hadley

Rain pelted the lead paned glass windows, making it too blurry to see out of. I sat back in my recliner, sipping fir needle tea and staring outside at the bleary trees beyond. For a summer rain, this was most welcome since lately it had been so arid. For me, it felt like a premonition, and it had me anxious.

I took another sip and set my tea down. The urge to pace and set items to rights clawed in my veins. Instead of cuddling up and taking a nap, I wanted to be busy. Prior to sitting in my recliner, I had reorganized my kitchen and pantry until Aysel told me to take a break.

But something was amiss. I felt it; the tangible, energetic, electric feel of something brooding made the hairs on my arm stand on end. Thunder rippled across my house with the yellow gnarled fingers of lightning following the sonorous clap.

I glanced outside out of habit only to see nothing. The sharp crack of a tree breaking, followed by the shaking rumble of it falling didn't help my nerves. I twirled a strand of hair with my left hand. My fingers thrummed on the recliner's arm. Part of me wanted to consult the tea leaves, scry, or even read the runes. But I couldn't force myself to do it. I didn't want to know *this* future.

Go take a shower, Aysel prodded from her spot by the toasty fireplace. *Wash away the fear and come out with a new perspective.*

She was correct. Despite that, it felt like water couldn't wash this away. I stole a glance at Mahak asleep on his perch. For the last two days, he'd been lethargic. I knew my time with him was ending. He was about to pass on and it killed me inside. Part of me felt dead already like a dagger was already protruding through my heart. There was nothing I could do to save him. I wasn't that kind of witch.

Mahak had been my first familiar when I came into my powers at six. He'd been my best friend, my greatest companion, and confidant for the last fourteen years. Seeing him slowly fade was difficult. It pained my heart fiercely. I didn't want to let him go, yet I had to allow him to pass on to the Goddess.

Maybe this is what has me so upset, I reasoned. But even that logical explanation couldn't shake the dread from my bones. Taking the hint from Aysel's pointed look from her snuggly bed, I headed down the hallway toward the bathroom with the clawfoot tub in the corner.

I stared out the window, wondering if I could see the forest or anything of importance. The rain was so heavy,

I saw nothing but water blurring any visual of outside. The light of day waned, making the thunderstorm appear darker and more foreboding. Forks of lightning flashed in between the bangs of thunder.

I started the water for my bath and went to my room to grab the runes. Divination was one of my specialties. I just disliked fucking with it. I didn't like the powerful visions where my head snapped back and it was like I was living the actual moment, seeing everything reel in slow motion, having people talk to me and I respond. Once the vision faded, I was sapped of energy for hours; and unable to prevent what was coming to pass.

You can't run away from your talent, my mother's words echoed in my ears. I couldn't suppress my gifts either. I've tried, only to earn the disappointment of my mother and former coven; and the shakes from my powers needing release.

Taking the runes, I went back to the clawfoot tub. I quickly shucked my clothes, the cold prickling my bare skin. I lit the white candles lining the bath and watched them flicker for a moment. I threw a handful of blessed salt in the bath to cleanse my aura for a better reading. I quickly got in, sighing at the warmth enclosing around me and pulling my eyelids down.

Hey, Aysel griped, *put me on the side table. I wanna help.*

Reaching over the side of the tub, Aysel hopped in my hand, and I put her on her padded perch by the tub. She batted her long lashes, staring at the water in the tub.

Whatever happens, she whispered, *don't pull out of the vision.*

I nodded, grabbing the bag of runes from over the side of the tub. My hands shook. The cream velvet bag felt heavy. I took a deep breath and closed my eyes. Licking my lips, I uttered a prayer under my breath.

Goddess Moon shining bright,
Help me hone my inner sight,
Make my vision clear and true,
Show me what I need to do.
Be it cards or stones of old,
Show me what I need to know.

I opened the cream bag with my right hand and poured the stones into my left. The stones heated, feeling like fire and I flung them into the water, keeping my eyes clenched closed. My entire body shook despite the warmth of the tub. I was terrified to open my eyes. I didn't want to know what the five stones I chose had cast.

Biting my lower lip, I opened my eyes and looked. My head snapped backward. Snippets of a forest flitted through my mind's eye. A giant castle that once proudly stood was now demolished. Pixies, minotaurs, faeries, and others once plentiful in the world were now mere legends. My vision circled around the fallen castle, where I saw the backside of a rushing waterfall and a small dirt trail. Then it faded.

My vision took me away from the fallen castle to the west. The moon, in all her splendid glory hung bright in the night sky. The air was stagnant, nary a breeze and hot. The forest where I lived surrounded me, and so did the golden eyes of werewolves. I stood before the forest with Aysel in my hands. Somehow, I knew Mahak was dead. Bright silver-gray eyes of vampires came from my left. Their translucent hollow stare sent a shiver up my spine.

"Come," one hooded vampire spoke.

His voice was firm, brooking no room for argument. His face, shrouded in darkness, only his lips were visible from the black cloak he wore low over his head. I shook my head, backing away from him, but I found myself on a precipice.

"Kill her," Keres demanded.

I swallowed, unable to tear my eyes away from her sudden appearance. The Supreme of the Black Ash Coven wanted me dead long before this moment. Keres despised my mother, despised what I am, and coveted it all the same.

The vampire stepped in front of me. "Come," he demanded again.

Cloaked in moonlight, fire surrounded me.

"Come," he snarled, lunging for me.

I summoned my magic to my hands, but somehow, I wasn't fast enough. He got a hold of me, enclosing a hand around my throat while someone else bound my hands in iron. I screamed, unable to defend myself. He bit into my neck while I continued screaming against the icy fire rushing through my body as the vampire drained me.

Sucking in a lungful of air, my head snapped forward. I sat in the bathtub shaking as if I had been in a freezer. Aysel perched expectantly on the end table with Mahak beside her. Relief flooded me when I saw Mahak, peppering my eyes with tears. I hadn't much longer left with him.

I sniffed, leaning back in the cold water. "We need to leave here," I whispered.

My head pounded, and my throat felt thick. Whatever the vision meant, I knew for sure that I had to leave. My survival was imperative on that part. I wasn't sure if I was envisioning my death, but I was certain if this came to pass, I would wish I was. What got me confused was seeing the old castle of Kadia.

Over sixty years ago, the castle was destroyed in the Hell War. Alpha Evander Akselsen and his wife Zuri destroyed the old castle and everything in it to remove the evil lingering there. Together, those alphas killed the God of Death and released Elohi from his oath. But what did any of that have to do with me? Why was I being shown that place?

This will come to pass, Mahak stated in his droll tone. *I'm sorry for leaving you at such a pivotal moment. But... I'm tired, Hadley.*

Tears welled along my lashes, trickling down my cheeks. I scooped Mahak in my arms and held him close as I cried. "I know. I love you so much. Thank you for all the years together, for your patience, loyalty, kindness, and for teaching me. I'm going to miss you eternally."

I love you too, Mahak cooed. *It's been an honor to be by your side.*

I snuggled him closer to me. His beak clacked against my cheek. "Let me know when you're ready to go. I'll give you some herbs to help carry you into the next life."

Thank you, Mahak said, heaving a weary sigh. *You've been an excellent partner. I'm grateful for the years I've got to spend with you.*

"Same here," I sniffed. "Is there anything I can get for you to eat?"

Not today.

I set him on the end table. He stretched his legs, giving a huff as he ruffled his feathers. Mahak turned, staring out the window. His beak opened and closed, head swiveling in different directions.

You hear it too, Aysel asked.

Mahak bobbed his head. *The trees are whispering. This is no ordinary storm.*

I collected the runes from the bottom of the tub and stuck them back inside the velvet sack. My hands shook. I carefully got out of the tub, every limb in my body shaking from what I saw in the vision. Something huge was forthcoming. I felt the electric tendrils in the air. It was slow in coming, but it was moving. *And that vampire...* I shuddered.

"What are the trees saying?" I asked Mahak, staring at the floor.

I shook my head clear of my rising fear. I needed to be rational. I had more than myself to think about.

The old barn owl hopped closer to the window ledge. *The trees are crying*, he whispered. *They're sad. The Supreme of the Willow Coven has passed.* Mahak gasped, looking at me with wide dark brown eyes. *Keres killed the white witch!*

Aysel glanced from Mahak to me, *what's your plan, Hadley?*

I shook my head, wiping the lone tear trickling down my cheek. "We'll be safe, I promise."

I closed my eyes at the horrible news, but I wasn't surprised. There was upheaval in the Black Ash Coven since my mother died. Some of the coven members despised Keres, while others adored her. I feared her. Keres made her intentions known. She wasn't above killing her own kind to collect their soul, for a witch's soul was the essence of their power. Keres craved power; she thirsted for it. Due to Keres's hunger for power, the Supreme of the Willow Coven banished her from their lands and any witch from my coven. Until now.

Chewing on the inside of my cheek, I walked naked to my bedroom, putting on dark denim jeans and a black t-shirt. I forwent the bra. They were a nuisance anyway, and I wasn't endowed enough for them to pose a huge problem. I was a baby b-cup at best.

My wet hair slapped my back, creating a large wet spot of uncomfortableness, but I ignored it. Keres was on the warpath for power, and I was her eventual target. So far, I had kept myself fairly well hidden, my home spelled and secured with whatever new incantation I could think of to block her and others; but Keres would know it was me. And she would find a way to collect my soul.

I swallowed, getting out a map from the top shelf of books near my cauldron. Even though many races of paranormals had gone extinct since the Hell War, there were some still alive that may help to hide me. I just had to find them quickly.

I sighed, blocking out the eastern half of Quivleren since going there would be unwise. I could skirt around the large city of OKimma, but if I was caught, my grandparents would kill me. Between the Black Ash coven taking over the western half of the city and the dragons still occupying the eastern half, no matter who found me, death was certain and for different reasons.

My father was a well-known and powerful dragon, and my mother, a high priestess witch, a noble supreme. In a different world, they were a match made in the heavens, blessed by the moon, and Goddess above. Here, in reality, it got them fucking killed. And me, their procreation, on the run from a former coven who wanted my powers for their benefit and the dragons who wanted me dead because I had their blood and magic. Not to mention between here and the east side were numerous vampire covens and somewhere, the largest wolf pack.

Damn it all, I cursed, snapping the book shut. The options before me were not the best. I could go to the Utah Mountains and chance my luck with the remaining minotaurs or go southwest to the Pamola Mountains to find the werelions. The werebears in the Scirwode Forest were out of the fucking question; between my ex-boyfriend being one and the witches preying upon them for spells, it would be a snowy day in hell that I got help. That left the Riodhr Forest as a possible option too. No matter what I chose, I would be hunted.

Hadley, the mouse softly pried, sitting back on her hind legs, and worrying her paws. *What are we going to do? Do you have a spell book for vampires?*

"I don't, but we're leaving," I softly replied, picking her up. I glanced around for Mahak who was not to be found. More than likely, he was back in the bathroom watching the storm. "After Mahak feels it's time to go. Then, we'll head to the Riodhr Forest."

Aysel nuzzled against my palm. I smiled wanly, stroking her soft face. Thunder cracked over my house, coupled with the gnarled tendrils of lightning flittering through the windows to brighten the dark outside world. Mahak hooted in delight.

His happy hoot echoed from the bathroom. I grinned, heading back to scoop him in my hands. Any moment I had from him this point forward would need to be treasured; for when he passed away, hell would be on my doorstep.

Five

Brooks

I grumbled as I walked through another city in the northern part of Quivleren. I spent the last two fucking weeks tracking her in whatever place I thought logical for a witch to be. Her scent was ingrained in my head, yet finding her was troublesome. From what Keres mentioned, she was a divination witch and would be easily apprehensible. Nothing about finding her thus far had been easy.

Rubbing my temples, I continued through the larger city of Nukpana. Some of my men came with me to cover the area more quickly before we went back west to search. It was frustrating to constantly come to dead ends. It was even more frustrating that all I had to go on was a lock of her fire-red hair. I was getting to where hiring a damned dog would prove more fruitful.

I strode down the sidewalk, turning right on a street. My mind kept reeling from what Keres promised me: Toan Castle. I found it surprising. In my experience with the heathen wretches, they never willingly did anything or gave anyone something without payment. This was suspicious, but I was willing to take this risk to get back what my family once had, prior to it being stripped from us. To have it back would mean everything to our coven.

I cracked my neck to the side and kept walking, wandering aimlessly in search of a faint whiff of this witch's wheat fields and sunshine scent. I kept Keres's promise from my mind for the time being. I refused to put too much stock in her words. Even though following through with her demands was my intention, I wouldn't just hand her what she wanted. If anything, I was a man of my word and I expected the same from someone in her leadership position. However, I was prepared to eat the bitch and kill witches to get what I ultimately wanted; damn the treaty or not.

Releasing my clenched fists, I stopped at the side of the cobblestone walkway near an alley. A slight scent on the breeze smelled familiar. I proceeded toward it. I had no leads anyway.

Taking her stock of hair out of my pocket, I sniffed it again to remind myself of its distinct scent. It was similar. Curious, I followed the breeze. *I am like a fucking mutt*, I thought, disgusted with myself. Like the wolves I greatly despised, the scent of a person was distinct. I could smell it, just not to a wolf's particularly intense capability. It was the person's blood I could tell the most. And with this lock of hair, the blood from the hair follicle provided the scent.

She smells... she smells pretty. Blood type AB negative, I deduced with a smirk.

I turned left, heading down the cobblestone, passing under a storefront with wrought iron lanterns outside. I paused outside of a large bookstore, whipping out my cell phone to tell the others via text that I caught her trail. She was near.

Opening the door, I went inside the bookstore, browsing the sections along the perimeter to determine her location.

"Thank you, Zennia," a woman's soft voice said. "I've been looking for this forever."

"You're welcome."

I crept forward, curious about the interaction, but more so to the smell. Somewhere along the line, it had changed. I kept getting mixed notes filtering in with the raspberry vanilla candle burning near the front desk.

Frowning, I kept to the side of the bookstore. A woman with dark brown hair left the building with a paper bag in hand. The store clerk, a blonde woman, hummed while putting books in a stack. Squinting, her name tag read Zennia.

I perused the bookstore, acting the part of an interested buyer when I was just trying to catch a whiff of whatever I smelled prior. Whatever it was I caught outside the store was now lost.

"Fuck," I mumbled under my breath.

Zennia glanced up. "Something the matter, sir?"

"Sold out," I said, pointing.

She smiled wanly. "Just got more in."

Fuck...

"Thanks," I replied, going up to the front of the store. I dropped a bill on the countertop. "I don't need change."

I tilted my head to the side, looking at the wall behind her. I wasn't one who knew lots regarding witches, but I knew an altar when I saw one. Mostly, I tried to veer from witches and their forked tongues.

"Thank you, sir," she said brightly, sticking the book in a bag.

"You're welcome," I said, taking the bag from her. "Do you know where I can get a divination reading?"

Zennia peeked over her shoulder, noting my stare and finger point behind her.

"I do them," she smiled brightly. "What kind of reading are you asking for? Love? Finances? General?" she prodded.

"A general reading. I'm also hoping to get a spell and maybe a potion," I lied. "Are you the only witch in Nukpana?"

She sniffed. "No, I'm not. Chela does spells. She's on the south end of town next to the ogre bakery. And the witch who just left the store, does potions and divination. She lives out of town on the forest's edge."

"Thank you," I replied evenly. To cover my ass, I continued, "Can I get my reading?"

Zennia brightened. "Sure," she said, reaching under her countertop and pulling out a deck of cards.

Oh. My. Fucking. Darkness... I plastered a fake smile to my face. *Fucking card games and they call themselves witches.* I kept my face impassive as she shuffled the large deck. She hummed, mumbling something under her breath regarding a fucking moon, true words, and a clear path. My impatience flared, and it took a lot of effort to mask my indifference to this parlor trick.

"I've never had a vampire ask for a reading before," she said sweetly. "What made you ask?"

"Morbid curiosity," I deadpanned, staring at her deck of silver-plated cards.

She laughed. "Didn't think vampires had that."

"Didn't know witches did this," I said pointing to her deck.

5 cards came flying out of the deck and landed on top of the counter. She put the rest of the deck to the side and aligned the cards in front of her.

Zennia's face scrunched. "Interesting how these cards came to play."

I stared at the black and silver deck. *I'm a blessed idiot*, I grumbled at myself, masking my face even further to not allow my annoyance a hint of showing.

"Two of cups," she stated. "You're desiring partnership, some unity in your life, perhaps?"

I blinked. *Like fuck I was.* Women were troublesome. Vampire women were sleazy and finding a decent one took a damn century. *Literally.* I considered humans, turning one, and marrying her, but humans were worthless. They weren't scared of the paranormal any longer, but their lack of fortitude, honesty, and loyalty was something that bothered me. With my luck, I would turn another one and she would fall for someone else too.

"King of Wands," Zennia continued. "You're a leader or about to be one but facing many challenges leaving you lost and confused about what to do. And the Four of Swords reversed," she paused. "You're burned out over something, yet restless to get back to it to get it done. Seems like you're involved in a troublesome task. So, take a step back and get a different viewpoint."

"Is everything in this child's play set a this or that?" I mocked.

This pissed me off. Staring at a card deck about life was fucking dumb. How the fuck was it going to do anything but play on emotions? It was like humans who claimed to speak to the dead. There were fakes, then there were necromancers who could *actually* fucking do it. And Zennia was a fake witch.

I slapped a crisp bill on the counter just to be done with her. "Have a good day," I said, turning on my heel.

Aggravated at myself for being curious and the time wasted on said curiosity, I stormed out the door. But in the end, I had two leads. Upon exiting the bookstore, I called the four who came with me on a group call.

"Two of you head to the witch on the south end of town by the ogre bakery. The rest come with me into the forest. We're getting a witch today."

Six

Hadley

I leaned back in the bathtub and stared blankly out the window. My entire body was numb despite the hot water and the calming lavender floating candles. Tears silently rolled down my cheeks as I sank lower into the water. Mahak passed away several nights ago in his sleep. It killed me as I held him, watching him draw his final shallow breath, knowing there was no way I could cease it from happening.

Glancing out the window at the setting sun, my entire body shivered. What my vision had warned me about was coming to fruition. After burying Mahak near his favorite tree outside, I couldn't seem to drag myself to venture into the forest. Something unseen was preventing my presence, and it irked me.

My gaze roamed to Aysel, sitting on the end table by the bathtub. Her small body was curled up contentedly. I floated in the tub. Closing my eyes, I summoned magic to my hands. The bright orange orb came willingly as I cast it out to reheat the tepid water.

I wasn't the best with my magic. I feared it. Scared of what I know it could do and the destruction it could cause. Essentially, I feared myself. My power was the reason Keres wanted me so badly and part of why I went into hiding. Keres wanted my loyalty, for me to take a blood oath and bind myself to the coven and her, so she could use and manipulate my powers. Since I ran, she wanted to kill me for my soul; to have access to my magic and everything that made me the witch I was.

Or the witch I'm not, I hollowly bit out at myself. The love my parents had irked Keres, for she too, wanted a dragon mate. And me being... well, me, irked her even more. I wasn't the witch my mother or Keres wanted me to be. I wanted a simple life amongst society, giving the beings of Quivleren what they desired, be it a potion or a reading. I wasn't looking for love, understanding that most feared or didn't care for my kind. Even though those of the Willow Coven fought alongside most of the paranormals in the Hell War, being a witch still bothered a lot of beings.

You're going to turn into a prune, Aysel said, yawning.

I smiled. "It's an old wives' tale."

Still, we should pack to leave here. Mahak warned us something was coming. We should take this seriously.

Sighing, I popped out of the water. Outside, the sun waned more, casting a golden light on the trees, and making it appear like the entire outside world was glittering splendidly. Birds chirped sonorously, calling to their families to come to bed before the world turned dark.

I got out of the bathtub and dried off quickly. "Is there anything you wish to take?" I asked, slipping into a pair of jeans.

Aysel shook her head. *Just one of Mahak's feathers.*

I nodded, putting on my bra and pulling on a black t-shirt. "He left us several of his feathers," I said, sniffling. "I miss him."

I miss him too.

Pulling on my hiking boots, I laced them up tight and quick. Standing in front of the mirror, I noted my haggard, saggy-eyed face and prayed to the goddess above that no one would recognize who I was. Using magic, I dried my hair and styled it in such a way, Aysel could bury herself inside the strands safely. Putting her in my pocket worried me. If I fell, I was scared of squishing her.

Picking her up off the end table, I set her on my shoulder and allowed her to pick her way through the style to situate herself comfortably. Her small tittering brought a smile to my face.

"Are you comfortable?"

Yeah, she replied, settling in. *Your hair is soft.*

"I try to keep it that way for you."

Aysel squeaked happily. *Thank you.*

I grinned, heading out of the bathroom to my bedroom to grab my never-ending backpack where I could fill it with whatever I wanted and would still have space; and thankfully, it never weighed over five pounds. I quickly stuffed it with a few changes of clothes, my mother's necklace, runes, cards, and tea leaves for divination. I finished my backpack with my potions, cauldron, and some books to help me rebuild my new home, wherever I decided it should be. I grabbed all that I could think of. My mind felt frazzled.

"Are you ready?" I asked.

Yes, Aysel replied, squirming in my hair. *Go out the back. Someone's coming to the front.*

I peeked carefully out the kitchen window, seeing a hooded figure come toward the door. The spells I had in place to sound alarms weren't alerting me. My insides went cold. *Vampires.* It had to be. I spelled my entire house to alert me when another witch, dragon, or wolf was coming. I didn't have a spell for vampires. The Black Ash coven had those.

"I'm a moron," I growled at myself.

Aysel squirmed. *You're not. It's been a lot the last several years. And their kind had no use with us, especially after the treaty. Plus, Keres has the book you need for bigger spells. The virgins hand you used in the last spell helped ward against vampires and wolves. However, there's over three vampires here, so it's null.*

I nodded morosely. She was right. Since witches and vampires were on non-speaking terms and had no physical interaction either, it was logical for me at the time to ward my house against those I knew were pertinent threats.

"You're right," I replied, backtracking toward the back of my house.

My sweet little mouse had only come to me three months ago. It was then I knew Mahak was on the downhill slope toward the end of his life. For a witch, a new familiar would come to them, assigned by the Goddess, and blessed by the moon, when their current one was nearing death. It was a normal occurrence for a witch to have several familiars over their lifetime. I just wasn't ready to say goodbye.

I peered out the back door window. Everything appeared quiet and undisturbed. My insides jittered. Backing away from the door, I went toward my room. Aysel quaked, burying herself as far as she could inside my hair.

I gently shut the bedroom door and ripped a book off my shelf regarding teleportation. I could do it; I just wasn't the greatest. I wasn't the best at much, except for divination and potions. Mahak warned me that my timidity about my magic would be my greatest hindrance. He was right.

Biting my upper lip, I skimmed through the old leather book until what my eyes were looking for forced me to pause. Pounding came from my front door. A male voice crooned to me, beseeching I open the door and let him in; that he was only here for a potion. My gut twisted in knots, telling me otherwise.

I chewed my bottom lip, reading the long spell. Some words had worn away and were unreadable. I summoned my magic into my left hand, swirling it into a compact baseball sized orb. The fiery magic rattled inside the ball, not liking the compressed state.

The front door clattering made me jump. Men entered my home. Bile rose in my throat.

Fire magic and full moon glow,
Take me where I need to go.

I swallowed, pausing to listen to see how close they were. My hands shook. The magic swirling in my hands intensified, rattling against the tight constraints I held it in. My nervousness got the better of me and now I was forced to start the incantation over.

Fire magic and full moon glow,
Take me where I need to go.
Far away or some place near
Keep me safe from what I fear.
Nestled deep in the forest green,
Goddess Moon don't let me be seen.
I cast this spell with purest heart,

Please take me from this dreadful part.

I finished, throwing the ball of magic at the ground. The orb burst open as it collided with the wooden floor. The door to my bedchamber burst open. The dark cloaks of the vampires from my vision vehemently glared back at me. One stood in the doorway. His bulky figure taking up the entirety. I could only see the lower part of the vampire's mouth.

"Come," he commanded.

Go, Aysel squeaked.

I leaped through the open portal. The magic snapped shut behind me like the clap of a car door shutting. My magic spit me out in the middle of a forest. The tall trees swayed in the crisp wind; their branches rustling and groaning.

Where are we, Aysel asked.

"Not a damn clue," I replied. "Do you smell any wolves or bears?"

No, she replied, sniffing the air. *Let me ask around. Put me down a moment.*

I put my hand by my hair and waited for her to plop into my hand. She scurried across my head and into my hand. The darkness of the night prevented me from seeing in front of my face.

My nerves were jittering. I'd just come close to death. I took a deep breath, setting Aysel on the ground. Bringing my knees to my chest, I cried. The stress of the situation and narrowly escaping fried my nerves. I had to find the Mother's Amulet. I needed it now more than ever. It was my only salvation. If I had the amulet, no witch could ever kill me, no vampire could bite me; it would protect me from those I feared most.

We're in the Riodhr Forest, about a mile from the lake, Aysel said, upon returning. She crawled up my leg and perched herself on my knee. *We need to get moving. A shrew told me witches were spotted around here.*

I nodded, picking her up and setting her back on top of my head. Not knowing what coven the witches hailed from, it was best to heed the advice. I hurriedly masked my scent and my magic.

"Where shall we make our new home?" I whispered.

In a tree, Aysel replied, tucking herself by my ear. *No one would think of finding a witch in a tree.*

"What about caves?"

Eww! Why would you even think that would be appropriate? You are a witch, not a troll. Plus, in a tree, we can see them coming.

I swished my head from side to side, conceding. "Tree it is."

I walked carefully through the woods, still unable to see the hand in front of my face. I was scared of using magic to see, scared of who or what might see me moving in the darkness. The vampire's icy stare pierced my mind's eye, reminding me of how close I had gotten to death. If he were ever to find me again, I knew I wouldn't be escaping.

Seven

Brooks

I sat in her cozy little home, picking apart all that she'd left behind. There wasn't much besides large furniture, like she knew we were coming for her. The fear in her blue orbs elicited a smirk from me. Her blood would be running hot in her veins, the adrenaline making it sweeter for me to suck dry. But now that she teleported, finding her would take a little while unless I either got more of my coven, hired a wolf, or bought a search spell. Witch's magic was sometimes a bitch to track. And the witches themselves were awful to work with.

I sat in her blue recliner and steepled my fingers. Already I spent two weeks away from home looking for her. I cared not to waste more time hunting her down. Already I was bored with the hunt. The only thing keeping me going was the promise of Toan Castle and drinking a witch's blood.

I glanced around, noting the rising sun. I groaned, begrudgingly getting out of the chair and closing the blinds. The sun itself wasn't deadly, but the first rays of light were as they were the strongest. Being over two hundred years old, I still had a lot to live for. The joke made me smile.

"Lord Zygrath," my subordinate began.

I flicked my wrist for him to continue. The man bowed low at the waist. I rolled my eyes, not liking formalities on missions; they impeded getting to the point of the matter.

"Yes?" I asked when he didn't continue.

"Your brother has sent word."

I lifted my head, arching an expectant brow. "And?"

"Lord Lydon Zygrath states he's hired the local wolf Vukan, from the Nashoba pack," he paused, his lip curling. "And they are searching now for the missing witch in the Riodhr Forest. Lydon has provided him with your number."

I nodded. I'd called Lydon after the bookstore, asking for him to hire a wolf. Normally, I wouldn't ever ask for one, but I was over this damned excursion. There was one pack we had relations with since cash and access to our land to hunt was an ideal payment. But that's where our cordiality ended as I disliked the rabid mutant dogs regardless of this mutual exchange.

"Perfect. Tell Korbin and Eckard to stay behind with me. The rest of you may return to the coven."

"Yes, Lord."

I sat in the chair a moment longer before rising. So far, I had scoped out this witch's entire house and found nothing useful besides her name: *Hadley Birch.* I scoffed. It was such a typical witch's name. Every witch's last name was after some idiotic tree or flower. But whatever, it was the confirmation I needed to know she *was* the witch I was after.

I rolled my eyes, studying the picture of herself and the familiar she'd left behind. Instead of the stoic look most witches opted for in pictures, this witch smiled; the cheerfulness of her grin matched the fire-red of her hair and brought out her warm blue eyes. She had a pretty smile, despite the crooked eye tooth on the right side of her mouth. An ash-colored barn owl perched proudly on her shoulder. Hadley wore a cream-colored blouse, accentuating her slender shoulders and the light brown freckles dusting her face and chest.

I tilted my head to the side. *She was at the bookstore,* I deduced. *She must've cloaked her hair and facial appearance.* It was the only reason I could conjure why I had her scent, then missed it altogether. The amethyst eyes I'd come to recognize belonging to only witches were lost on Hadley. If I didn't have her scent or knew what I was looking for, I wouldn't have deduced she was a witch at all.

"She's pretty," Korbin's deep voice broke my scrutiny.

"She's okay," I retorted.

"You have an unhealthy penchant for raven haired beauties," he quipped, plopping down in her recliner and sighing. "She has a good taste for comfortable chairs."

I nodded. "I will give her that."

"Heyyy," Eckard said, taking the picture of Hadley from my hands, "she's a hottie!"

Korbin flicked his wrist as if to stress his point. I snatched the picture back, breaking the frame and ripping the picture from it. I shoved it into my pocket. I had her scent, but now I had something to compare it to, in case she cloaked herself again.

Eckard grumbled. "When do we leave to find her?"

"As soon as the sun gets higher. Vukan, the wolf from the Nashoba pack, is on her scent as we speak. I'm thinking we head back to Nukpana and see if the other witch can make a spell for us to track her too."

Korbin turned around in the chair and glared at me. "Can a witch track a witch?"

I shrugged. "It's worth a shot. I have her picture and a lock of hair."

Both Korbin and Eckard stared wide-eyed at me.

"How did you get her hair?"

"Keres," I groaned.

After losing the Hell War, the Black Ash Coven went into turmoil. Oriel was the coven leader at the time. She was the only witch I happened to remotely get along with. However, Oriel died years ago, and Keres took over. I loathed Keres. She made it well known, frequently, she desired to wipe the vampires out of Quivleren; especially after I rejected her three daughters. Unlucky for her, our coven numbers outshone hers.

Korbin nodded, "Keres must've stolen it off her head."

I said nothing. It was the same conclusion I came to as well. Whatever the reason for Keres wanting this witch, was of no concern to me. I had my own issues to deal with. The Eldest of our coven wanted to go to war with the wolves and I opted against it, earning scorn from my brother and some of my coven members. It's not that I didn't want war, I wanted to be tactical about killing them. And if the witches were still wanting to kill my kind, then war on two fronts would prove difficult. We needed allies and a plan, both of which were nonexistent.

"Let's get going. I want to be home by the weekend," I said, heading toward the front door.

Korbin groaned. "You have no thrill of adventure."

"I've had enough."

Eckard crossed his arms and pouted. "I was hoping to turn a human."

"Find a decent one to turn. The last one was a waste of a bite."

Eckard shrugged, answering a text on his phone. "She's clingy, but I really like her."

"She's ridiculous," I countered.

"Just because Senna decided not to do a blood-rite with you doesn't mean every woman is out to burn you at the stake. So what if she's clingy? At least she's loyal."

Korbin whistled low and turned toward the door. My body tensed. I clenched and released my fists many times, trying to stave off the monster in me from sucking him dry. I cracked my neck, feeling the sharpness of the pop tingle into my shoulders.

"Let's go," I growled, storming out the door.

The sun had risen to where incineration wasn't possible. I sprinted down the path and through the tree line, zooming past it all like I was in a video game driving a 200-mph car. Everything was blurry as I ran past, coming to the edge of town in a matter of seconds. I could have teleported but wanted to reserve my power for that special trick for later.

I paused on the outskirts, fixing my hair and clothing. Korbin appeared on my right, arms crossed and his constant dour expression on his face.

"He coming?" I spat.

Korbin shrugged. "In a moment. He's looting her house for a gift for his woman."

I nodded. I refrained from rolling my eyes and decided to head toward the place I needed without him. The spell store next to the ogre bakery the lady from yesterday mentioned wasn't a difficult place to find. It was at the very end of town, the last row of commercial buildings. It wasn't even seven in the morning and people lined up outside the bakery. The witch I needed, decked out in flamboyant colors, head scarfs and gold bracelets maneuvered around the sizeable crowd, opening her shop front.

Outside the shop front was littered with all kinds of plants and flowers, either in pots, stands, or hanging from the edge of the roof. How anyone could find the entrance to the store was beyond me. Plants were everywhere.

I opened the door and strode in, immediately wiggling my nose from the intense smells. The shop was pungent with the aroma of old moldy leather, dirt, dead flowers, and just overall uncleanliness. Cobwebs hung from everything. A thick layer of dust remained on untouched objects.

"How can I help you?" a woman purred from the right.

Her dark curly hair billowed behind her and touched her knees. Large, circular black glasses took up most of her face and made her eyes appear huge, like an owl. Bright amethyst eyes stared back at me with piqued curiosity. A red and gold headscarf held her giant curls from flopping in her face.

"I need a spell to locate a witch," I stated.

"I cannot help you," she replied, taking a seat behind a plant. "Your aura is malicious, and I will not forsake a fellow witch."

I crossed my arms. "She's wanted by Keres. Unless you wish to become her next target, I suggest you help."

The witch blanched. I smirked; my threat gave the witch pause to reconsider. The plants in the room writhed with the witch's souring mood. It was almost laughable. What could a fucking plant do to an immortal vampire?

She tilted her chin upward and sniffed. "And Keres hired you?" She questioned, a slight growl at the end of her words.

"We struck a bargain."

"Who's the witch?"

"Hadley Birch."

The witch's eyes widened. "I'll take my chances with Keres."

I arched a brow, not expecting to hear that answer. The witch turned her palms upward, wiggling her fingers. Green magic misted from her fingertips. The plants came to life, writhing and climbing upward and weaving throughout, locking themselves in a dome around her.

Rolling my eyes, I turned on my heel and left. I didn't want to eat her. Her blood smelled of smoke and other intoxicants. It would taste disgusting and be thick, like a milkshake. I wasn't a snob, but I wasn't desperate to eat either.

"Let's go," I stated, walking out the door.

The line to the ogre bakery dwindled slightly. Eckard waited outside with a bag of food and munching on a donut. He held out the bag, and I took it.

"Donuts," Eckard mumbled, then swallowed. "Where to next, Lord?"

Reaching in, I grabbed one. "To her house. She may come back."

"Did you find out anything?"

I nodded, taking a bite of the donut; I could see why the line was so long. Come tomorrow, I planned to send Eckard back for more.

I grinned darkly. "I found out plenty. "

Eight

Hadley

I paced the dirt floor of my new living room. Where we wanted to be up high, it wasn't plausible. The poor tree would be too tired from carrying the weight of our home. But the lovely oak granted me permission to live under her roots. So, here I was, six feet underground and in hiding for the last four days. The spacious one room dwelling housed all my belongings, mainly stacks of books, in one corner and a makeshift bed in the other.

Aysel and I teleported in and out of our new home. The practice allowed me to better hone my skills. And much to Aysel's delight, I'd been practicing my magic.

Knowing what I could do with it made me nervous. I didn't want to fight or kill anyone. However, if it came down to them or me, I chose myself.

I sighed, shaking my hands out at my sides. "I want to go back home."

For what, Aysel squeaked, exasperated. *Everything you need is here.*

"I need a book I left behind. It's hidden on the shelf by where I had my cauldron."

What's in it?

"It's a book inside a book. Looks like divination processes, but it's about controlling gifted dragon magic."

And you didn't think to grab it prior to all this, she huffed. *Come on Hadley!*

"No. I was trying to keep your tail attached to your opinionated high-maintenance body and my head on mine," I shot back.

I continued pacing, thinking of a way to grab it. The book would be useful to me as I progressed in learning more about how to control the magic. Even though it was about being gifted dragon magic, like the long-ago Queen Lyvia of Kadia castle, it would still be beneficial to me. Since I was a half-breed, any sort of information would be helpful for me to grow. I wanted to fight off whomever was coming after me, be it vampires, wolves, or more witches. I didn't want to leave myself helpless and vulnerable. The attack from the vampires coming to my house taught me just how placid I had been.

I ran a hand over my face to ebb the tears back into my eyes. I didn't want to cry. Not now. Not after coming so far on my own. I went from being under my mother's loving tutelage to being on my own with Mahak and hunted. From a young age, I was forced to grow up and learn magic quickly, knowing that having mixed blood could result in my death. It scared me. It made me afraid of myself and my abilities. Now, I was truly being hunted, and it forced me to choose between giving up or fighting.

I sat on the edge of the bed and covered my face with my hands. These past few days had been so hard, so draining. I exhausted my magic the first day, trying to create our new home under a tree, craft items, and practice various spells. For the next several days, I spent practicing magic and putting wards in place; wanting to be stronger and more confident in my magic and myself.

Come on my little bee, my dad's voice crooned in my head. *Know your power and what you can do. Be responsible enough to know what you can do with it and empathetic enough to choose what to do with it.*

My dad passed away when I was eight. He taught me a few things I could do with my magic. I still practiced them, reminiscing about time spent together. He was a good man, kind, and patient. His mop of dark brown hair always hung in his eyes. His long whiskers always tickled my cheek when he squeezed me tight and kissed the top of my head. He was tall, with the kindest dark blue eyes.

"Fuck," I muttered.

Aysel scurried from the stack of books over to me and climbed up my leg. *Sorry*, she huffed. *I'm scared.*

"I'm scared too," I said, holding her in my hand. "But we don't need to get persnickety with each other."

Aysel nodded. *Agreed. I'm sorry. If we need to go back for that book, then let's do it. Together.*

"I need that book and another. It's one my father left me."

Where's that one?

"Hidden under the stone plate where my cauldron sat. It has my family lineage, heritage, and more about my powers."

Aysel rubbed her face.

"Don't. Even. Start," I quipped.

I'm not saying a word, but look at my face.

I glanced at my hand, seeing her small furry face tilt to the right and her attempt at a scowl. I giggled. Aysel looked too damn cute. She was a complete contrast to Mahak as a familiar: more sarcastic, preppy, and did not take my indecisive nature well. Where Mahak understood my past, was sympathetic and just as annoyingly sarcastic, Aysel was more assertive. I needed it. I needed to hear it more, and I appreciated it about her.

"I understand. However, I gathered what I could and got us to safety. You can't fault me for that."

I'm not. But let's get this over with. There and back.

"There and back."

My bright orange magic swirled in my hands. I formed it into a perfect triangle, picturing my house in the middle of it, and cast the magic toward the center of the room. Stepping through, I came out on the other side in my cauldron room.

My old home was eerily silent, like the home itself held its breath. I peeked around the cauldron room, searching for anything that might've been tampered with. Everything was as it should be. Not even moving my feet, I quietly lifted the stone where my cauldron sat, snatching the book hidden beneath, and quickly replaced the stone.

Do you smell anything? I asked Aysel through our shared mind-link.

No, she replied. *But something is wrong.*

I nodded. Turning carefully on my feet to not make a sound, I reached to my right for the book on the top shelf. I took my eye off the door leading into the cauldron room to focus on getting the book. I softly grunted, standing on my tippy toes while quietly berating myself for putting such an important book on the top shelf.

My body was forced against the wall. Rough hands clasped around my throat, lifting me off the ground. Bringing my hands up, I created a fireball and cast it at the person holding me. The man was unphased, unaffected, still holding onto me. Gray smoke flittered toward the ceiling. His clothes smoldered, littering the air with the pungent aroma of burned skin and cloth.

I stared at the translucent silver-gray eyes of a vampire. His dark brown hair slicked back off his face in an old mafia style I saw once in a movie, gave him an ominous vibe. An afternoon shadow caressed his jaw line. A pristine navy suit and cream undershirt hugged his lithe form. Fresh skin appeared like water soaking into a cloth on his body.

My lips pursed. I figured my fireball would have at least shot him backward or have gotten him to release his hold. Out of all the paranormals I had prepared my house to protect me from, I stupidly was lax with vampires. Granted, the virgin's hand I just used was supposed to provide some protection against vampires, mainly wolves, but clearly it did nothing.

The man laughed. "Fire can't kill me, *witch*."

"I know more than fire," I shot back.

I'd had little interaction with his kind. Vampires kept to themselves, segregated from most of everyone in Quivleren. Witch-vampire interactions were limited and cordial at best, if it could be called that.

He chortled. "Clearly, you don't," he boredly replied.

I spat in his face. Using magic, I imbued my legs with it. Bringing my legs up to my chest, I kicked straight out. The man flew back and struck the wall. He grunted disgustedly when he dropped from the wall and struck the floor. My body trembled. Even my magic trembled as I cast it out to teleport and stepped through.

"Cute trick," the man stated.

I slowly turned around. His deep scowl made him appear creepier than intimidating. His skin wasn't pale as some others I've seen. He loomed over me, his muscles ready to tear themselves out of the fabric covering them.

He looked average, save for the eyes being a giveaway to what he was.

I swallowed. "What do you want?"

He tilted his chin down and narrowed his eyes. "Are my intentions not clear enough?"

My mouth went dry. Every bone in my body screamed to run and get away. But I was trapped. If I attempted to get away by teleportation or broom, he would easily follow. Vampires were quick sprinters but for limited short bursts. He could change into a bat and fly, whereas I could not. And in either his human or winged rodent form, his strength wouldn't lapse. I was fucked. There was no way around it.

He took a step closer. I held my ground, my stomach quivering. My body felt like I fell through a frozen lake.

"What do you want?" I demanded.

He smirked. "I don't want you, but what you have."

I stared at the book in my hands. I quickly released magic over the book, turning the pages inside blank. To my eyes only, the words would reveal themselves. The man glared at me.

"Here," I said, handing the item over. "This is all I have."

He laughed, flinging the book to the side. Before I could blink, his hand latched around my throat. Aysel scurried out of my hair, leaping onto the back of his hand, and bit him. The vampire flicked her off with his free hand.

His upper lip curled. "Tell me, what would you do without your familiar?"

My heart hammered in my chest. "What do you want with me?" I yelled.

Tears peppered my eyes. I loathed being toyed with. Clearly, I was useful otherwise he would've already bitten me and drank every ounce of blood I had in my veins. I peeked to my left, seeing Aysel on the ground breathing slowly.

Aysel? I queried.

She didn't answer.

His thumb caressed the right side of my throat. "Like I said, I want what you have."

I stared at him dumbfounded. *What the fuck did I have?* I had a cauldron, potions, books, herbs, items to do divination with. I had witchy things. Nothing in my house or in my newest home was worth spit to a vampire.

"Come now," he purred, obviously enjoying toying with me. "You cannot be *that* incompetent."

He held loftily onto my neck, firm enough where I knew escape was pointless yet soft enough that begged me to try. Something inside me snapped, and I stopped being scared. I was pissed. I was a lot of things, but incompetent wasn't one of those.

"Okay, you conniving egotistical flying rat," I seethed, stabbing a pointed finger into his chest.

His brows arched. A smirk caressed his lips. "Well," he cooed, "this is new."

"Wanna know what else is new? The way you're gonna be walking when I shove my foot up your dusty ass. You show up, unprovoked in my house, and hold me captive. What in the actual fuck do you think you need or want with me, huh?"

My magic sparked on my fingertips. I was fuming. My beloved familiar was dead, my other familiar hurt on the ground; everything I worked so tirelessly to protect was now in shambles. My entire life was uprooted.

The vampire grinned, his fangs elongating. "I want what Keres wants."

I blinked, not thinking he would tell me. I stared at his unsettling eyes and pushed into his hold. My magic continued roiling in my hands. "Well, tell her to shove it," I replied, sucker punching him in the jaw with magic behind it.

The vampire flew against the dirt wall. I held him there with my powers, begging the tree to help me in holding him. The tree obliged, wrapping her roots around his body.

"What the fuck?" the man growled.

The tree lashed another root around him. The vampire grunted; an arm pinned over his head. I dashed to Aysel, grabbed my backpack and the book flung against the wall. Staring at Aysel for a moment, I tucked her into the middle of my bra. She'd be pissed when she woke up, but at least she wouldn't fly out of my pocket.

"I'll find you," he growled.

I created a portal to take me to the other side of Quivleren. Casting the magic, I watched it swirl in front of me. "Bring a fucking army," I snarled, and stepped through.

Nine

Brooks

Once she disappeared through the portal she made, the tree let go of me, and I fell to the dirt floor. Laughter bubbled inside of me, spilling out to echo in the tiny, shoddy dirt room. I was surprised at the amount of force she put behind the magic in her uppercut punch. It was a mean right hook. I worked my jaw back and forth a bit as I stared at her barren hiding spot.

I smirked, impressed with her hard knock. "*Bring a fucking army*, the daring little chit," I hummed, walking around the small room.

Hadley was thinner than I expected, given her photo with full cheeks and plump lips; and tall for a female but not overly so. Even with heels, she would still be smaller than me. She was cuter in person than her picture. Feeling her blood rush through her veins when I grabbed her neck was thrilling. The fear in her eyes and the slight trembling in her body would have made her even more delectable to feed on.

Yet, she surprised me. Terror had danced behind her dark blue eyes until the moment I called her incompetent. Then all fear plumed out of her and the fury blooming in her eyes was charming. I chortled.

"Now I know what ticks her off," I mused.

I picked up a book she had left behind. This one corner of her dirt home housed a few stacks of books and a stand to keep them off the ground. Looking around the small underground hovel, she didn't take much with her when she fled. Even her makeshift bed in the corner was nothing but twigs for a base and layers of greenery for cushion. I shook my head, bewildered she didn't head to another coven or to someone else's house for better protection.

I huffed, peeking through another book; this one about teleportation. The words and runes inside the pages made my eyes swim, like I was looking underwater. Nothing made sense. I snapped the book closed and set it down.

"Witches," I grumbled, realizing she spelled it.

I turned the stack of books to get a better idea of what she was. The witch back in Nukpana mentioned Hadley did potions and divination. But according to the variety of these books, it seemed Hadley could do more.

I scowled, having had enough with her trivial books. Summoning what limited magic vampires had, I cast it and teleported back to her main house, landing myself in her bedroom. Her home had a charming, cozy feel to it that rankled me. It was too nauseating; random plants, items on the wall, no uniformity anywhere other than the light shade of green-gray paint. There was no black to break up the colorful globs of whatever one would call her house.

A *rainbow puke bucket*, I decided, glancing around her bedroom. I strode out of the colorful puke room and into the living room. Eckard and Korbin were in the middle of the room pacing and on their phones. My phone rang, blaring the tone I had set for Lydon.

"Yes?" I answered.

"Elders. You're requested," Lydon replied. "Now."

I slipped my phone into my pocket. "Let's get going," I announced, striding past them.

"Where've you been?" Eckard asked, slipping his cell phone into his pocket.

I smiled, hand on the front doorknob. "I found our little witch."

"And you let her get away," Korbin groaned.

I yanked the door open and strode out. "I now find myself enjoying the hunt."

I jumped into the air, shifting into a bat. The shift took over my body instantly, leaving behind a puff of black smoke in my wake. Unlike werewolves where their shift peeled over their skin like one would an orange, ours was cloaked in smoke. I never understood the reasoning behind it, but I assumed since our kind was created in Diomedes's Hell where it's always hot and smoky, it had something to do with it.

Sighing contentedly, I flapped toward my residence on the outskirts of Aiolos. I wanted to give the witch a false sense of security; lure her into making a move so I could manipulate her and the situation. My stomach quivered gleefully. Little did she know I put a small tracker on her, slipping it behind her ear when I had her by the throat. I could get her now if I so choose, but I wanted a hot shower and a moment to plan my next move, not only regarding Hadley but my coven.

I smirked, thinking of the fiery redhead. The feistiness in her was charming for a witch. Usually, the vile bitches were too haughty, solving their problems with flamboyant magic, a craftily worded spell, a damn plant, or something else ridiculous. This one used her fists.

"Let me guess," Korbin griped, catching up. "You're enjoying the cat-and-mouse game."

I nodded. "I am. I'm going to allow her to scamper off with her little mousey friend, figure out what she's up to, then eat her."

Eckard dramatically sighed. "Ten bucks says she's gonna leave another bruise on the other side of his face."

Korbin snickered.

"She's not," I replied evenly.

"Then why wait to track her down and eat her?"

I shrugged. "I want to do some deeper research on her besides what I've already done. Plus, I have a feeling our coven is about to get," I paused, swishing my head back and forth, "complicated."

My friends didn't say a word as we flapped in silence. I was fine with it. I knew they were irritated with me. After two weeks on the hunt for this witch, just to let her go, pissed them off despite me telling them I had a tracker on her.

My stomach jolted, thinking about her power and how it rippled through me as her punch connected with my face. The fact she decked me still made me smirk. All my other bounties cowered, cried, begged for their lives, yet she packed a punch. *She must be more than just a witch as Keres made her seem,* I decided. The thought had been ruminating in my head since I left her dirt hovel and puking rainbow home. There was more to her. I just had to find out what.

I made for a clearing below, growing irritated with flying home and it being too slow to my liking. I waited long enough for Eckard and Korbin to land and shift beside me before I teleported us back to the mansion. I hated teleporting, as it made me nauseated and used up most of my limited magic.

The house was buzzing with people. Servants flitted up and down corridors and stairs, fake smiles plastered to their blank faces while their pinched eyes portrayed their irritation. I knew the look well. They were on edge since the Elders were here. I couldn't say I blamed them. Exactly one third of them and I didn't get along.

"What the fuck is going on?" Korbin asked.

"Looks like the Elders are visiting."

Eckard groaned. "If it's Elder Ubel, count me out."

"It's probably him with Elders Ghiza and Rezon," Korbin spat. "They never go anywhere without each other."

My left foot didn't even have time to strike the first step of the stairs when I caught the Elders out of the corner of my eye. They glided from the right side of the hallway toward the large meeting room just off the stairs. Elder Ubel led the procession followed closely by his two faithful pets and Senna. My breath hitched.

I briefly closed my eyes and sighed. I hadn't seen Senna since she refused to do a blood-rite with me. Seeing her now, a fresh bandage covering her neck irked me. My hands clenched on their own accord.

"Shit," Korbin mumbled under his breath.

"Well, this meeting's fucked," Eckard quipped.

I nodded, striding up the wide stairs and toward the meeting room. Lydon met me at the top of the landing. The scowl pulling slightly at his brow had me raising mine. Lydon was not one to show the slightest bit of emotion besides glee to eat, whereas I played with the emotions of others. Humans called it manipulation. I called it a tactic.

"You're late," Lydon hissed.

"Anything to do with those three, and I will always be late."

My older brother huffed. "Let's go. Our *sire* is calling for us."

"Let's not disappoint, shall we?"

I strode ahead of them all, walking straight into the meeting room and taking the nearest seat. The meeting room was large, opulent to convey my father's wealth. My mother sat bejeweled beside him, offering me a tight smile. Nine Elders surrounded the long oblong table. Ornate silver backed mirrors lined the walls every few feet, the only reflection showing was Senna's until the blood-rite completed.

All the Elders were here, unless I miscounted, but why? My father was a lord, on the list to be an Elder. Until one of our kind died, my father wouldn't get the position. I crossed my legs over the other and leaned back in my chair, waiting for the shit storm to blow in. Whatever this spontaneous meeting was for had better be important, as they weren't set to meet for a while.

I peeked out of my peripheral at Senna. She stared at her lap. A deep burgundy satin dress hugged her lithe body. A light sheen of sweat covered her creamy skin. Her long raven black hair trailed over her right shoulder, held in place by an ornate comb. I turned in my seat to candidly look, wondering if what I thought to be correct happened to be true. I wasn't mistaken. A red line made its way from the left side of her neck where she was bitten and tucked itself under her satin dress toward her heart. My blood roiled.

My gaze flitted to Elder Rezon. The pompous elder leaned back in his seat and smirked at me. His oily black hair was slicked over his head, hiding the bald spot he had prior to his bite. He turned his head just enough to whisper something to the shrew, Elder Ghiza, giving away his own red lined bite mark. The woman I had loved, who refused me, took the blood-rite with him. In two days, when the blood-rite took effect, Senna would be a vampire and his mate for life.

Air angrily left my body. My jaw clenched to the point it hurt.

"Easy," Korbin whispered.

I lifted my chin slightly, tearing my vehement stare from Elder Rezon, and gave my attention to my father.

"Thank you all for coming," Lord Halvor Zygrath's droll, monotone voice began. "I've called you all here for very important and specific reasons."

"And *that* being?" Ubel hissed. "We weren't set to meet until August's full moon. This is the beginning of July."

My father dipped his head in acknowledgement of the Elder. "The first order I have is the passing of the mansion and title. I'm passing my lordship over to Brooks."

Ghiza scoffed, the impetuous action causing her vibrant orange wig to bounce on her head. "Honestly, you called all *nine* of us here for that?" she snarled, shaking her head.

The wig tilted to the right. I chortled quietly at the wrinkly bat. For a female vampire, age hit her with an ugly truck that reversed over her body a few times before screeching away on her face. It didn't help that her personality matched. I'd no idea when Ghiza came to be a vampire, whether born or eventually created, but she was a nasty woman; even centuries later, Ghiza was still fuming my father rejected her advances and married my beautiful mother.

"There's eight," Halvor replied. "Or has age forsaken you from counting?"

Eckard whistled low. I coughed, masking the laugh that escaped. My father scowled, ignoring her bouncing jaw. Halvor stared directly at Elder Indrek. My father's eyes pinched, a slight smirk twitched at the corner of his lip that would've been missed had I blinked. I crossed my arms over my chest and grinned. It was going to be a long night of chats and political bullshit I had nothing to do with.

"Furthermore," Halvor continued, his gaze fixed upon Indrek, "before I do so, I'm signing over the mansion's small army to you, Elder Indrek, as a faithful token to your upcoming war regime against the mutts."

Eckard made a soft explosion noise. "And here we go."

"Shut it," Korbin hissed.

"Now's not the time for war," Eckard retaliated.

I nodded, agreeing with his statement. I ran a hand along my jawline and grimaced. For centuries, the wolves and vampires hated each other. Like most wars, it began out of love where a werewolf female fell in love with the heir to our coven. The wolf's alpha found out and ripped her throat out before she could elope. The vampire, in his grief, slaughtered the alpha. Thus began a fucking war.

I couldn't care less about how it started, only that the wolves had tried several times since then to eradicate our line. I did not disagree that the mutts should be taken out, decimated as how they did us, if not fully destroyed. However, I believed Keres was up to something and Hadley might be the key.

Leaning back in my seat, I halfheartedly listened to my father and the other elders. My mind was wrapping itself around Hadley. There was something more about her than Keres was letting on. For why hire me when a mutt has a better nose? Why hire a vampire to get her soul when a wolf, witch or other being was just as capable? And why me *exactly* with promises of Toan Castle?

I got up from the table and strode out of the room while Halvor and the other elders spoke about war.

Checking my phone, Hadley's tracker had her stalled outside the town of OKimma. I breathily laughed. If she thought to hide there, or anywhere, she would be sorely mistaken.

I took the stairs down and to the left, heading to the other side of the mansion where my office was. After a bit of research, a quick shower, and a nap, my hunt for Hadley Birch would be much swifter this time.

Ten

Hadley

"Fucking vampires," I seethed under my breath. "I don't know which race I dislike more: wolves or vampires."

Vampires, Aysel replied.

"Why vampires for you?"

Mutts can be trained, she giggled. *In all seriousness though werewolves are much more aggressive and animalistic. Vampires want to mind control you. I don't like that.*

I snorted, trudging through the thick underbrush toward Kadia Castle. *I dislike things about both races, but the cunning manipulation of vampires seems to take the cake for me*, I mind-spoke as I went through a leafy bush. *Wolves have some decency and honor to them, which I admire.*

I had the feeling I was being watched, but I couldn't pin-point where. I felt Aysel's head turning movements as she sat perched on my head, snuggled inside my messy bun. We had been walking for hours toward Kadia Castle. But ever since last night, we haven't stopped feeling on edge. And being in this forest only made the feelings worse.

You never say hate, Aysel finally replied after a moment. *Why?*

Hate's a strong word. And I feel when it's used, it has power. So, I reserve it for those who truly deserve it.

Aysel scrambled out of my hair and plopped her small face down over my forehead. She smiled at me, hanging onto the strand of hair that fell in my face. I lifted my hand up in case she fell.

I love that about you, she said approvingly. *You're so gentle.*

I smiled wanly. *Thank you.*

Aysel climbed back into her spot in my hair. *Do you know where-about the Kadia Ruins are? I get we can't teleport since we don't have a clear picture of what the castle looks like. It's just*, she squeaked, *this is taking so long.*

I have an idea of where. From what I found in an old map, it's in the northeast corner of Quivleren tucked between where the Zilar River meets the Espowyes Mountains and the Xylia Forest. I just hope I find it soon. I don't like the vibe I'm feeling.

Aysel sniffed the air. *I smell and hear nothing if it helps.*

I didn't reply. I couldn't pinpoint what I felt. It was a multitude of emotions. However, the biggest one I felt was anxiousness to get through the forest and to the ruins of the old castle. Before the Hell War broke loose, the former Queen of Kadia castle, Lyvia, was a human; gifted the second heart from the Dragon Queen, kept slaves of different races in her dungeon, though slavery wasn't her worst crime. Queen Lyvia murdered and committed genocide of a multitude of races. Fortunately, both Lyvia and the Dragon Queen were killed during the war, though not before both queens decimated several species, forcing most into hiding and some into extinction. The great dragon, Holdur, became the leader of the dragon colony. From what I understood, he still was.

My head snapped to the left, hearing a twig break. I held my breath and peeked in front of the tree blocking my direct view. Several black-tailed deer rose, eyes staring wide and noses twitching. I let out a slow breath, pressing forward like I never saw them.

The valley surrendered to the will of the woods. The trees and shrubs took over the land, enclosing it as it once was, where not even the paved road seemed to exist. I crossed over the broken chunks of pavement, heading north instead of following the dilapidated road. Every creature followed a path. I didn't want to be found following it.

The sun danced between the darkening clouds, not giving way to the time but announced a thunderstorm awakening.

We need to find shelter soon, I softly spoke to Aysel.

Aysel sniffed the air. We're good for a while. Did you mask your scent for wolves?

Yes. And my magic. Why?

I smell wolves... And... something else.

"Shit," I muttered. "Hang on."

Staring at the tree ahead of me, I called magic in my hands and shot it at the ground. I blasted upward toward the nearest biggest branch forty feet off the ground. Landing on the branch feet first, I began the tedious assent toward the tippy top of the hundred plus foot giant red sequoia.

Moments later, wolves ran between the trees. I let out a long, slow breath once they passed by me. Every nerve in me rattled; even more so now than before when I felt something was off. I finally understood why. I was being hunted.

There was only so much magic I could do to defend myself, only so many spells and so many tactics. I was smart, but not physically strong; not like those who were after me. I was feeble in comparison. My fingers thrummed on the rough bark as I contemplated my next move.

I needed to get to Kadia Castle. I had to inspect the ruins, to try to find the amulet that was supposedly hidden within. It was imperative to my survival.

I stared in the direction I swore Kadia Castle happened to be. I saw nothing beyond the treetops, but north and a bit east, was where I needed to go. I felt the way deep in my core that I was in the right direction.

Glancing below, the wolves had gone. I let out a breath and began my tedious, slow descent. I didn't want to just leap and garner their unwanted attention. Plus, there was no way to get down with magic that wouldn't be noticeable.

I don't see or smell them, Aysel encouraged.

Thank you. To be safe, I'm still not going to use magic.

I was grateful to my familiar for her help. She was a sweet mouse, thoughtful yet direct. She was exactly what I needed at this moment in my life. Mahak's wisdom would have been beneficial to me, and I sighed, depressed he was gone. I missed him dearly.

Upon getting to the last branch, I leaped into a bush not far to the left of me. I clambered out of it and proceeded in the direction where I last left off. I sent all kinds of prayers to the Goddess and the universe to protect me while I journeyed.

My mind kept reeling back to what that vampire had said: *I want what Keres wants.* It made my blood chill. Every fiber of my being panicked. Keres killed my mother, taking her soul, her very essence of being a witch and tainting it, consuming it into herself for more power. And if that vampire wants what Keres wants, then finding this amulet was critical.

I shook off the chills creeping up my spine. *Now is not the time to bitch out,* I chastised myself. My mother, the former leader of the Black Ash Coven, would have skinned me alive for hiding as I have now and for the past several years. I wasn't the witch she desired me to be; I didn't stand up for myself often and didn't flaunt what I could do. I wasn't into the super dark magic Black Ash was known for compared to the Willow Coven with their light and cheerful kindness. I was just me, a mixture of both the darkness of my ominous witchy mother and the light of my dragon blooded father.

I let out a slow breath, trying to keep it quiet so wolves couldn't hear me. Knowing wolves were in the woods, I paused often to look all around me. The last thing I needed would be to encounter the tick infested mongrels. They were overly territorial, and I cared not to deal with them or their sniffing noses, even if they couldn't detect me by smell.

I have a feeling we're getting closer, I said.

Aysel turned upon my head, her nose twitching and whiskers tickling my hair. *We are. I can't smell any of them.*

Cool. Let's hope it stays that way.

I hustled toward the ruins, wanting to be there before the sun set. I did not wish to be in the open elements where wolves prowled. I stopped on the edge of a clearing, holding completely still like a deer caught in a car's headlights. I wanted to turn to my left yet refused.

Every muscle in my body urged me to keep completely immobile.

Hadley, Aysel trembled.

Yeah? I swallowed.

How good of a sprinter are you?

I took third–

Oh awesome–

To last in high school track.

So... so, you're slow, Aysel deadpanned.

Slow-ish. I wasn't as fast as a lion, but I have endurance. Why? What do you see?

I see several wolves watching us and for some reason, there's a bear too.

Shit... That's how they must've found me. Have we been spotted-spotted or are they just trying to figure out what we are?

Oh no, Aysel paused, swallowing. *We're fucked.*

I swallowed. I knew they wanted me to give chase. They were counting on me doing so. Using magic would be a dead giveaway to who I was if they were even looking for me. I was at a loss for what to do. My stomach rumbled loudly, and I cringed. I couldn't remember the last time I had food. But leave it to my body to remind me now while I was in dire straits.

I'm going to keep walking and pretend I never saw them.

Aysel huffed. *Gee, what a plan.*

That's all I got, I countered, walking toward my intended destination. I peeked out of my peripheral to find them following at a distance. I closed my eyes and chastised myself for being careless yet again. I needed to protect myself from all enemies at this point, not just the main ones who knowingly hate witches.

Aysel wriggled in my hair. *And what happens if they just come and try to eat you?*

Then I'll sprint and hope for the best.

Ya know what... Aysel huffed. *Nope, I'm not gonna say a thing.*

I grinned. *If anything happens to me, I want you to know I love you and thank you for standing beside me and for everything else you've done for me.*

Aysel went silent, and that was fine. I felt her tuck herself safely inside my mop of hair. I peeked again out of my peripheral, seeing them closing in on me. I was stuck and too tired to teleport. My nerves rattled; everything in me felt jittery from lack of food, water, and so much exertion.

I trudged forward through the clearing and into a thick crop of woods. I stumbled over rotting logs and whatever else was in my path. My ass was dragging, yet I pushed onward. The wolves and single bear followed, slowly closing in.

I cast magic at the ground and shot into the air. I feebly grabbed a tree branch. Below, the animals, now shifted, stared angrily at the tree. The four men glared up at me. I couldn't help but grin. My time was running short before they athletically climbed it.

I swung my backpack around, digging it in to see if I had any food, and was disappointed when I found nothing. The tree shook violently. The men rocked the tree back and forth. I giggled at their attempt to knock me loose. Unless they found an alternative method, my ass was staying put.

I looped an arm around the tree and dug through my backpack. My fingers wrapped around a vial of Retching Monster, and I grinned. Looking down below, more wolves joined the efforts of knocking me from the tree. The bear shifted, roaring up at me. His massive paws struck the tree, knocking chunks of bark and flesh away with a single swipe.

Shit.

Hadley, Aysel exclaimed nervously. *What are we gonna do?*

How do you feel about flying?

Eleven

Hadley

I threw the vial of Retching Monster down at my enemies. The bottle exploded on a branch, showering the wolves and bear in an expanding blue ooze. I giggled, watching the goo erupt to cover a forty-by-forty-foot area. The men freaked, yelling to get away when it was too late for them. The men collapsed to their knees, vomiting uncontrollably. I grinned. They would puke until they passed out. Other than that, there would be no long-term effects.

Seizing my opportunity, I leaped off the tree branch. As I fell to the ground, I used what energy I had left in me to cast magic, hoping to slow my fall enough without causing injury. My body met the dry fir-needle floor in an inelegant belly-flop where not even my magic could fix the landing. Groaning from the impact, I rolled to my feet and began sprinting north.

Is that your definition of flying, Aysel cried. *It was more like awkward falling.*

Ya know I'm not a vegan, right? I peeked behind me, not seeing the men follow. *Do you smell anything?*

Aysel popped out of my messy bun. *More wolves to the east. Isn't that where we're headed?*

North, then a bit east, I huffed. *But honestly, I lost track of direction.*

I have no comment. Are you gonna mask your scent to bears?

I shook my head. *I'm saving my energy to find the amulet.*

Wolves howled to my right, and I panicked. My side ached like it was being crushed by rocks. My body felt trance-like where I'd gone into a stupor while running because I couldn't think of anything else to do but run. Peering to the east, the sun glowed a deep orange. I trembled. Night would soon envelop me, and I knew the damn vampire would be back.

Got anything else in your backpack, Aysel asked.

I shook my head. *No, I don't.*

The howls got closer; their triumphant sound sent shivers up my arms. I pushed branches out of my way only for them to come slapping back in my face and against my body. I labored for breath, striving to reach the other side of the forest before the sun fully set. I glanced up toward the treetops, attempting to gauge how much sunlight I had left, only to see the incoming darkness while the sun faded, lighting the heaven in a deep reddish orange.

I pushed harder, seeing the edge of the forest come into view, giving way to more of the fading sunlight. I shoved myself through the low-lying brush with a huff and a grin. Between the leaves, I caught glimpses of rocks and a clearing. I whacked the last piece of a tree out of my way and took in the castle. I'd finally made it. The ruins I was desperately searching for laid before me.

Moss and vegetation covered the broken stones and wood. A dark, foreboding evil emanated from the ruin. I swallowed, not liking the vibes I was getting, but then again, most everything these days made me leery. I was jumpier than a cat in a room full of rocking chairs. Hesitantly, I went toward it, not knowing what lurked inside. Howls sounded eerily closer, making the hairs on my arms stand on end.

I glanced behind me. "Fuck it," I muttered and rushed for the safety the ruins provided.

I passed under the crumbled archway. What I believed to be a wooden door lay crushed to the side, half eaten by termites. The marble floor boasted cracks in various places. Trees dared to grow between the crevices futilely, not gaining a modicum of ground. Dirt and leaves covered various corners of the floors while lizards climbed the walls in safety from my presence.

"We made it," I whispered to Aysel.

She didn't reply. Her tiny body shook inside my messy bun. I swallowed my trepidation and pressed on. Somewhere in this dark, depressive ruins lay the Mother's Amulet. I swallowed, licking my lips as I went through what I believed to be another archway.

Climbing ivy covered the walls. Furniture, somehow still holding together, decorated the outliers of the rooms, pushed up against the walls. Pictures hung awkwardly, covered in slime and whatever else nature had in store.

Aysel popped her head out of my hair, looking all over. I felt her tiny paws go to the left and right of my head before settling down on top.

Hadley?

Yes, I replied.

I don't remember you having a small clear block behind your ear.

A *block?* I paused in the middle of what I believed to be a sitting room and checked behind both my ears. Sure enough, something was behind the top of my left ear. *Ouch,* I hissed, pulling it off. *It's a tracking device. It has to be.* I stared at it. The blood in my veins iced over. *He's gonna get me. I know he is.* Tears slipped out of my eyes before I could fully comprehend my newfound situation. This entire time, that bastard knew where I was, where I was going.

Let's find the amulet, Aysel encouraged.

I wiped my face and strode through the castle, being careful about where I walked and what I touched. Once upon a time, there was an upper level; however, now there wasn't anything to identify it ever existed. I walked toward the back of the castle since most of everything else was destroyed. A rushing burst of air caught my attention, and I strode toward it. The roar of a waterfall made me curious, and I walked carefully to where the sounds beckoned me.

This is the back of the castle, I told Aysel. *Beautiful view.*

The cliff dropped straight down into fir trees. It had to have been several hundred feet before the tops of the trees came into view. Peering to the right, I squinted and tried to find the trail my vision told me was there, but didn't see a thing. I threw the tracking device over the edge and spun on my heel.

I walked back in, trying to deduce where to start. Since the upper level was demolished, leaving the bottom level to search, but even here, it seemed ridiculous to even try. There was so much vegetation suffocating anything it could touch. And if it wasn't the vegetation, then the condition of the deteriorated building made searching harder too. I walked to the west side, where one hallway was intact; not even a cracked wall or shattered glass pane window could ruin this side.

It has to be here.

Sure, Aysel replied. *Let's just find it and go.*

I wanna go home, I pouted. *And we can once I find this amulet.*

I don't feel any magic or beasts near us.

She could have spelled it and hidden it away.

Aysel groaned. *I don't think Lyvia was ever keen enough to do that.*

I shrugged. What the hell would I know about it anyway? I flipped my backpack around and dug for a flashlight that was nonexistent. I cursed myself. I was so under prepared for things it was alarming. I made my home fool proof against dragons, humans, witches, and wolves to name a few, but failed against vampires since our races never interacted and I stupidly never deemed them a threat. And earlier, where I masked my scent against wolves but failed to mask it against bears. I have failed at protecting myself; just thinking solely of the immediate threat but never the lurking others. How I was even alive was an unexplained miracle.

I huffed. I had no flashlight and hardly any energy left to keep going. Since I had no energy, any magic I used would be weak and drain me more. I was fucked. I'd carefully planned my house with charms, spells, potions, whatever the hell I could to keep me safe, yet I was lax in thinking about other species. I was reckless, thoughtless. Even if I never meant to be.

I pinched the bridge of my nose and willed the tears to go away. I rolled my left wrist and snapped twice, bringing an orange ball of light to my palm.

If something happens while I do this, run away, and do not help me, I ordered.

I sat down on the dirty floor, crossing my legs. I bought my backpack around, hoping what little energy I could mooch off my belongings would help me. I rolled the magic in my hands over the other until I could see the crackling orb I created behind my closed eyes.

I envisioned a silver string emerging from my heart and penetrating the orb. In my mind's eye, the silver string formed a loop inside the magic orb. I held the vision there, ignoring the world around me to get this right. I had one shot.

What was lost, is now found,
As my magic circles round.
Whether you are hidden far or near,
I call you now to come meet me here.

I repeated the spell three times, invoking the laws of three as I pictured the amulet inside the silver loop of magic. Nothing came. I held onto the magic, forcing my mind to keep steady the silver loop as I waited for the amulet to make itself known. I called out harder, repeating the spell while manifesting what I believed the amulet would look like. My magic began waning as I tried to hold it. Aysel lent me her magical strength, causing the magical orb I created to flash brightly before everything fizzled out.

"Fuck!" I screamed, laying down on the cold floor.

Tears seeped down my cheeks on their own accord. My heart withered. I had staked so much on finding something, but there was no amulet here. It was gone. If it was here, hidden with spells or not, it would've appeared, or I would've had an inkling to where it might be. But I had nothing.

"You were a tricky one to find."

I glanced up, staring a cocky man in the face. His shoulder-length brown hair fell forward. His comrades, staying in their wolf form, surrounded me as did the singular bear. The man in front of me stood, hands on his hips, as his green eyes pierced me.

"Come with me."

"No," I snorted.

"I didn't ask."

"Neither did your parents when they asked for you, but here we are."

He chortled. "Aren't you... *amusing*."

I smiled sarcastically. "That's cute, but you're the bigger joke. Now, if you'll excuse me, my home is calling."

I got to my feet and swung my backpack over my shoulders. The wolves took a step toward me, and I tried to sneak my way past them. One wolf snapped his jaws at me.

"Down boy," I commanded.

The wolf bared its teeth, nudging me in toward the other man grinning broadly at me.

Aysel, are you ready? I asked the quaking mouse.

I don't have enough magic and neither do you, she angrily retorted.

What the fuck are we gonna do? It's not like I'm quick enough to outrun them.

You'll have to sacrifice the energy in your mother's bracelet to teleport.

I stared at my left hand where my mother's beloved red jasper and rose quartz spelled bracelet had remained for the last decade. I closed my eyes, not wanting to depart with it or use the energy inside to get away. With my luck, I would fail.

"Are you done with your antics?" he growled.

"Oh, I've been waiting for you this entire time."

He smirked, crossing his arms over his broad chest as he rocked back on his heels. "Are you going to come willingly, or will I need to use force?"

"Define willingly."

He strode up to me, his green eyes roving my body. I felt disgusted by him being such a blatant creep. He smirked, cracking his knuckles.

Ugh wolves, I complained.

"You've a mouse in your hair," he remarked, surprised.

"She's my friend," I replied, brooking no room for argument.

The man grabbed the backpack on my shoulder and wrenched it off me. He threw it over his left shoulder then threw me over his right. I yelped as I hung over his body like a sack of potatoes. I felt violated, angry. I felt like a failure and a complete, utter loser. I wanted a bath to get rid of his musty stench.

"Call the bloodsucker," he announced. "Tell him we have his pet."

"Person," I corrected. "I'm a fucking person, not a pet."

The man hummed, amused. "Fine. We have the witch. Better?"

"Yes, thank you."

Another man shifted and strode forward, binding my hands and feet. I lay over the leader's shoulder, knowing escape at this point was pointless. Wherever I was about to be taken, I was determined to escape the first chance I got.

Twelve

Brooks

I walked the pathways through the manicured garden outside our estate home, lost in thought. Quiet gurgles of the nearby fountain filled the silent void. Korbin walked beside me, offering support. My mind was blazing. The Elders and my father were in current talks about war with the werewolf packs. While I didn't disagree with war, something niggled in the back of my mind to keep the witches in our peripheral. Keres was up to something, and it involved the witch I was after. There was more to it than just that, I was sure of it.

Earlier this morning I had attempted to do some research regarding the red-headed witch but was interrupted when Senna walked into my office. Her excuse of *"being lost"* and *"wanting to talk"* irked me. She damn well wasn't lost and there was nothing to discuss. Her abysmal arrival forced me to leave my sanctuary. It was nearing dusk, and I hadn't returned yet.

I discovered some things about Hadley, as in where she grew up and went to school. Other than that, it was like she didn't exist, but I wasn't surprised. Since the Hell War, finding pertinent details about anyone became difficult. War had a way of eradicating information. Still, what I was able to find had her associated with the Black Ash Coven. From the notes, she was well-liked and exceedingly smart.

If she's so well-liked and smart, then why does Keres want her dead, I thought, making another round around the gardenscape. My phone vibrated, alerting me to the tracking device. I checked the tracking app on my phone, watching as Hadley made her way northeast.

"Looks like she's heading for the old castle ruins," Korbin remarked.

I nodded. "Let's get ready to go after her."

Korbin clapped me on the shoulder. "Are you going to fulfill what Keres wants?"

I shook my head. "No. I want to know what's so special about this witch first," I replied, following Korbin. "Keres wants her for a reason. Why else offer us Toan Castle? I don't trust the bitch, but if she wants Hadley so bad, then there must be something about her I can utilize or exploit."

"Makes sense," he nodded, tugging the back door open.

I stepped through, heading to the right. I caught sight of Senna out of my peripheral and refrained from curling my lip. I kept walking toward my study like I had never seen her. She was nothing to me now.

My mind reverted to Hadley. In the brief moment we met, she surprised me by her force of magic and her unwillingness to use it. She was more interested in getting away than fighting. I found it odd, but let it go. However, it's been on my mind most of the day.

My legs mechanically carried me toward my study. I'd just stepped through when the phone in my pocket blared. I peeked over my shoulder, noting Korbin right behind me with an expectantly arched brow.

I slammed the door shut and answered. "Yes?"

"It's Vukan," the wolf growled.

"Do you have her?"

"I do. She's safe."

"Where *is* she?" I demanded.

Vukan chortled. "You must really want her. That surprises me."

"Tell me where she is."

"Or what?" Vukan's deep voice challenged. "Be satisfied with knowing we have her."

I clenched my teeth until my jaw hurt. I hated dealing with wolves. But if he got a hold of Hadley, then it would all be worth it.

"I'll bring your money," I finally said.

"I don't want money this time."

I took a seat in my office chair. "What do you want?"

Vukan snorted. "I'm thinking about claiming her for myself."

My blood boiled. I heard a female yell in the background. I could only assume it was her. It disgusted me how wolves would just sniff something and claim it. I wouldn't be surprised if they tried pissing on it too.

"That's going to be a problem," I snarled.

"I don't see how it is," Vukan rebuked. "We have her. You don't."

"What do you want in exchange for the witch? More hunting grounds?"

Vukan breathily laughed. "Your loyalty."

I arched a skeptical brow and bit back a laugh. "I'm listening."

"We fight for each other's loyalty. Winner gets the witch."

My hand clenched. I worked my jaw back and forth debating on how to respond; more or less, how badly I wanted this witch.

"Where do we meet?" I finally responded, venom in my tone.

"Kadia Ruins and whenever you get here. Just make it quick," Vukan smugly replied, hanging up.

I tilted my head back and laughed. Glancing to my left, I noticed Korbin sitting in a chair in front of my desk. Eckard was behind him, leaning against the other vacant seat. I quickly filled them in on the conversation I had with Vukan as I debated on how to kill him. Granted, wolves were strong with crushing jaws and a good weight behind their attacks. In any fight our races have had over the years, each was able to land decimating blows. However, I was a true blood, and much stronger than those created like Senna.

"Should we bring others?" Eckard asked.

I nodded. "Bring a dozen and tell them to lurk in the shadows. We leave close to midnight."

Eckard spun on his heel and left. Korbin sat back, relaxed in the chair, staring at me with a conniving smile.

"What are you planning?" Korbin asked.

I leaned back in my seat and huffed a smug breath. "Eradication. No fucking *whelp* is going to threaten me."

"And you're only taking a dozen? Nashoba has more than that."

I shrugged. "We'll see how strong they are when I rip their throats out and burn their bodies."

"I'm not doubting you, but have a few more on stand-by."

I flicked my wrist, allowing him to secure more. Korbin nodded, rising from his seat to leave, and I did the same. After giving an order to meet out front of the estate at thirty minutes to midnight, I strode out of my office, making my way toward my room on the third story.

I hadn't even made it to the first level of steps when Senna sidled up alongside me. Ignoring her, I pressed on to my room. There was nothing she could say to me to convince me to forgive her for what she'd done.

"Brooks," she pleaded.

Normally, her soft call would make me pause. Now, all I cared to do was walk away since seeing her, even hearing her voice made me fucking pissed and forlorn at the same time. I held out my hand to my side, not wanting her to follow me further.

"Please," she called, sniffing.

I stopped in my tracks. "There's nothing you can say to me, Senna," I spat.

"Why did you just give up on me?" she cried. "You just let me go! Like I meant nothing to you at all!"

I rounded on her. "Give up on you? That's pretty fucked to say considering I begged you not to leave. But I wasn't going to stand in your way. I wanted you to choose me of your own free will."

"How dare–" she began screeching, but I cut her off.

"How dare you!" I snarled. "I didn't want a bitten whore to fawn over me for another bite and a quick fuck. I wanted a mate. I wanted you to choose me, to choose us of your own free will. I wanted to build a life with you. But I wasn't going to back you into a corner and force you to choose. I loved you more than that. Now I can't even stand the sight of you."

I glared into her swirling silver-hazel eyes that were slowly changing with the blood-rite. I backed away from her, turning on my heel.

"Brooks, I did this for you," Senna continued, wailing like an idiot.

I laughed, walking away toward the next level of stairs. "Fuck off, Senna. You're a waste of a damn bite."

For so long, her deceit and rejection stung. I thought she loved me, but she loved power. I could only give her the title of Lady Zygrath until I could inherit or lay claim to a bigger title. Clearly, what I could give wasn't enough. It pained me to be looked over by a woman let alone a witch who couldn't even make a fucking potion.

I made it to my room and punched the wall beside it. My fist went straight through the lath and plaster wall. The sharp crack of my knuckles breaking made my anger dissipate some. I flexed my hand, setting the bones in place. Not like doing so really mattered to my race; we healed quickly. I walked to my bed and laid down on top of the down feather comforter.

Senna broke me as a man. I gave her my heart, every ounce I had in me. For nothing. It was all for nothing. I didn't want the loose women in my coven, so I dared to hope to find a mate outside of it. And it brought me heartache.

"That went better than I expected."

"Hello sister," I grouched.

"Come now Brooks, you need to get back out there."

"Fuck. No. Nyura."

I could feel her pout. "I have a friend–"

"Nope!"

"I found a mate for Lydon," she persisted.

I scoffed. "I wouldn't call her a *mate* just yet. Lydon just likes her tits."

"The witch does have a nice ample pair."

I wasn't about to comment, so I sat up and stared at my sister. "What's going on? You never seek me out."

"Father wants me to move up the date of the blood-rite to Elder Indrek's son to secure the true blood's lineage and affirm his position since Indrek has sway over the rest of the Elders."

"And you want me to join your cause in saying no? Why? You wanted to do this with him."

Nyura nodded, making puppy eyes at me. "Yes, I want you to join my cause. And I don't want to blood-rite with him anymore. Lydon won't come between Father and I as he's next to be Elder."

"I'll do what I can," I promised her.

"Thank you." Nyura replied, tucking her dark hair behind her ear. "See you later."

I nodded, lying back down. Her footsteps faded as the door to my room snapped shut. I was finally alone again. I ran a hand over my face as I stared at the ceiling. Images of Hadley flitted across my mind. My hands clenched. Somehow there was more at work than what I was noticing, and I swore she was the root cause of it all.

I sat up, putting my elbows on my knees. I raked my fingers through my hair. "Time to see how wicked one little witch can be," I said, striding toward my shower.

Thirteen

Hadley

"**F**uck," I grouched.

An iron cage surrounded me. While the metal itself was harmless, it prohibited me from using magic. I sat cross-legged, munching on a burger and fries they made me and sharing some with Aysel. The wolves were kind enough to give me food to eat and water, but that was as far as their kindness went.

The leader, Vukan, from what I gathered, made a comment about me when he was on the phone with someone. I had no idea who wanted me other than the vampire dude, unless there was another race who wanted me besides Keres. Either way, the wolf desired to claim me as his and like hell that was going to happen. But Vukan's continual and random comments throughout my capture made it clear: I was theirs.

I watched warily as wolves paced outside of my cage. I polished off my meal and downed the bottle of water. I left water inside the lid for Aysel. We were still at the Kadia Ruins for whatever reason. I was surprised as I figured they would want to take me back to their pack; more eyes on the captive, more wolves to defend against outsiders.

I squinted to peek through the holes of my cage. Night came on quick. It felt as though the graying of night after the color of day bled away, had come quicker than normal, but then again, I was inside a cage with limited vision. Thunder cracked overhead, unleashing a torrent of rain. I shuddered. While I liked the rain, I didn't want to be wet. I wanted a warm place to sleep, a cozy blanket and to be left alone.

I moved to a corner where the holes weren't, hoping it would help stem off the rain. I pulled my knees to my chest and tried to make myself seem small. Aysel stayed tucked in my hair, not speaking to me. I couldn't rightly blame her after all the shit I drug her into, all my indecisive moves, the lack of forward thinking, and just downright stupid choices. I warded against those who I knew were threats but never once stopped to think about other races. I was lax. I was careless and thoughtless. And now it bit me so hard in the ass, I was surprised I still had an ass to sit on.

Tears fell from my eyes, that were intermixed with raindrops. I sniffed, tilting my head to the side. Footsteps approached, and I ignored it. The cage had random holes all around it with the floor being solid. Water spilled through the holes in the roof, soaking the floor.

A loud, crinkly sound overhead caused me to jump. Looking up, a tarp rested over the cage to cover the holes.

"Better?" Vukan's deep voice asked.

"Yes," I replied, swallowing the lump in my throat. "Thank you."

"Are you cold?"

My eyes narrowed; not that I could make out his form in the darkness. "Why are you being kind?"

"Didn't realize I was supposed to be a prick. Just because you're my captive doesn't mean I'm overly cruel or must be."

My face fell. I had no response to that. His visceral emerald eyes practically glowed as he peered inside my cage.

"Yes, I'm cold," I finally replied.

"Scoot back to the corner and I'll give you a blanket and a towel. Don't try anything. I really don't want to hurt you."

I did as he requested, going back to the far corner of my dog kennel. The door opened, and he tossed in a blanket and towel as promised. I unfolded the towel, sopping up the water where I sat. Once it was dry, I tossed it in the opposite corner. Unfurling the blanket, I wrapped it around my body and covered my head so Aysel could dry off and be warm.

"Thank you. I appreciate your kindness."

"You're welcome," he softly replied.

The man huffed outside the door. Rain continued splattering the tarp, and it had me wondering why he was just sitting outside in the rain. It seemed stupid.

"What did you do to piss off the vampire coven?" Vukan asked.

I blinked, realizing it *was* them who wanted me. For what reasons, I truly didn't know beyond what that one said to me: *I want what Keres wants.* Keres wanted my soul to gain my magic and power. But what the hell would a vampire want with any of that?

"No idea. They came out of nowhere," I finally answered.

He laughed. "I've a hard time believing that."

I didn't reply. It wasn't worth it. If wolves could sniff the truth out like they claimed, then he could sniff away. I couldn't care less. I scooted down in my cage and laid on my side. If I was to remain in here, then so be it. At least I was fed, dry, and now warm.

Aysel wriggled in my hair and came down to rest on my shoulder.

Everything okay? I asked her.

I wanted to apologize, she replied despondently.

About what? You've nothing to apologize for.

She nuzzled against my cheek and plopped down on the floor. I couldn't see her nor hear her padded footfalls over the din of the rain. Aysel climbed up and rested herself on my neck.

I'm sorry, Hadley, for being so mean to you.

My brows furrowed. *You haven't been mean.*

I was. I've been mean to you and I'm sorry. I haven't been a good familiar to you since the night of the attack.

I reached over and cupped her, holding her against me. *It's okay. We all get scared and say things in the heat of the fearful moment. Let's work on communicating better and move on.*

Aysel sniffed. *Thank you.*

I love you, Aysel. I want you to know that.

I love you too.

I snuggled down into my blanket, since there was no way out of this mess. The rain pattered on the tarp above my head, lulling me to sleep. My eyes felt heavy, and I struggled to keep them open, but somehow, I did. I felt like I had stared off into space for hours when it might have only been minutes, but I was scared to fall asleep.

"You okay?" Vukan asked.

"Yes," I replied, my voice raspy.

"Do you need to go to the bathroom?"

I shook my head, though he couldn't see. "No, thank you."

"If you need anything, let me know. Okay?"

"Okay," I whispered. "Thank you."

"You're welcome."

"Alpha," some deep voiced wolf stated. "Lord Brooks Zygrath is here."

I heard Vukan leap to his feet. "Let's do this. Bring her out. I want to make sure I got the right witch."

The door to my cage groaned open. The same wolf who'd spoken to Vukan, deep voice beckoned me to come out slowly. I did so, hissing at the tightness of my sore muscles from being cramped in such a small space.

"Hands," the man ordered.

I gave him my hands, feeling the weight of the iron binds. Magic, of any kind in Quivleren, was blocked by iron. I closed my eyes, feeling all the gusto to escape puff out of me quicker than a dandelion wish on a breeze. Once the shackles were in place, I tried to keep the blanket on me and over my head to keep Aysel dry.

"Here," he offered, fixing my blanket.

"Thank you."

He didn't say a word as he gently pulled me forward through the darkness, making remarks about watching my step. I could barely make out the Kadia Ruins through the dark shadows. I walked behind the man leading me. Rain gently patted my head, slowly seeping through the blanket to coldly kiss my hair.

Several large fires lined the perimeter of the circle where I stood. Someone must've gotten their hands on a magic spell because there was no way these fires would have lasted in the amount of rain pouring down without fizzling out. Their shadowy glows afforded me a dim and distorted view of those around me. I quaked in my shoes. In front of the man guarding me stood the same vampire who came after me.

Vukan snapped his fingers. I was pushed forward to stand beside the werewolf alpha. I shivered at the icy, unnerving stares the vampires in front of me gave. The leader of the vampires strode toward me. I took a step back but was met with Vukan's hand on my shoulder, prohibiting me from the action.

"Don't show fear," he encouraged.

I swallowed down bile.

The vampire glossed me over, then yanked the blanket off carelessly. "I told you I'd find you," he gibed at me

"But *you* didn't," I countered, straightening.

Vukan chortled. "This is why I want to claim her."

The vampire lord curled his lip but said nothing to the alpha. Instead, his unsettling silver eyes peered bitterly down at me.

"I brought a fucking army," he sneered.

"At least you listened to that part."

"Indeed," he replied unamused. "Hand her over Vukan, and your mutts don't have to die."

Vukan growled. "That's a cute threat, Brooks."

"It's a fact."

Vukan smirked. "Let's see it then."

Peering over his shoulder, Vukan called for someone to have hold of me. A calloused hand gripped my shoulder, pulling me backward and away from the pair.

Brooks hissed, bearing elongated fangs. I stared wide-eyed as three-inch fangs protruded out of his upper teeth. It was sickeningly gross to me. His skin turned a mottling of gray and white, somewhere in between death and disease. Muscles bulged out of chest and abdomen, splitting the pressed suit he wore. Wings erupted out of his back, sounding like a cracking branch as they unfurled. Brooks's fingers elongated with sharp claws at the end. I swallowed, not having seen a vampire take this form before, and I didn't care to ever again.

Vukan and the others around him growled and shifted. My jaw dropped. It was like their shift and fur peeled over their body like an orange. Their wolf forms were the size of a cow. I blanched, taking several steps back until I hit the metal cage. Whatever battle was about to ensue, I wanted nothing to do with it. If I could escape without being noticed, I would; then I would teleport back to my house, spell everything to ward against everyone, and live for the rest of my life inside the safety of my house.

Brooks and Vukan circled each other until Vukan lunged. I closed my eyes, not having the stomach for gore and violence; but I could not tear my eyes away. The mighty werewolf's teeth sunk into the flesh of the vampire. Blood sprouted from the open wound on his arm. My mouth dropped open. Brooks clamped his clawed hand around Vukan's neck and flung him off. With speed I couldn't even track, Vukan's body was thrust into the side of the decrepit castle, smacking the stone so hard, the structure rattled.

Hey, can you find me a metal pin, I asked Aysel. *I'm gonna try to pick these cuffs.*

Aysel squeaked from inside my hair. My brows furrowed. She hadn't squeaked in fear since I've known her as a singular response. My skin crawled. I peeked over my right shoulder, seeing a vampire standing beside me. I jumped, taking several steps to the left.

The vampire smirked. His chocolate brown hair swept low over his silver eyes. A slight smirk coiled at the edge of his lip.

"Hadley Birch?" he queried.

I couldn't find an answer to give. By the gleam in his eye, he already knew who I was. The fucker was just toying with me. My mouth opened on its own, but nothing came out. I attempted to summon magic to hands, hoping maybe the chains weren't full iron. Nothing.

Brooks laughed. "Magic cannot solve everything, little witch," he menacingly purred.

I took a step back and gasped. Vukan tackled Brooks to the ground. His wolfish jaws clamped around the neck and shoulder, tearing into the vampire. The squelching sound and bones crunching made me cringe. Brooks screamed in pain. I squeezed my eyes shut at the sound. Brooks slashed a clawed hand at Vukan's throat. The wolf dodged, moving behind the vampire while holding tenaciously onto the squirming beast. Brooks snarled, somehow gaining his feet. Cautiously, I opened my eyes and glanced around. Everyone was occupied with one or more opponents.

Aysel. I paused, waiting for a response. *Aysel!*
She squeaked.
Come on, we need to leave.
You're bound in iron.
I know. Just find me a pin so I can pick the chains.

I glanced around again, ensuring everyone was occupied. With Vukan tearing into Brooks's arm, I dashed toward the Kadia Ruins. I peeked behind me, seeing Brooks's hard silver eyes on me. I pumped my legs harder.

I dodged around two vampires, tearing into a wolf. The wolf howled in agony as the vampire clawed through his chest, exposing his rib cage. The beast quickly succumbed to death. I tore my eyes away, refocusing on the ruins mere yards from me.

A piercing screech rent the chaotic din of the air. My body shivered. Bile climbed into my throat. Whatever that scream was for, I felt like it was for me.

"Hello Hadley."

I yelped at his sudden appearance. "Goodbye Brooks," I replied, darting to the side.

He snagged my arm, whipping me around and forcing me to the ground. His large, booted foot pressed into my chest, giving a constant pressure despite my futile struggle to move and breathe. His wings folded back into his body. I scrunched my shoulders; the squelching sound, like sinking my hands in slime, made me want to gag. Ever so slowly, he looked like the semi-handsome asshole I'd previously met.

"Little witch," he purred.

"Icky bat!"

He smirked. "Come," he commanded, grabbing my chained hands.

My head snapped backward.

Hadley, Aysel called, frightened.

I stared upward at the vacant sky and held my breath as a vision overtook me.

Fourteen

Brooks

*T*his *is new*, I thought, watching her eyes roll in the back of her head. I let go of the crazy witch. She fell backward in a heap to the ground, striking her shoulder on a rock. She was clad in iron, so there was nothing she could do now. Even her pathetic little familiar couldn't help her. But if she wanted to convulse on the ground like a worm with her eyes rolled back in her head, far be it from me to stop her dramatics.

I glanced down at her. Hadley's back arched almost unnaturally; her mouth slightly agape. She looked pained.

I softly kicked her leg with my booted foot. She didn't move.

"Hey... Sleepy head," I teased, knowing in the brief interactions how she loathed my condescending demeanor.

Fur plowed into my body. I hissed, regaining my former shift with wings and elongated claws. Vukan grabbed my collarbone, his teeth sinking into my flesh. I went to rip him off, but he dodged. I snarled, gaining my feet with him hanging on the backside of my body. Grabbing his head, I sank my clawed fingers into his flesh and ripped him off; his body flying over the top of mine while I held onto his head.

The wolf thrashed, getting out of my vice-like grip. Not waiting for Vukan to gain his feet, I charged him, plowing into his side. Using both hands, I sank my fingers into the back of his neck, slowly digging past his fur and into his skin. Vukan attempted to twist out of my grip, but I hung on, forcing my fingers further into the bloody meat of his body. The aromatic waft of blood, rich in iron, tingled my nose and I salivated, driving my claws deeper. The thirst, the stomach clenching pain of hunger to feed surged in me.

I felt the vertebrates of Vukan's neck and grinned. Vukan kept thrashing, trying to dislodge my permanent grip. Putting my weight behind it, I pressed into Vukan, enclosing my hands around the cusps of his bones. The wolf sucked in a breath, going limp as I slowly separated his head from his body. A delightful crack permeated the lawless fracas of battle.

I bellowed to my coven, announcing my victory over the alpha. The other wolves howled in lamentation. I could give a fuck. They should've known better. I knew there was a wolf out there who would eventually be my demise, but it wasn't this prick.

Erratic movement caught my attention. I whipped my head to the left, seeing Hadley attempt to sneak off again. I growled, shifting back into a more appealing form. Tossing the wolf's head aside, I dashed after her, getting in front of her before she could blink. Her startled scream made me grin.

"Hello again."

"Goodbye forever," she said, terror lacing her voice.

I grabbed her chained hands, holding them tightly. Her face paled. Her entire body convulsed in a shiver.

I arched a speculative brow. "Did anyone bite you?"

"No. Why? You wanna drink me dry yourself?"

I scoffed. "Absolutely not."

Hadley's face scrunched, her keen blue eyes narrowing on me. "Then what's your deal?"

"Like I said before, *little witch*, I want what Keres wants."

She wrenched her hands free from me and I smirked. She took several steps back, shaking her head.

"You're an idiot," she whispered.

"Oh?"

"Do you even know what *she* wants?"

"It makes no difference to me what her motives are so long as I get what I want at the end of this deal."

I crossed my arms and watched her face fall and become even more pale. I glanced beyond those of my coven who survived. The ground was littered with bodies of dead wolves and a few vampires. Come morning, as soon as the light of dawn struck the vampire corpses, they would return to ash.

"Holy shit," Hadley turned around and murmured.

"Not even the holiest of shits would save you."

Hadley rounded on me, the fire in her eyes I admired in her before, returning. I grinned. I liked a bit of a feisty fight before I needed to kill. I would stop at nothing to get

Toan Castle back, but this brief pause to goad her would be enjoyable.

"Then eat me already," she growled.

I shook my head. "I'm having too much fun."

"Didn't your mother ever tell you not to play with your food?"

I laughed while the others around me chuckled. "Why just kill you? There's no joy in ending things between us so quickly."

"I didn't know you could feel such emotions."

"I might be a walking corpse, but I do feel."

Hadley rolled her eyes. "I would say you're more of a walking, used menstrual pad."

I tilted my head to the side. To say I was amused by her would be an understatement. Her full-on glare, brows pulled low over her blue eyes, her skin shining in the moonlight. It was adorable. She was a cute, spry little thing, much more beautiful in person than in her picture.

I took a step closer, watching her eyes change from annoyed to fearful. I grinned, elongating my fangs. Her back foot pivoted. Instead of taking a step back, she stepped toward me, making me smile further. I was having more fun than I ought to.

"A used menstrual pad?" I replied, mocking her, as if her claim wounded me. "Is it because I'm such a pussy? Or is it because I'm bloody intolerable?"

Hadley crossed her arms over herself. "Both."

"That hurts my heart."

"Just get to the point."

I sighed, taking another step toward her. I didn't tower over her. Hadley was tall for a woman, maybe five foot six, but I was still more than a head taller. She tilted her head up, the fire in her eyes dissipating and replaced with trepidation.

I took her chained hands in mine, feeling her pulse race through the thick iron shackles. She swallowed, tears welling at the corner of her eyes. Her glassy eyes in the moon's light were enchanting. It took everything in me not to slurp her up now. Eating her would be delightful. I loved criers. Their tears coupled with a racing pulse and pleas for their life was enthralling. I gave a quick jerk of my head, popping my neck to snap myself out of the carnality I wanted to bestow upon her.

Grabbing her chains tighter, I yanked her to me. Her ample chest pressed into mine, her breath coming in ragged pants. Her red head tilted back, blue eyes staring so wide, I could make out the furrows and crypts in her irises. The scent of her hair wafted up to me, smelling exactly like the sample I still had in my pocket, and something else. She was an adorable woman, though one who stood in my way of what I wanted most.

I grabbed her chin, forcing her to look at me. "I have questions about your Supreme that you *will* answer."

"I won't," she sassed.

"I think you will," I growled, tossing her backward toward two of my brethren. "Stick her in the vault. Separate the witch from the familiar hiding in her hair."

Hadley wrenched her head back and forth, screaming for the mouse to run. The little mouse hiding her hair leaped from her and onto the ground. I laughed, watching it try to scurry away.

"Got it," Korbin replied, holding the furry creature by the ear.

"Let her go!" Hadley cried, struggling. "Let her go! Please, please, please! Just let her go."

It was pathetic watching her squirm. Rolling my eyes, I turned my back on her. Shadows appeared on the horizon line, indicating dawn was around an hour away. The gray light hadn't graced the treetops yet, but the sky was slowly morphing.

I teleported back to my mansion home, no longer giving a single fuck about Hadley. We had her, and whether I was going to give her over to Keres was up for debate. Either way, Toan Castle would be mine and Hadley Birch sucked dry.

Fifteen

Hadley

One of Brooks's men grasped me tightly around the upper arms. Hissing from the bruising pain, I fought back unsuccessfully. Quickly, one of Brooks's men clamped an iron shackle around my neck. The click of the lock grinding into place sent a shiver up my spine and made my skin pebble at the cool temperature of the metal. The cumbersome piece made me feel smaller than I already felt.

Aysel, I called.

She didn't answer.

Aysel?

My throat constricted. Tears stung my eyes and nose. I couldn't bear to lose her too. It was selfish of me to want her near me so I wouldn't be alone when I died, or whatever was ultimately supposed to happen to me. My demise was imminent. So long as iron was on me, there was no getting free, no magic, no hope, no anything. And so long as Aysel was near me, she too, was a target.

I'm here, she replied, groaning.

"Ugh, it moves," a vampire complained, tossing her into a sack he tied about his waist.

I shot him a chilling glare but said nothing. There was no point. Three vampires shifted into mule sized bats. One grabbed me by the shackles around my waist, lifting me into the air. I sucked in a breath, not liking how the metal dug into my skin. With each flap of his leathery wings, the chains moved, chafing against my body until the fabric tore and it dug into my bare skin. I sharply gasped with each movement, closing my eyes to stem the pain.

"You're fine," he grouched. "It's a short flight."

I opened my eyes to shoot daggers his way, and retort, but nothing was forthcoming. My breath hitched with each flap of his wings. I wriggled a little until the pain was more tolerable. Then my mind went blank. Peeking down, I was dangling above the treetops some three hundred feet above the ground. My eyes swam, so I clenched them shut. Heights and I weren't friends.

Hadley, Aysel called. *It's going to be okay. Keep your eyes closed.*

I whimpered, strongly disliking heights. The vampire jostled me and laughed. I sniffed, covering my face with my hands. The pain from the chains nearly killed me. Mostly, I hated myself most for putting Aysel in danger.

What did you see in your vision? Aysel pried.

Flames... Death and flames.

What else?

I shook my head, not having the desire to discuss it right now. I needed to process it, analyzing everything once I was locked up and alone. The eeriness bothered me. I couldn't shake the memory of his touch. The way it spread through my body like icy fire. It felt as if I was being burned alive, electrocuted, and frozen in a glacier all at once. It was the most inhuman touch I'd ever experienced, and I cared not to ever again.

My head had snapped backward on its own, forcing my gaze to the stars. The emptiness of the night sky it all mocked me. My eyes went to each constellation for answers, believing the oncoming vision was related. But I was wrong. Those specks couldn't save me from being eaten. Their freedom mocked my own. Their brightness dimmed my heart, crumpling it to feel absolute pain.

When Brooks released me, it was like my soul was free. Only I began convulsing. I couldn't stop myself from shaking. I couldn't breathe. The heady mountain air lingered in my throat, burning it with its teasing promise of life for my body. I couldn't inhale. I couldn't do anything but shake as a vision of what was to come played out like a stiff reenactment of a movie scene.

Hadley, Aysel began.

I shook my head at the memory of Brooks and the vision replaying violently in my mind. I wanted it out of my head. There was nothing I could do to stop it replaying over and over. The world was fucked. I was fucked. There would be no escaping the demise set forth by Keres. Not even someone as mighty as Zuri or powerful as Evander could stop this. Quivleren will fall. Quivleren will come to heel in the name of Keres.

Hadley!

Tears seeped from my eyes. I had failed. I couldn't find the Mother's Amulet. I couldn't find the one fucking thing I needed to keep myself safe from others, from being killed and my soul taken.

My head fell against my chest as tears splattered on my skin. *I'm so sorry Aysel.*

I meant that apology with my entire being.

What did you see? Aysel prodded.

When Brooks touched me, it was like I could see what he was planning to do. I've long known wolves and vampires had been at odds. Now it seems the vampires plan to eradicate the entire race and are moving forward with that plan. But Brooks is leery of Keres. Which he is right to do. Then, it was as if Brooks saw me and that I was trying to see into his plan and he cut me off. I paused, shaking my head. *The vision was replaced with flames. Everything was burning and Keres's laughter echoed in those flames. The dragons took to the air only to be struck down by something... Something massive, even bigger than the dragons themselves. There's more, but I'm struggling to recall it...*

Aysel gasped. *Do you think Keres is trying to unlock her?*

My body chilled. *By the Goddess, I hope not. Not even the Gods know where she's located.*

Aysel guffawed. *Elohi does.*

Elohi hasn't been spotted since the Hell War, I reminded. *And even though Zuri killed Diomedes, I also really doubt the demon is truly dead.*

The mouse squeaked and my head snapped to the right. The vampire who had her must've done something. I couldn't see where she was, only able to make out the silhouette of the beast.

You okay, Aysel?

Yeah, she huffed. *He just tightened his grip on me.*

I'm sorry I dragged you into this. I should've left you elsewhere, so you would've been safe.

I would've followed you. Granted, it would've taken me forever with my little legs, but I'd have found you.

I nodded. I knew she would have. She couldn't stand to be in a different room from me. Even when I asked her for a moment alone, it was hard on her to grant me a respite; even more so with Mahak gone. The love Aysel had for me made my heart swell and all the while shatter at the predicament I got us into.

The vampire banked to the left and descended. A large outline of a building came into view with dots of symmetrical lanterns outside the building. The closer we got, the more bile churned in my stomach. I wanted to puke.

I closed my eyes as the bat descended toward the top of the building. I felt his claws let go. I sucked in a breath as I tumbled to the ground, scuffing my bare skin on gritty concrete. I was yanked to my feet by the shackle around my neck. I swallowed hard and coughed, trying to clear my throat from being choked.

I didn't want to open my eyes and see who all surrounded me. I didn't want to know. Nothing mattered. I wasn't getting out or escaping.

My eyes pried themselves open. I finally took in the building's top, noting outdoor sitting areas with metal fire pits and several vampires taking a stroll around the perimeter. Their gleaming smiles in the lantern light made my stomach churn. I was in their lair, and I was fucked.

"Welcome, Hadley Birch," Brooks crooned. "I had to ensure your new living arrangements were specific to you."

"How considerate," I sarcastically mumbled.

A vampire handed Brooks the pouch containing Aysel, and I glared. Aysel squeaked in the bag. I tried to take a step forward but was quickly reminded I couldn't move. I fell backward on my ass. Brooks made a sarcastic, condescending noise while his silver eyes jovially glared at me. Tears peppered my eyes, not so much at the noise, but the fact I couldn't get to Aysel.

Brooks smugly laughed. "I'll take good care of her."

I swallowed the lump in my throat. "If you kill her, I'll kill you."

Brooks *tsked* his tongue. "That's no way to help your predicament."

"Quit being a prick," I growled. "Unless you wanna do the world a favor and prick yourself on a wooden stake."

The vampire beamed. "Aren't you full of flavor?" He crooned, reaching out and cupping my chin.

His clammy touch sent a chill through me. It wasn't as dead as the first time. My head thankfully didn't snap back with a vision. Brooks grabbed my chin harder when I attempted to wrench it free.

"Life is full of choices, so here's one for you. We can either work together or I can eat you," Brooks's hard voice stated. His eyes roved mine; a softness lingered at the edges of his irises, making me wonder why he was being such an asshole.

I stared up at him. "Eat me," I softly answered.

Brooks scowled, taking a step back. "Put her in the vault, Korbin."

Korbin shoved me forward as he walked in stride on my left. He guided me around a sitting area toward a rooftop door. I went to reach for it, wanting to get to where I needed to be. I wanted a moment alone. I wanted to process my next moves if I had any left to make.

Korbin swatted my hand away. "I'll get the door."

"Really? Chivalry?" I asked, turning toward him.

Korbin guffawed. "I can be mean."

I kept silent. I didn't want to see his mean side. The scowl deepening on his dark countenance made me question why I even said a word to him. His skin was darker than Brooks's. With dark brown hair swept to the side, he stared at me menacingly with deep silver eyes. I swallowed. I had seriously fucked up by talking.

He smirked, "Walk."

I strode down the polished hardwood hallway. Old, gilded chandeliers hung from the ceiling with old-fashioned light bulbs. It was rustic, yet beautiful in an updated way. Potted plants, sitting in stands, stood outside some doors. Evenly spaced between doors, demilune tables held marble statues of what I could only assume were vampires. No pictures hung on the cream damask wallpapered walls. It was quite stunning.

"Turn left," Korbin ordered.

I did as bid. Straight in front of me was another plain and solid dark wood door. Korbin got it, revealing an elevator.

"If you comply with whatever Lord Zygrath asks of you, you may be able to leave here alive."

I entered the opened elevator and stared at the expanded metal floor. I wasn't about to reply to that. And I seriously doubted if I complied, I would be allowed to freely leave.

Aysel, I called.

I'm okay, she replied. *I love you, Hadley.*

I love you too.

Tears peppered my eyes and silently fell down my cheeks. It felt like the final goodbye I had to the last being who loved me. My breath hitched as the elevator glitched and jerked to a stop. Korbin gave a breathy laugh but said nothing as he took my chains and led me down a dimly lit concrete hallway. Wherever I was, this entire place was solid concrete.

Korbin took me to the first cell on the left, ushering me inside. A twin sized bed with a pink quilt folded on the end was the first thing to catch my attention. It was snug against the left side of the iron plated wall. A nightstand with a lamp already lit was to the right of the bed, giving a mediocre bit of dim light. A toilet and pedestal sink were to the far right, thankfully hidden by the door to offer a modicum of privacy.

Korbin carefully spun me around, undoing the chains around my hands. "The one around your neck stays."

I nodded. "And what about Aysel?"

His brows furrowed. "Your mouse stays with Lord Zygrath."

I swallowed the lump in my throat. "Please don't hurt her. So long as I'm in iron she can't do anything for me."

Korbin arched a disbelieving brow. "Sure," he replied, pushing me back into the cell. "Aysel will be fine."

The cell door clicked. My heart immediately startled by the sound, pounded so hard while I struggled to catch my breath. Korbin's soft footfalls stepping away made tears seep out of my eyes. Aysel was gone, and I didn't believe a word of what Korbin said.

My eyes swam as I looked around the room. Everything got bigger without me realizing between the door shutting and looking around the room, I had crumbled to the ground. The cool concrete soothed my flaming skin. Tears leaked into my hair.

Aysel? I called, wondering if I could communicate.

I waited a few seconds. Nothing.

Aysel?

I cried harder. Earlier our bond was still intact despite the iron, which eluded me to why that was. Now, there was nothing. I was alone. I was certain Brooks was doing this to see if he could break me to be more compliant. It was working.

I took a deep breath, feeling cold air enter my lungs. I gasped, like in those brief moments, I'd somehow forgotten how to breathe. Flashbacks of the vision I had when Brooks touched me came back in weird, jumpy scenes. Dragons were flying, taking to the sky in droves. Elves, long thought to be extinct since the Hell Wars reclaimed their forest and cast shimmering white magic to envelope where they were. Vampires battled wolves either in their shifted forms or with primitive weapons. But the vampires were losing. Keres stood at the top of some tower, laughing maniacally as dark purple-smoky magic seeped from her hands. I scowled, trying to understand it. One thing remaining consistent throughout were the flames licking at the edges of the movie-reel visions. Then, as quickly as the vision replayed itself, it stopped.

Aysel? I tried again.

I craved her insight into whatever my vision might mean. I licked my lips and sniffed. She wasn't going to answer. I blinked hard, trying to get the tears to stop. It tore me inside to not hear her, to not have her close.

"Aysel," I whispered, my voice cracking. "Stay safe, wherever you are."

I wiped my nose on my arm, not caring that my arm now felt disgusting. I never felt more alone. Groaning, I rolled to my knees and staggered to my feet. Somehow, despite an iron walled room and iron around my neck, I had visions. My brows furrowed, trying to understand it.

Perhaps it was because I was a mixed breed, that the iron didn't suck the life force from me instantly, and that's why I could communicate with Aysel and have visions. The weight of the room and the iron shackle felt like thousands of pounds on my body. It was soul crushing. So how was I able to do this?

Exhausted, I curled up on the bed. I stared at the side table with the lamp. There was nothing else I could do but sleep and wait. The fear I once had slowly dissipated. Why I had been so fearful of Brooks was beyond me. I always ran and hid, but it got me here. I couldn't do that anymore. I couldn't be meek or timid.

Never again, I vowed to myself. *I'm going to face this head on. I'm going to be assertive... I can do this.* Whenever an opportunity presented itself, I was destroying Brooks. I may die, but to die trying was better than at the hands of Keres.

Sixteen

Brooks

I stared between the mouse on my desk and the camera in the vault. Hadley deadpan stared at the lamp on the nightstand. Tears stained her flushed cheeks. I groaned, leaning back in my chair. If all she was going to do was cry, then there was no damn need for a camera.

I glared at the mouse. The stupid little thing watched the screen intently. My gaze went back to the witch. Her words from earlier repeated like a plague in my mind: *eat me*. The way she said it, so full of despair yet an unshakable resolution in her statement, caught me off guard.

I rubbed the stubble lining my jaw. I hadn't notified Keres that I had her little wicked runaway witch, as I wanted information from Hadley first before I killed her. But it begged another question, how truly terrible was Keres for a witch to beg a vampire to eat her? Not only that, but for the witch from Nukpana to want to take her chances with Keres to defend Hadley also had the wheels in my head turning. From the brief interaction I've had with Hadley, she was more scared of herself and the outside world. She was undoubtedly afraid of Keres.

A small squeak jerked my attention to the mouse in the glass cage. The brown rodent deflated, staring at the camera depressed.

"Hey," I said, flicking the glass cage.

The mouse jumped, scowling at me. I gave a breathy laugh, amused at this little disgusting thing.

"Can you understand me?"

It nodded.

"Are you able to communicate with Hadley?"

The mouse shook its head.

"Good," I replied, patting the top of the cage. "If you try to escape to help her, I'll know. Then I'll kill you both."

The mouse scowled, making chattering sounds at me. I chuckled, striding out my study doors and toward the meeting hall. Since my father announced his self-appointed title as Elder, with none contesting his ascension, the other elders and Senna hadn't left. Instead, they planned for war against the werewolves. The deliberation on whether to attack the wolves or wait would take days on end. Seven out of nine elders had to come to an agreement. To my current understanding, only four agreed to attack.

The meeting doors opened at my arrival by two men on either side. The lights were off while the projector on my immediate right illuminated the wall. I turned left, heading down to the very end to take a seat. A map of

Quivleren displayed large purple circles with 'W' in the middle of them, labeling the known wolf packs. Triangles dotted the map, labeling each vampire coven.

I refrained from groaning, only half listening to the droll, monotonous blathering voice of Elder Welden as he droned on regarding the packs, their alphas and whatever else he apparently "*knew*" about them. My father turned in his seat and glared at me. I gleefully waved, further earning his ire.

"We all need to attack here," Weldon claimed. "This point here is where they are weakest as it's–"

"I disagree," Elder Nefen stood, using a long stick to point to where the covens should attack first. "To attack their strongest pack, not even their fortress, head long without considering the outlying packs will result in our decimation. We must prepare better for war. We should wait."

I nodded. Murmurs of disagreements fiddled through the divisive air. Compared to the other corpses, Elder Nefen was a seasoned veteran, his family having been warlords for generations. Many centuries past, Elder Nefen's family served as the right hand to the Vampire King. When the war between the vampires and wolves broke out, many were pissed the King refused to attack immediately. Instead, he planned a thought-out extermination of the wolves. Sadly, a member of the King's family staked him through the heart. Before anyone thought to attack, the council of the former king established the Elders and various coven sects. To me, it was asinine to have so many leaders and covens scattered throughout Quivleren. To ultimately divide our forces, to me meant, to be easily conquered. Even alphas of different wolf packs came together in solidarity in times of need, while ours just bickered.

I sank in my seat, twirling my thumbs. The vexed discussion would last for a while, build in turbulence then fizzle out to where they'd pick up where they left off, only to do it again. It would take another week, if not longer, for them to conclude whether to attack or wait for a firmer plan.

The door opened to the lithe silhouette of Senna standing in the frame. I watched her stride over to Rezon. My heart went cold. Senna passed in front of a mirror, showing the completed blood-rite with her reflection non-existent.

I forced my gaze to my father, watching him in deep conversation with Elders who wanted to postpone the attack to better plan; and thus far, was the winning side of the debate. The projector turned off and the main light came on.

"Brooks!"

My head snapped to the left, seeing Elder Rezon rise from his seat and stare directly at me. The room silenced.

"For what cause have you joined our private discussion? It's quite churlish of you to be here when no others' offspring are present."

I stood, straightening my jacket. "I'm here to better be of service to our coven. Should the Elders decide to postpone, I'll have training sessions commence, and supplies gathered for the impending attack on the dogs. Or should it be decided to attack now while under prepared, I will get my brethren ready for war to the best of my abilities. Is this not for the same reason your mate is here? To be of sufficient aid to our cause?"

"It is quite sufficient, Lord Zygrath. I admire your dedication and thank you for being here," Elder Yulene's gentle voice added. "I vote to postpone the attack. Our brethren need time to prepare."

"I second this," Elder Nefen added.

Rezon sat back down. His silver eyes locked on me with vehemence at being trounced. My father smirked and dipped his head at me. I straightened at my father's silent show of approval. I retook my seat, running a hand over my jaw to hide my smirk. Rezon was just a childish prick playing leader. The only thing that corpse knew was how to be eloquent, gaining him popularity.

One by one the Elders voted, leaving Elders Ubel, Ghiza and Rezon the only ones desiring to attack now. Even the spineless Weldon agreed to wait. Before Rezon could pull me aside, I strode out of the room and went back to my office. My watch was alerting me to abnormal movement concerning the mouse; plus, there needed to be one more vote to wait to attack. It was stupid.

Upon opening the office door, my eyes locked on Hadley's mouse on top of her cage. I sped to my desk, clutching the disgusting creature in my left hand and squeezing.

"Didn't I warn you?" I snarled.

Movement on the camera caught my attention. Hadley stirred. A stricken gaze fixed on her face as she peered around, calling for her mouse.

"Aysel, huh?" I crooned, gripping the creature tightly.

The mouse squeaked, sheer panic in her beady black eyes. It tried to wriggle out of my hand, garnering a laugh and a tighter grip from me. Hadley screamed for the creature, the sheer frustrated panic, her frantic search and screams making me grin. Her hands wrung in her hair, tugging on the ends.

"I thought you couldn't communicate?"

Aysel shook her head.

"Seems to me like you can."

Again, the mouse shook her small head. I squeezed tighter as I looked at the camera. Hadley screamed, beating her fists on the door for someone to let her out. Blood streaked across the metal. The witch shrieked in pain as her left wrist snapped from her relentless pounding. She crumbled to the ground, weeping, holding her twisted appendage close to her chest. I squeezed the mouse even tighter as I peered at the camera. Hadley's back arched unnaturally, one hand grabbing her throat.

"Interesting."

I dropped the mouse back in her glass cage, this time setting a heavy book on top. The mouse laid on its side, wheezing. Hadley laid on the ground, breathing just as Aysel. I laced my fingers together, stretching outward and cracking them.

I monitored the camera as I paced in front of it. There was something about Hadley I couldn't quite figure out. She was so demure, skittish of her own self and shadow, yet feisty enough when it came to defending her mouse or intelligence. Even before, at her house, when she used her magic against me, it was like she was afraid of herself and what she wielded.

Using my office phone, I dialed Korbin.

"Yes, Lord Zygrath," he answered.

I nodded, knowing he was around certain people otherwise he wouldn't have greeted me thusly. "Grab a box and the mouse, then head to the roof. I'm getting the witch."

"Yes, sir."

I hung up. Rolling up my sleeves, I strode out of my office and toward the vault where Hadley was held. I had to decide whether Hadley would be worth keeping alive. So far, it seemed she might prove useful.

Seventeen

Hadley

I laid on the floor, breathing heavily until I was certain my lungs would not explode. Whatever had just happened, I was certain Aysel tried to escape and got caught by that fucking bat. Whoever squeezed Aysel tighter, I was going to hurt them. The bond between my familiar, and I was linked through our souls. If she was in trouble or hurting, I felt the same pain she did; except death was different since our souls would disconnect before the passing of one of us.

I rubbed the ache in my heart. Mahak disconnected from me a few hours before his passing, not wanting me to lose myself in grief. His passing still ached, though I could only imagine how much more I would have hurt had he not done that last kindness for me.

Sluggishly, I rolled to my side and sat up. The pain in my chest finally dissipated to a dull ache. My left wrist throbbed. I tried not to look. I knew the moment I did, the pain would be worse; and if the bone was in the wrong direction, I'd pass out. I hadn't the stomach for blood or gore. I didn't enjoy seeing people in pain.

I stumbled back to the bed and laid on top of the sheets completely drained. My eyes fixated on the ceiling fan above my bed. They had locked the fan in a clear box with slits cut through to allow air circulation.

My body felt so heavy. Since being on the run, lack of food, water, and sleep, I felt like I could sleep for days, yet sleep continued to elude me. I pushed the iron collar up toward my chin. The chaffing metal ground into the base of my neck and began to hurt. I swished my head side to side, trying to see if I could adjust it to a comfortable spot, but it didn't work.

Groaning, I swiped my good hand over my face. The grinding metal of the cell lock being turned caught my attention. The metal door yawned open only to clang shut. I glimpsed the vampire lord out of my peripheral and groaned again.

"What do you want?" I griped at Brooks.

He stepped further inside the cell. "I came to see how you were faring."

"Oh, what a bleeding heart you surely *don't* have."

He softly laughed, striding toward the middle of the room. "Are you hungry?"

"I'm quite alright actually," I lied.

He smirked, dipping his head as he strode toward me and kneeled in front of me. I sat up on the bed, glaring at him. His silver-gray eyes bore into mine like he was trying to deduce if I was worth keeping alive. The hardness I have gotten used to in his gaze was lacking for a moment. It made me wonder what game he was playing or if he really disliked playing the hard ass.

"Come with me," he demanded, his eyes searching mine.

"For what purpose?"

I was curious, but not enough to truly warrant me wanting to go with him if I could help it; though the look in his condescending eyes spoke of no choice was to be given. If he wanted to show me all the ways I couldn't escape, then he was a prick more than most. Already this iron collar would be sufficient to keep me here since using magic was now pointless; and I severely lacked the physical strength to hold my own against him.

"Don't you want to say goodbye?" he smarmily asked.

My fist connected with his jaw. The man was a rock. I winced, shaking out my hand. My direct hit left a mark on the side of his face. I couldn't care less if I had two broken wrists, but to tell me Aysel was dead was too far.

Brooks stood, laughing as he rubbed his jaw. "I was trying to be kind, but if you do *not* wish to say goodbye then so be it," he finished, turning on his heel. "I respect your wishes."

"You're a terrible creature," I seethed, tears welling at the corners of my eyes. "Your *kindness* reeks of cruelty!"

"So heartless of me to personally come and get you? I get it. But again, I ask you if you wish to say goodbye."

I got off the bed and stood behind him. "Ready when you are," my voice cracked. I wiped the falling tears as I followed him out of my cell.

"Good. I have a stop to make before I take you to your rat."

"I have a mouse. I'm looking at a rat."

"None. Of. That." Brooks booped me on the nose, enunciating each word. "Especially up there. I don't want to fight anyone wanting to protect my honor just to keep someone like you alive."

Brooks firmly grabbed my upper arm, leading me out of the dungeon area, through some twisting halls, and down a different corridor. The cream damask wallpaper coupled with the lights and the dark mahogany wood throughout revealed the opulent prestige of vampires.

Mirrors hung on the walls intermittently, allowing more light in the hallway. I stared at one as we strode past, noting his lack of reflection and my very dirty appearance. I saw in that quick glimpse that my hair was disheveled and ratty, my clothes were torn and muddied, and scratches lined my face and arms from my ordeal in the forest. I looked like shit, but it matched how I felt.

Korbin stood at the end of the wall way, hand on the door as he waited for us. He stood tall, stoic, holding a small black box in his hand. I squinted, trying to see if I could deduce movement. I couldn't. My heart was immediately in my throat. I wanted to puke.

I rationalized Brooks was just being an asshole while my mind raced with possibilities of what it could be, and my breath caught. He slapped me on the back, rocketing me forward. He caught me before I fell. The sharp movement forced me to inhale.

"You okay?" he asked smugly.

"You're despicable!" I hissed.

Brooks shrugged. "At least I put that *thing* in a box. I wanted to flush it, but didn't want to risk clogging my pipes."

I growled, clenching my hands at my sides. "And you think by doing this, it's going to win you my compliance?"

"No. Not at all," he said, leaning in and brushing stray hairs out of my eyes. "It's supposed to break you," he whispered, bringing his lips close to my ear.

He spun me around, shoving me forward. My legs mechanically moved, following Korbin blindly. My mind was racing. I tried calling out to Aysel, hearing no response. Tears welled, but I refused to blink and let them roll. Everything in my body was icy. Mindlessly, I flexed the fingers on my good hand, but they felt detached from my body.

The afternoon sun beat against the top of my head. The summer warmth in the breeze caused me to shiver. The top of the roof looked like a fancy member's only club with cushy lounge chairs and seating areas with heat elements, metal fire pits, and lanterns.

Brooks grabbed my upper arm, leading me to a ledge on the far side of the rooftop away from others. I peeked over, spying a small drop off and a lazy stream curling behind and away from the mansion. The drop was at least a hundred feet, perhaps a touch more; and the stream was too small to launch myself into it. There would be no way to viably escape.

Brooks cleared his throat, snapping my attention back. He held the black box over the ledge, beaming. His eyes glared into mine, full of malice and delight in my misery.

"Say goodbye, Hadley."

I couldn't move. At one point, I had sucked in a lungful of air, but I hadn't recalled the last time I inhaled.

Brooks shrugged. "Suit yourself," he snidely remarked, carelessly tossing the box over the ledge.

Snapping out of my head, I swung at him.

Brooks caught my fist in his hand. "I'd hate to break your other hand."

"Then break it!" I growled.

Brooks laughed. Somewhere, my growl turned into a scream. Rocking my head forward, it connected with his nose. I shoved Brooks out of the way, diving over the side hoping to grab the black box before it hit the ground. I didn't want Aysel to be destroyed like that. She deserved better. She always deserved better than being my familiar.

My body hovered in midair. I didn't understand how or why, but I didn't care. My eyes fixated on the box smashing against the ground. I screamed again, my voice sounding so distant, even to me. Everything moved in slow motion. I swore I could count the seconds in between the box smashing and my next breath.

My backside slid against the rough concrete of the roof. Korbin stood over me.

His large, booted foot kicked me in the side. "Breathe."

I glanced between Korbin and Brooks, their haughty eyes narrowed on me. Brooks pinched his nose, using his other to wipe the blood off. I gasped; air finally entering my lungs made my eyes flutter with relief. He breathily laughed, sitting on his haunches while he stared at me.

"Lock her back up," Brooks hissed, harshly patting my cheek.

It wasn't quite a slap, but enough to get me to pay attention and be pissed about it. Korbin's wide hand locked itself around my broken wrist. I yelped, quickly swallowing down the tears. He dragged me away. The bare skin on my legs burned from the rough concrete.

I peeked back at Brooks. His observant hollow stare scrutinizing me. His malicious smirk brought out the ire in me. This was all a ploy to see what I would do, to see if it would make me more compliant.

Korbin stopped. "Get up and sit."

I carefully rolled to my side, groaning as I did so. My legs shook. The pain from being dragged, my wrist, and kick in the ribs, made my entire body quiver uncontrollably. I got to my knees, forcing myself to rise the rest of the way. Korbin kicked me square in the chest. I rocketed backward, landing in a cushioned chair.

"Should've gone faster," he quipped.

"Fuck... Off," I rasped.

In a blink, he was to me, yanking my head back by my hair. "Quit being difficult. I don't enjoy doing this."

I snorted derisively. "Just eat me and get it over with. I'm not going to comply."

I leaned my head back against the cushioned head-rest and sighed. I felt so defeated that everything I did was pointless and stupid; I was always three steps behind. But the topping on this shit-tastic cake was I'd no way of knowing if Aysel was alive or dead. It was probably a good thing this metal collar was around my neck. If ever it came off, I would truly know then.

My head lolled to the right. Around a dozen vampires occupied a section of the rooftop bar. Their intimidating gaze studying me. One licked their lips, and I laughed. If that idiot thought it was going to scare me, he was sorely mistaken. I was far from scared anymore. I was just exhausted.

"Honestly, what the fuck do you want?" I despondently groaned.

"Tell me about your Supreme," Korbin demanded.

I sighed, turning my head enough to glare at him. "She's evil."

"Every witch is," Brooks added. "But I need more than that to let you live."

"You weren't ever going to *let me live*," I retorted condescendingly. "Whatever you believe Keres will give you in exchange for my life just proves you're a fucking dumbass. You're so old your brain is dust."

Brooks laughed haughtily, looming over my head. "I was planning on allowing you to live."

"Oh, how gracious."

"Just tell me about your Supreme. That's all you have to do."

I huffed. "As. *I've. Said*," I bitterly enunciated. "Keres was *never* going to give you whatever she promised you.

In fact, I'm certain she's currently conspiring against you. She's power hungry. She'll stop at nothing until she takes it all, every witch's power, everyone's soul, all of Quivleren. And you're stupid enough to help her."

"How does a witch even take another's power?" Korbin questioned.

"Their soul. I'm going to assume she told you to eat me so long as she gets my soul?" their blank faces said it all. "She wants my power, the essence that makes me a witch."

"Seems like a fair trade to me," Brooks stated, grabbing me by the throat.

Eighteen

Brooks

I lifted her off the seat by her throat. She didn't fight me. I wasn't sure what I expected from her really, but just to stare off, unphased and calm, wasn't it. Even her pulse was steady. No fear danced in her eyes like it had before. She was just... complacent; like she was dead inside.

My fingers adjusted around her throat. I held her still while a shiver crawled up her spine and shook her. My mouth salivated, feeling her pulse through my fingertips. The hunger in me stirred. It'd been years since I've tasted a witch. Their blood was enigmatic, emotional, yet powerful.

I shook my head, stemming off the urge for a touch longer. I didn't want to eat her; not yet anyway, since there was more I could learn from her. I dropped her on the couch.

"Why does Keres want you dead?"

Her glassy blue eyes slid over to meet mine. "Does being dead also make you deaf?"

"Come now," I crooned, looming over her. "We can be friends if you just answer me."

Hadley sighed, defeatedly staring off; she pushed against me until I finally took a step back. She rubbed her neck, tilting her head back to look at me fully.

"Keres wants my soul to make her more powerful. She'll take my soul, have it enter her body, thus gaining my power. What she wants *exactly*, like what drives her forward besides power, I don't know. But I wouldn't trust whatever she promised you. She'd rather see you dead before fulfilling a promise." She pulled her hair off to the side, exposing the side of her neck. "Now, let's get this over with."

"What is Keres planning?"

Hadley clenched her good hand, growling under her breath. "I guess being dead does make you deaf," she snarled. "Lemme see if you can understand this. I. *Don't. Fucking. Know.*"

"But you're a witch," Korbin interjected. "Don't they share things with you?"

"If I was a part of their coven, sure. But I'm not and haven't been for years. So," Hadley clasped her hands together, wincing at the broken one. "I don't know what she's planning. All I know is she loves power and will stop at nothing to have it. Which leads me to this: when you eat me, do *not* collect my soul. Don't give it to her."

"Why not? It was part of the deal we struck," I said nonchalantly. "So, you must know something. What is it?"

"I don't know."

"I'm getting quite tired of this."

"As am I."

"What is she planning? What does she want?"

Hadley laughed, shaking her head. Her laughter turned rancorous, garnering the attention of others on the rooftop. Her cornflower blue eyes squinted. For a moment, I was hoping to catch a glimpse of the evil I'd come to find in most witches, yet hers held nothing but exhaustion.

She leaned back in her seat. "Question, are vampires like werewolves in which you can somehow smell lies on a person?"

My lip curled. "Eww, no."

Hadley erupted into laughter. "Eww? Eww! *Pfft*, that's hilarious."

Anger roiled inside of me. I lashed out, grabbing her by the throat, squeezing my hand just under her chin. Her heartbeat pulsed under my fingers. I lifted her out of the chair. She didn't struggle, no kicking, no fighting. It was strange to me. I expected something from her, yet she was just limp. Her eyes never met mine. Squeezing harder, I pulled her to me, where our noses touched.

Her eyes lifted, finally meeting mine. "Don't give her my soul," she softly squeaked out.

"Why not? What else do you know?"

"You're... a dumbass."

Korbin snorted. "She knows nothing. Just eat her."

Hadley choked, finally kicking her feet somewhat. Her small hand wrapped around my wrist. The other one was too broke to do anything and dangled at her side. She was a small witch. Her voluminous crazy red hair made her head seem small. Her appendages were lithe, like it was nothing but literal skin and bone. Hadley kicked, trying to wrench herself free. Finally, there was some vivacity in her.

The thrumming of her blood under my fingertips exhilarated me. Her pulse quickened. I latched onto her broken wrist with my free hand. Her eyes widened. A scream tried to escape but couldn't.

I squeezed her broken wrist while letting my grasp around her throat drop. Tears crawled out of her eyes to slide down her face, leaving muddied tracks in their wake. Spinning her around by her wrist, I pulled her into me, where her back was pressed against my body. She tried to hike her shoulders up, but I wouldn't let her.

"Then *you* are nothing."

Grinning, I wrapped my other arm around her, pinning her arms down at her sides. Taking a leg, I wrapped it around hers while my free hand pushed her head to the side. Hadley tried to push against my hand. I laughed at the weak attempt.

The thrill of being able to eat a witch sent shivers up my arms. I sunk my teeth into her neck higher up to avoid her collar. The softness of her supple flesh brought a smile to my face as I fed. Her blood tasted of iron, sage, and an underlying hint I couldn't place. Was it cinnamon? Perhaps, as the last witch I tasted had that same spice, but there was still something more. Whatever it was, I craved it. Her blood was delightful, filling, and vibrant. It made my body quiver and pants tighten with erotic hunger.

I sucked another mouthful and pulled off her for a moment. I savored the taste on my tongue and swished it around in my cheeks to revel in it. Her blood was rich, intoxicatingly so. There was still more to her blood I couldn't place. It was delightful, whatever the flavor happened to be. It was potent, powerful, energizing my entire body to where it felt like an electric hum. I licked the side of her neck where the blood dribbled. My lips hovered over my bite mark, wanting more but afraid to kill her. I wanted more than just this one bite.

"Finish me off," Hadley rasped, her legs giving out.

Supporting her weight, I tilted her head back and turned her toward me. I was surprised she could still speak after how much I drained off her.

"Keres... cannot have... my soul," she breathed, her eyes rolling up in the back of her head.

Hadley laid limp in my arms. I gently helped her to the ground and stepped over her.

"Get a medic," I instructed Korbin. "Fix her wrist and stick her back in the vault."

"Yes, Lord Zygrath," Korbin replied.

I strode off the rooftop, past the throng of people watching my exchange with the witch. Keres must want Hadley's soul due to whatever it was in her blood. My tongue slid over my teeth, trying to place the flavor of her. I couldn't tell much other than she wasn't a full witch. She was mixed with something, but it wasn't a wolf or a bear.

Peeking over my shoulder, Korbin hefted her over his shoulder gently. He was tender with women, regardless of their origin. So having to be rough with Hadley in front of our coven really upset him; he'd be sulking for hours. Granted, it irked me too having done this in front of the coven.

I grumbled, pulling at the skin on the back of my neck; turning around as Korbin strode down a different side of the rooftop where he would head to the onsite medic. To me, it was stupid we had one, but since we employed some humans, they needed one.

I snorted derisively, heading toward my office. Her blood tingled through my body, making my skin buzz and my head feel foggy. It enriched my eyesight, making colors more vibrant. I could see the pulse of those pesky living human servants without having to grab hold of them to see it in my mind's eye. It was magnificent. To test out how her blood made me feel, I teleported to my office. It was quicker.

"Interesting."

I sped from one side of my office to the other. It was quicker. I tried jumping in the air and it was higher than normal.

"Very interesting."

I went over to the glass cage where her damn mouse was. It laid on its side, panting. It seemed whatever I did to one of them, the other somehow felt. I assumed that with the iron around Hadley's neck, it would prohibit whatever dumb bond they had. Iron prohibited magic. So how could they feel each other's pain?

"Hey," I said, tapping on the glass, "wake up."

The mouse roused, staring at me wearily. Its nose wriggled, little silver whiskers moving side to side.

"Can you feel Hadley's pain?"

Aysel nodded, her small beady eyes glaring at me.

"How?"

The mouse closed its eyes as if I asked it something stupid. I rattled the cage.

"Hey, quit being rude! Is Hadley's blood mixed with elf or lion?"

Aysel shook her head.

"Faerie or sprite?"

Again, the mouse said no.

"I know it's not a wolf or bear. So, what is she mixed with?"

The mouse turned her back on me, bedding down and tucking her head away.

"Damn rodent," I cursed, heading out the office door.

If she wasn't one of those, that left little room for other paranormals in Quivleren. No matter, her and her blood were safely tucked inside my walls. Now that I somewhat knew why Keres wanted her so badly, I wasn't about to give her up until my coven was inside Toan Castle. Then the witch could die.

Nineteen

Hadley

I groaned, sitting up in bed. I felt like I'd been crushed by a tree. My entire body ached. My neck hurt to move, and my eyes swam. The last thing I recalled was asking Brooks to finish me off.

"Ugh," I complained, rubbing my eyes.

My left hand felt heavy and scratchy. I forced my eyes open, studying my hand. A dark purple hard cast covered my arm up to my elbow. Someone signed the cast, though I didn't bother to study whom it was.

I dangled my feet over the bed, feeling the urge to move and relieve myself. I felt groggy, like everything in me was overly sore and stiff. I craned my neck to the side, hoping to pop it, but the metal collar prohibited the action.

"Dammit."

I rubbed my neck, feeling the bandage that went over it. I remembered Brooks had fed on me. My lip curled in disgust. I wanted nothing more than to wash it all away, but there was no shower in this room; only a toilet and a small sink that hardly trickled enough water to wash my hands. I took in my surroundings, hoping to find Aysel hiding somewhere, but didn't see shit.

"Morning, sleepyhead."

I turned slowly to my right, spying Brooks in the corner.

"What the fuck do you want now?"

"Well... It's technically night, but I came to see how you were faring."

I rolled my eyes. "Bullshit."

Brooks sped toward me, cupping my face. His hands were warm. It caught me off guard since before they were ice cold and caused me to have a vision. His eyes roved over my face; his gaze, softer than before, as if he constantly warred with himself about what to do regarding me. Like times before, he seemed unsure of how to treat me. His lips tightened, pursing slightly while he continued staring intently at me.

Scowling, I wrenched my face from his grasp. "What do you want?"

"I came to offer you clothes and a hot bath in exchange–"

I shoved him away. "Seriously?!"

"I'm trying to show hospitality," Brooks stated, holding his arms at his sides.

I took several steps away from his open show of neutrality. Like Diomedes's Hell, he was trying to be hospitable. I backed up against the cold wall. I was fucked. I was in no shape to defend myself if he wanted to feed on me again.

"What do you want?" I angrily asked. "You're not here to play hostess."

Brooks chuckled, crossing his arms. "What's in your blood? Is that why Keres wants you?"

"Yes."

"So, what are you mixed with?"

I laughed. "Not telling."

"I figured," he sighed dourly. "Which is why I hate to do this."

Brooks reached into his pocket. I held my breath. Tears already peppered my eyes.

"Oh... So, you know what this is?" He vilely crooned, holding a fist out in front of me.

Slowly, he opened his palm, revealing Aysel bound with black electrical tape. Covering my face with my hands, I cried; in part from relief she was alive, the other in fear she was about to be taken from me again. I felt like such a useless witch.

"If you want her to live, you'll comply."

I shook my head. "NO!"

Brooks clucked his tongue. "And I was making such progress."

"I will never tell you what I am."

Brooks threw Aysel across the room. "Ugh... mice disgust me!"

I screamed, bolting to her. Aysel hovered in the air, squeaking, and shaking. I went to reach for her but couldn't. Brooks held out his hand, holding me still with his power.

Brooks laughed. "But you will. The collar you wear, like the bitch you are, is made from pure iron," he tittered, striding past me. "You cannot touch magic. You cannot use magic. Nothing you do will save Aysel unless you comply and answer my questions."

Tears gushed freely down my face. Not once in my life have I ever used the word hate against another being. I strongly believed words had power, just as much power as I had. But this man, I was coming close to hating.

"Now, Hadley Birch, what are you?"

"A witch," I snarled.

"Aysel told me you aren't a sprite, a faerie, or elf. By the blood I tasted, you aren't a wolf, lion, or bear."

"You'll have to suck me dry. I'll never tell."

Brooks shrugged. "That's okay. I'll call Keres. I don't give a fuck if you die now or later. You mean nothing to me."

"Kill me."

"Oh no... I'm going to feed on you for a while before I do that." He strode up to me, patting me condescendingly on the cheek. "Come, my pet."

I spat on him. The moment I got free was the moment I would use every ounce of power in me to kill him. Even if I died in the process, I was taking him with me. Brooks Zygrath was as good as dead. I've never felt such blatant hatred for a person in my life; even when Keres was hunting me, I disliked her immensely, but not to the point of the hostile animosity I felt for Brooks.

"Aww," he purred, "hate me, don't you?" Brooks grinned broadly, putting a hand on my shoulder. "Now, how about you come with me, *hmmm*?"

I took a step back. Brooks dug his fingers into my shoulder. I cried out, my knees buckling as I went to the ground.

"Being agreeable would be easier on you."

"I will not!" I ground through gritted teeth.

Brooks shrugged as he lifted me off the ground with the same hand digging into my shoulder. Yelping, blood trickled down my shoulder from his vice-like grasp. He shoved me forward. I stumbled, but remained on my feet.

The metal door containing me opened. Korbin waited outside the door with another male vampire to his left. I stalled in the door frame, not wanting to move another inch. Going into the middle of a vampire coven wasn't something I desired. At least in that room with a locked metal door, they had to open it to get to me first.

"Come, Hadley," Korbin said softly.

"No."

Brooks shoved his way past me, heading up the hallway. "Get her bathed, dressed and fed. She smells like shit," he called over his shoulder. He held Aysel by the tail out to his side, dangling her in the air. "If you do anything stupid, the mouse dies."

Tears slid down my cheeks. My heart ached at the same time, burning with an intense loathing for that brown-haired prick. My entire body trembled with the rushing emotions I felt; relief Aysel was alive, and that Brooks was gone, anger at being imprisoned here and treated so poorly, but mostly intense sadness for being such a pathetic witch.

"Come, Hadley," Korbin said again, putting a hand on my arm.

"Don't touch me!" I yelled, shirking away.

"I'm sorry. I'm sorry," Korbin held up his hands. "Follow me."

I shuffled behind Korbin. The other man behind me cleared his throat and poked me in the back until I moved quicker. I was exhausted with the adrenaline wearing off. Walking behind them wore me out. My feet felt like they had bricks attached to them.

I sighed, wiping the drying tears off my face. The only consolation I had now was that Aysel was alive. Knowing she was breathing gave me something to fight for. I would get us out of this. Somehow, someway, we would leave here alive together.

"So, what are you?" Korbin asked, opening the door. "You're more than just a witch."

I stared at him unresponsively. While Brooks was an outright prick, Korbin was decent-ish. I wasn't about to fall for his nice guy tactic to reveal details about myself. I was exhausted, not stupid. I snorted, walking through the door.

Korbin got ahead of me, leading me down a different hallway and to the right. Vampires strode around gracefully, muttering amongst themselves and not giving me the time of day. Several vampires huddled in a cluster, dressed more ornately than the rest we had passed. The servants, however, stared wide eyed at me like I was something to be feared.

The hallway broke off, where we could turn left or right or go straight down a set of carpeted stairs. Korbin turned to the right, going down the hallway. Doors were on my right while a dark oak railing was on my left. The mansion home of the vampires was beautiful, though I expected nothing less. They were vain about everything.

Korbin turned to the right again, heading up another set of stairs. "Lord Zygrath wants you near him."

"How about no?"

"How about you don't have a choice," the man behind me quipped.

I planted my feet, refusing to move. Even though a bath and food sounded magnificent, I didn't want to be near Brooks. I'd rather rot in my cell.

"Move, Hadley," the vampire grouched.

"Be nice, Eckard," Korbin admonished. "Come on, Hadley. It's a bit further."

"Are you hoping to turn this witch just to fry Brooks's ass?" Eckard asked.

Korbin scoffed. "Nope. After watching the one you've turned, I've decided to wait a decade or two."

Eckard mumbled under his breath behind me.

"What does it take for you to turn someone?" I finally broached.

I was curious about how it was done. It made me worried if Brooks's bite would turn me. I hoped not. I had plans to never be a vampire. Plus, I wasn't sure I could be one with the mixed blood I had if I ever desired to be a vampire.

"It's done when the moon is high in the sky. You must drink not only the blood of the person who bit you, but the blood of a bat directly after. If one is done and not the other, then you're a half blood who dies by any direct contact with sunlight. If the ritual is performed correctly, only the first rays of dawn and the final of sunset kill you," Korbin offered. "However, you don't need to concern yourself with your bite. You won't turn."

I nodded. "Thank the Goddess for that."

Korbin stiffened, stopping outside a door. "Head inside. This is where you'll stay until Brooks is done with you."

"Oh, joy."

Eckard shoved me inside. I stumbled, falling on a rug. I hissed at the pain jolting up my left arm after trying to break my fall. The door behind me slammed shut. I rolled to my back, laying on the soft shaggy carpet. Light streamed through the curtains, offering a glimpse of the room I was now confined to.

Oak crown molding marked the difference between the light green walls and the white ceiling. I rolled to my feet, noting the same dark colored hardwood floors. A chair sat in a corner to my left behind the door. To my right was an open doorway leading into a tiled bathroom. The bed was in front of me, perfectly centered between two large windows.

I strode to the window, glaring at the iron bars on the outside blocking my escape. I hissed, wanting to slam my fists against the glass in defiance. Instead, I hung my head.

Trudging to the bathroom, I stared at the steaming water in the clawfoot tub. An assortment of soaps lay on a silver tray over the end of the tub. A small trash bag with tape lay beside the soaps for me to cover my cast. I shucked my clothes, eagerly stepping to the warm liquid.

I stood there, staring at the water. *Do I dare?* I questioned. If I was dead, Brooks couldn't drink my blood, nor Keres could have my soul. If I was dead, this nightmare would end, and Aysel would be free of me and my pathetic choices. I could solve everything if I killed myself.

I sat in the water cross legged and stared at the warm swirling blue water. *Do I dare?* My head battled with my body. My body was tired of fighting, of running, of uselessly and painfully failing time and time again, while my head begged me to keep pushing forward. But... I was tired. Not one damn thing I had done thus far actually panned out for me. I was useless and pathetic.

I leaned back, wondering if I was the length of the tub to make this decision easier. I was. I closed my eyes, floating in the tranquility while I decided.

I sighed, forcing myself under.

Twenty

Hadley

I came up sputtering and angry while tears slid down my cheeks. My entire body vibrated. My stomach roiled. Bringing my knees up, I rested my head against them and cried. I felt so trapped and alone. Even when I left the coven, and my friends, I was alone, but it didn't feel this hard.

"I'm such a pathetic idiot," I whispered to myself.

Drowning wouldn't solve my problems. My soul would be trapped in my body for two days. It would be long enough for Keres to extract it and use it for whatever purpose. Brooks would still get my blood. I felt chaotic and out of control. Between Mahak passing, the vampires, wolves, and now being trapped in an iron collar inside a vampire coven, made me feel emotionally frazzled and drained; I felt like I was spiraling.

I sniffed, wiping my tears. "I can do this," I breathed. "I will be okay. It's an obstacle, not a life sentence."

I laid back in the water, trying to calm my racing heart and mind. I needed to find a different perspective. All this time I had been thinking solely of my survival, but not of how to truly live. And I strongly believed, because of that, it led to me being stuck here.

You're a powerful witch, Hadley Kaida, my mother said pointedly. *You can only run so far until you're called to stand.* She was right. I ran and ran for years. I ran from my coven, not liking how they treated their own and viewed the world. It didn't help that Keres killed my mother, Oriel. I was pathetic, always fearing my shadow, myself, and the world around me; running from it all like I would somehow be protected if I used the right spells and performed the right rituals. Now I was being called to stand up for myself, to use and wield the powers I was gifted. It was just going to be harder now wearing this collar.

I sat up, grabbed the plastic wrap off the tray for my cast. Somehow, my cast was still dry. Once wrapped, I reached for the bar of soap with my good hand and rubbed it all over my hair. My mother used to admonish me when I refused to practice magic beyond what I felt was necessary to survive. She pushed me to do the magic my father's blood bestowed upon me, pushed me to understand that I was more powerful than her, than others; that I was special and hiding my abilities would be my downfall if I didn't comprehend its magnificence and darkness.

"You were right, Mom," I whispered. "Now I gotta stand."

I washed my hair, face, and the rest of my body to where my skin felt stretched, then I got out. Seeing the murky water I left behind made me gag. Striding out of the bathroom, I noticed clean clothes stacked on the end of the bed while a meal was beside it covered by a silver dome.

I dressed quickly, just in case the sneaky twerps were spying on me. It creeped me out to know there was a possibility I was being watched. The black short-sleeved dress had a band going just under the bra line, then flowed out from the body. It was comfortable, and I appreciated the forethought in color.

Most beings, especially humans, assumed witches wore black because they used dark, sinister magic; that the black clothing represented our wicked fucked up souls or something. In truth, it was because black absorbed all the colors in the spectrum and allowed for purer magic to be cast. Of course, other witches wore different colors, depending on their abilities and specialties. My mother wore a shit ton of purple as her specialty was spells and potions.

I smiled wanly, thinking of her dark plum outfits and matching eye shadow. How she wadded her red hair up in some messy bun and bedecked her arms in so many stone bracelets I used to think her arms would start dragging like a troll. Oriel was a lovely person inside and out.

The light from the window shining on the silver tray caught my attention. I stared at my reflection in the silver dome. My eyes were dark and tired. Water crawled down my face from my messy hair.

"You know, you can eat your food instead of staring at it," Brooks said.

My head snapped to the left, already annoyed and glaring daggers at him. "What do you want?"

"Is this how you're going to greet me from now on?"

"More than likely."

He rankled me more than I should allow it to. I couldn't stand him or his smug face. His chocolate brown hair was slicked back to one side, looking freshly gelled and wet with comb marks still present. He changed his attire from the last I saw him. A dark navy suit and cream undershirt hugged his muscular frame while bringing out the silver in his eyes. He looked rather dashing; and the thought of finding him attractive rankled me.

"How cute," he smirked.

Then he opened his ugly face and spoke, I thought.

"I've missed our conversations." Brooks sighed dramatically, taking several steps toward me.

"This is just getting old. Tell me what you want."

"I want to know what you are, why Keres is after you, and what your coven is planning."

"I'm a witch," I growled. "Nothing more. Keres wants my soul to have my power, and I don't know what the coven is planning."

Brooks darkly laughed. "I've a hard time believing that."

"That's because you're dumb."

"Take a stroll with me."

I sat on the bed, lifting the lid to the food. "After I eat," I said, lifting my chin.

Brooks dipped his head, going back to the far side of the room. He took a seat in the chair, leaning back with one leg perched over the other as he stared priggishly at me. I rolled my eyes and gave my attention to the food on my plate. Meatloaf with mashed potatoes, green beans and a roll greeted my eager eyes. I instantly salivated. The word starving was an understatement. I dug right in, eating slowly to savor every bite. I wasn't necessarily stalling for time; I just wasn't overeager to go on a walk with an idiotic corpse.

"If you eat any slower, your food will get cold," Brooks admonished.

"Sounds like a you problem, not a me problem."

"Tell me about yourself," Brooks commanded.

I snorted, shaking my head while shoving the entire roll into my mouth. I took my time in chewing while I analyzed him. Brooks wore no ring on his finger or jewelry of any kind. His eyes locked on me. In all our interactions, he was observant of every move I made. He leaned forward, elbows on his knees as he steepled his fingers. He seemed eager to converse with me.

"I'm twenty years old. My favorite color is orange," I offered, wiping my mouth. "I love to cook and curl up in my chair on a rainy day to enjoy just watching the storm."

"Why did you live in that house?" Brooks asked, jerking his thumb toward the door.

I scowled, rising from my seat. "Where else would I live?"

He shrugged. "I dunno, maybe with other witches, if not your coven. And why are there two covens?" he strode to the door, holding it wide open.

"Why do you have nine?" I countered.

I knew what he was driving at. I wasn't falling for it. The smirk on his face confirmed his foiled plan.

"Fair point."

"Black Ash is dark magic. Well," I paused, walking out the door. "Not necessarily dark, but they like to perform animal sacrifices, use blood and body parts to imbue their spells and whatever else they are doing, to make it more potent and powerful. The Willow Coven is the opposite and uses plants."

"Interesting," he said, gently tucking my broken hand into the crook of his arm. "Does this hurt?"

I shook my head. "What about you? Why are there nine covens?"

Brooks's countenance darkened. "At one point, we had just one ruler: the vampire king, but he was murdered. During that time, the damn mutts took over

Toan Castle, and our numbers were decimated. We were forced to divide and rebuild. I would like to have one coven again. Nine is just stupid."

He turned down one hallway. Servants bustled everywhere carrying laden trays of food and drink items. He took us past them, going out a swinging door and another shortly after. The sunlight struck my face and made me flinch. I squinted until my eyes adjusted.

I stood in the center of an atrium. Large, beautiful windows encased in oak wood polished off this brick and wood space. Directly to my right were trellises hosting different climbing flowers. In front of me, a brick walkway twirled its way through the room. A trickling waterfall was somewhere in the room, giving a soft and calming cadence to the area.

"Walk with me," Brooks said, leading me down the path.

I strolled in tandem beside him, rolling my neck from side to side. "You need to be careful in how you deal with Keres," I offered.

"How so?"

"She's more powerful than you think. She didn't ask you to hunt for me randomly. Keres is more than likely plotting something against you."

"And how would you know this if you weren't in direct communication with her?"

I snorted. "Huh, your brain must be super dusty, full of ash from too much sunlight. I haven't spoken to a member of that coven since I left when Keres killed my mother."

"Who was your mother?"

"Oriel Birch."

Brooks patted my casted hand, offering me a sorrowful look. "She was a good witch."

"You knew her?"

He nodded, leading me to a bench and helping me into my seat. "She's the one who demanded the truce between our species and created the documents."

He thrust his hands into his pockets and kicked back on his heel. His eyes went back to the softness I had caught glimpses of since being in his presence as he stared off at a wall. Finally, he took a seat beside me, leaving ample space between us.

"My mother," I sniffed as an image of her popped into my head, "she was a wonderful, kind person. I miss her a lot." I paused, taking a deep, cleansing breath. "After Keres killed Oriel, I fled, knowing I'd be her next target. It didn't take her long to order a bounty on my head. She promised serious cash to whomever could get me. No other witches took the bait, believing bad karma would befall them if they forsook a fellow sister. I've been hiding outside of Nukpana ever since."

"You've done well for yourself. Made it, what, three, four years?"

I shrugged, pushing my drying frizzing hair out of my face. The collar around my neck itched something fierce. I rolled my neck again, trying to adjust it better.

The door across the room squeaked open. My eyes snapped in the direction. A beautiful raven-haired woman dressed in a dull gold dress walked in tandem with an older vampire. His hair glistened in the sunlight, looking as if he dunked his head in a pool and slicked it back. The woman was gorgeous, darker skinned than what I pictured most vampires to be with an air of grace and elegance about her.

Brooks immediately stood pacing in front of me. "So how... how did you–"

"Get caught so easily?" I interrupted, trying to peek around him.

His wide, muscular frame blocked my path. "I wasn't going to say that."

I arched a brow, curious who those vampires were that had him irritated and not wanting to be seen by them. He turned his head slightly, his jaw clenching and posture becoming more rigid with each advancing step the couple took. I tried my best to hide the smirk at finding something which rankled him.

Leaving my seat, I began walking down the path again. "When are you going to collect your bounty?"

Brooks deflated slightly. "Soon."

I withheld a breathy laugh. He was so interested in me and what I was that I doubted he would turn me in soon. He wanted to glean what he could from me, but I wasn't about to give in.

Nodding, I continued along the path mindlessly. The aroma in here was soothing save for the company to my right. I closed my eyes, wondering if, despite my iron collar, if I could summon magic. I pictured the magic in my mind's eye, willing it to come to my hands. The magic fizzled, trying to flicker to life. A tiny spark emerged, combusting spontaneously like a match then dousing itself just as quickly. The collar on my neck rattled.

"What are you doing?" Brooks hissed.

"Just thinking."

"Of what? How stupid you can be?"

I kept silent. Despite the iron collar, I could summon a flicker of magic. Perhaps this collar wasn't completely iron? Or perhaps the dragon in me was immune to it? I was determined to try again when I was alone in my room. I was escaping here. Damn the consequences of it all.

"Come with me," Brooks commanded, holding open the door for me.

Twenty-One

Brooks

I sighed in relief when I made it out the door and away from Senna and Rezon. Their presence rankled me. The way Rezon lifted his square chin triumphantly at me, got under my skin quicker than I cared to admit. And Senna... That bitch fawned over that powdery waste of life, latching onto his arm like he was the one who rescued her, destroyed every jagged piece of my heart. Damn myself, I still loved her.

I shook my head. *No, I don't love her. I miss what we had and the future I built for us in my head.* The women in my coven tended to be more than a little free with their loyalty to their spouses. I never appreciated that. I appreciated it even less when they would attempt to lure me to their chambers like I didn't have a clue what they were up to.

So, I went out to find my own spouse. Senna was a barista at a coffee shop not far from our mansion. I hate coffee, still do, but for her, to get to know her, I drank every cup of whatever she brought me. After a year of dating, I finally felt it was time to introduce her to my family, to bring her into our folds. I was absolutely in love with her, her vibrancy, her charisma, her everything.

Senna left her coven and the coffee shop while I provided for us. I found us a home on the outskirts of the mansion since I knew she preferred cozy places as a witch. I even started a garden for whatever witchy thing she did.

Somehow in the mix of me collecting bounties from those who have wronged my coven and the other outlying covens where the elders resided, Senna fell out of love with me and in love with Rezon. I didn't know this until I proposed. She wanted whatever Rezon promised her while I wanted her to choose me, to choose us.

Damn witches, I griped. I tugged Hadley along, dragging her to my office. She stumbled. I caught her before she fell. Her slender hands slid up my arms. Even with my long-sleeved dress shirt, I felt the warmth of her. Her hands shook as she put them quickly down at her sides. I scowled, finding myself missing the intense warmth of her touch.

"Sorry," she softly offered. "I wasn't paying attention."

I nodded. Honestly, I wasn't either. My head was elsewhere while my feet dragged me where I wanted to go. I said nothing, just opened the door to allow her passage. Hadley stepped inside, crossing her arms over her chest. The afternoon sunlight kissed her bronze skin, making it almost match her hair. She paused, turning to look back at me. The way the natural light shone made her blue eyes fiercely bright. It gave me a moment to truly behold her. She was a beautiful woman.

Grumbling at myself, I dug into my coat pocket and pulled out her bracelet. "Here," I said, holding it out. "It had to be removed for your cast to be put on."

"Thank you," she murmured. "This was my mothers."

Again, I nodded, gently taking her elbow while continuing my path to my office. Her presence was oddly quieting for me. Despite her situation, she had a rather calming presence. Her voice, like her personality, was soft, like a gentle summer breeze, delicate on the ears and soothing.

Hadley trudged beside me with her head down. Her hair frizzed, creating a wispy halo on her head, blooming like a flower with each drying strand. *I need to get her a hairbrush*, I decided.

I turned to the left, going through the huge archway that led to an open sunroom and sitting area. Cushioned high-back chairs with loveseats were sprinkled throughout and clumped into small sitting areas. She stopped following, choosing instead to gawk. I tugged her along, earning a glare for my prodding.

"Don't you ever just stop and take a moment to admire what's around you?" she complained under her breath.

"Not when I live here."

"Well stop," she ordered, her voice exasperated. "Take a look up there," she said, pointing with two fingers.

I glanced at her hand, then at her. "Why?"

"There's a swallow family nesting in your rafters for starters. Also, the ornate stone with the chiseled in filigree work dates back a few hundred years. It's beautiful."

I snorted, shaking my head. "Come along. My patience is wearing thin."

"You're certainly on the path to getting me to be compliant."

"Trust me, I don't need some cordial small talk to get you to be compliant."

Hand on her elbow, I led her out of the sunroom to the left where my office was on the outside cusp where the sunroom met the hallway. She struggled to keep up with my pace and it irritated me more than her frizzy hair. I wanted answers so I could wash my hands of her. Korbin got the door to my office for the both of us, shutting it sharply once we all entered.

"Sit and don't move," I ordered.

Hadley nodded, tears already rolling down her cheeks and bottom lip wobbling. I rolled my eyes, taking a seat behind my desk as Korbin stood behind the witch. The little mouse tried climbing up the glass, going as far as attempting to jump, only to smack its pathetic head on the cover. Hadley dipped her head, staring at her feet.

"What's in your blood?" I asked.

"I'm a witch," she sniffed, not meeting my gaze.

"No, you're more than that. What's in your blood?"

Hadley moved the hair off her neck, wincing when strands got caught in the collar. Her eyes lifted, narrowing on me. "I am *just* a witch," she growled.

"Hadley," I paused.

Korbin gathered her locks in his hands, piling it on top of her head in a pony. I sat back in my seat and groaned.

"Really?" I asked, glaring at him.

Korbin shrugged, taking a hair tie off his wrist, and securing her locks in a wispy, messy ponytail. I pinched the bridge of my nose. *Fucking hell,* I groaned. I strummed my fingers on the arm of the chair, waiting for him to take a step back from her. Korbin finished, turning to his heel to stand by the door.

Even with the hair tie, her hair was even more of a frizzy mess. Her eyes were locked on the mouse in the cage. I glanced at the collar around her neck, not seeing it rattle. Her hands were devoid of any swirling magic. *They must be communicating somehow*, I deduced. Hadley's tears had dried, staining her cheeks with a watery trail.

"What else is in your blood? I'm not stupid, you know."

"Could've fooled me," she mumbled.

I removed the cover containing her beloved pet, sticking my hand in, and catching the furry creature. "Final time," I hissed, clutching the mouse tightly. "What is in your blood?"

"What difference would it make if you knew? Tell me that," she growled, rising from her seat.

"The difference is whether I let your rodent here live or die."

"You were going to kill us both anyway."

"Maybe I will. Maybe I won't."

"*Pfft*," she giggled. "You, sir, are utterly predictable. You try to break me, literally, then attempt to gain my trust by a bath, food, and a somewhat amiable conversation, and now back with the threats. Hell, your eyes never match your actions. Just fucking follow through for once! You wanna eat me, then do it. You wanna kill me, then do it," she snapped, striding toward me. She leaned over my desk, jabbing two fingers into my shoulder. "Do. It!" She enunciated. "Perhaps this is why that woman from the atrium left you; because you're a fucking spineless prick."

Korbin's jaw dropped. Rising out of my seat, I strode to stand in front of her. I tossed the mouse over my shoulder, hearing it *thunk* to the ground. Hadley did not break eye contact with me. Instead, she doubled down, puffing up and rising on her toes.

The chain around her neck rattled. The bracelet I had stupidly given back to her glowed like fire in her hands. Lashing out, I grabbed her by the collar, lifting her off the ground until her feet dangled and kicked. She gasped for air, the magic continuing to glow.

"I'll follow through, *little witch*," I growled, my fangs elongating.

"You," she choked, sucking in a hard gasp. "Better!"

She swung her feet up to kick me in the chest. Already having played that game with her, I flung her back toward Korbin. She skidded across the ground, crashing into the corner of the bookcase with her broken wrist tucked under her. The collar on her neck cracked.

Hadley smirked, pulling at the collar. The iron lock rattled. Magic, vibrant red, swirled in the palms of her hands. The bracelet she had exploded in her right hand, cutting her fingers. Shards of stone and glass erupted all over my office, breaking some of my antiques.

"I might be scared of what I am, terrified of what I know I can do," she raggedly breathed. The collar clattered to the floor at her feet. "But at least I can follow through when it calls for it."

"So can I," I growled, shifting.

I launched at her, grabbing her by the waist. She attempted to skirt around me to where her mouse lay against the wall. I sunk my claws into her, eliciting a scream. Hadley attempted to drag me along with her feeble march toward her pet. I laughed, further digging my nails into her supple flesh.

I grabbed her right side, just under her rib cage and spun her around. Her backside pressed into me. Swirling magic entered my body, making my arm heat intensely, though it was not enough to force me to let go. Hadley writhed in pain as I sunk my fingers in deeper and pushed her head to the side.

"I can follow through too," I purred in her ear.

"Prove it," she gulped.

I hovered over her neck, feeling her pulse quicken. Her heartbeat made the vein in her neck pulsate rhythmically. She stilled in my arms, her body turning somewhat limp. Blood dripped down her body, forming a small puddle at her feet.

Pushing her neck further to the side, I hovered over her goose pimpled flesh and bit, putting force behind my bite to hear her whimper. Hadley went limp in my arms as I fed on her blood. With the collar gone, her blood was even richer, creamier, full-bodied like wine but still something more. I tasted the same heady flavors of sage and iron, but whatever she was, it was a magnificent smoky, blackberry whiskey type of zest.

I forced myself to pull off before I truly killed her. She was right though; I wasn't about to let her die. This witch was enigmatic.

"Lord Zygrath," Korbin called from the door.

Glancing over, I finally noticed the phone pressed against Korbin's chest. I laid Hadley on the floor and shifted, quickly straightening my attire. Korbin handed me the cell phone and a napkin.

"This is Brooks," I answered, wiping off my face.

"Brooks," Keres purred on the other end. "I'm waiting."

I peeked over my shoulder, staring at her pale, limp form on the ground. Her blood made wet spots on her black dress prominent and stained my Aubusson rug. Her hair frizzed everywhere, standing on end even in the ponytail from all the static. Freckles danced from one pale cheek to the next. I swiped a hand over my face and looked away.

"I'm still hunting," I hissed, turning away from Hadley. "So, wait," I finished ending the call.

I flipped the phone back to Korbin. "Stick her in her room."

"What about the iron collar?"

"Leave it off."

"Lord," Korbin began skeptically.

"Leave it off," I commanded, going out my office door.

Twenty-Two

Hadley

I wiped a hand over my face. My heart felt heavy. My entire body felt heavy, and sore. Opening an eye, dark shadows pranced across the dark green wall. The faint light of the moon coupled with the bars on the windows made me groan.

Sitting up, I checked myself over. The cast on my left hand was a different color now, though it was a bit too dark for me to tell. I rubbed a hand over my neck, feeling it was devoid of that horrid collar, instead sporting a bandage.

"Eww," I moaned, remembering Brooks feeding on me.

The memory made me shiver. Groaning, I got out of bed and plodded to the bathroom. The light came on automatically upon me entering the room. I flinched at the bright lights. Squinting, I noted a black t-shirt covering my upper body. Hesitantly, I lifted the shirt, seeing fresh bandages cover my abdomen. The orange cast on my left hand was vibrant. My hair was still in a messy ponytail that was slowly falling out.

"Aysel?" I called out and waited.

Nothing answered me.

"Aysel?" I tried again.

I tested the connection of our souls, seeing them attached with an amethyst chord. Biting my bottom lip, I went on the search for her. The light to my bedroom came on. I ripped the sheets off the bed, turned the pillows inside out. I ransacked the room, calling for my beloved familiar.

Aysel, I called again. *Come on, you're freaking me out!*

You're freaked out? She quipped back. *I'm in a black bag that smells like dirt!*

Where are you?

Gee, I dunno, she snapped. *Buried somewhere.*

I'm sorry. I'm sorry. Give me a moment, I placated.

Sitting down in the middle of the room, I crossed my legs. I rolled the magic in my hands over the other until the crackling orange orb I created rattled in my hands. Closing my eyes, I envisioned a silver string emerging from my heart and penetrating the orb. In my mind's eye, the silver string formed a loop inside the magic orb, where I pictured Aysel inside that loop.

What was lost, is now found,
As my magic circles round.
Whether you are hidden far or near,

I call you now to come meet me here.

Aysel formed inside the loop. I held out my hands and ended the spell. Opening my eyes, Aysel laid on her back, breathing laboriously.

Thank the Goddess Above that worked, she huffed.

I cried, bringing her up to my cheek to snuggle. *I'm so happy to see you. I love you!*

I love you too but, ugh! How can you stand to hug me? I smell so bad! she squeaked. *And we need to leave. Brooks found out what you are.*

I'll pee then we'll leave.

Pee later!

Ignoring her, I hurried to the bathroom and relieved myself. I wasn't going to hold it and hope for the best. Hurrying back out, I went to the closet and scrounged around for jeans. The only thing in the closet was a black short-sleeved dress with a fitted corset, so I grabbed it, quickly getting dressed.

Fuck the shoes, I told Aysel. *We need to go.*

I can help. Your energy is sapped.

I feel so drained, yet electrified. I don't know why I feel so... icky. Like all my nerves are frazzled. I can feel my magic, summon it, but it feels so chaotic.

Because that creep ate you! Aysel squeaked, sticking out her tongue.

I paused, staring at her. *That was cute!*

Now's not the time!

Smiling at having her back, I picked her up and stuck her in my hair. I fixed the bed, putting it back together to resemble my sleeping form. Using magic, I spelled the bed to rise and fall like I was still asleep.

I carefully tip-toed to the door, using magic to mask my scent, magic, and movement. I let out a long breath, feeling even more drained. Every time I used magic since Brooks fed off me, I felt even more lethargic.

The door opened slowly inward. I pressed my back against the opposite wall, poking my head out to see if anyone lingered. With the coast clear, I carefully creeped out into the open. The mansion was eerily quiet. Moonlight softly filtered in through skylights in the ceiling and from windows.

Padding down the hallway, I turned to the right and crept down the stairs to the main level. Voices sounded from the right. I ducked on the other side of the stairwell, hiding beneath the railing.

The beautiful raven-haired woman I glimpsed earlier strode down the steps with an ugly, jowl-jawed man on her arm. My jaw hit the floor.

Holy Goddess that's Senna! I said to Aysel.

Isn't that your half-sister?

Yes, but I don't claim that nasty. I replied, glaring as she walked blissfully past me.

Why is she nasty?

She's really mean. She stole a lot of my things. But anyway, she bound herself to the coven then clearly mated with a vampire. It's not that it's not allowed, but if I'm going to break an oath to my coven for a man of any species, he better be kind, compassionate, as well as decent to look at.

He aged like an avocado, Aysel giggled.

I quickly clapped a hand over my mouth to keep myself from sputtering with laughter. Once they were out of view, I skated along the wall toward what I remembered to be the outside. Turning the corner, I noted the door to Brooks's office on my right. I went toward it, silently crossing the open marble floor to get there.

What are you doing? Aysel cried.

Snooping for answers as to what the vampires are doing.

Who cares what the answer is!

I want to know... For leverage purposes.

Carefully, I opened his office door and crept inside. The smell of cleaner hit my senses first. His desk sat in the middle of the room with two black chairs in front of this enormous oak desk. A floor to ceiling bookcase was behind the desk. I tip-toed behind the desk, spying my backpack underneath. I snatched it, flinging it over my shoulder.

I flipped through his notes, looking for any familiar names or anything to give me an indication about myself being hunted or what was to be gained from my death. I saw nothing. Grumbling under my breath, I continued to rummage through his desk.

A map was at the very bottom of the pile. Wiggling it out, the entire map of Quivleren had circles and triangles in different areas. From where the circles were, I deduced they were wolf packs. The Nashoba pack near Kadia castle had a circle with an 'X' through the middle of it. A gold star on the westside of Quivleren, to the west of Aiolos signified where I happened to be.

They must be wanting to go to war again, I said to Aysel.

Do you think it has anything to do with you?

It's possible depending on what Keres promised Brooks.

I set the map down, tucking it back under his giant messy pile of papers. Carefully, I pulled out the upper right drawer, wincing when it squealed.

"I'm surprised it took you this long to attempt to leave," Brooks quipped.

My head snapped up, seeing Brooks in the cushioned seat in front of his desk. A smug smile split his face. Korbin and the other guy who had locked me in my room before were stationed on either side of the door. Straightening, I said nothing. I didn't make a move to leave. Their fast reflexes would have me caught before I took two steps anyway.

"Wanna tell me what's in your blood?" he asked, strumming his fingers nonchalantly on the arm of the chair.

"What do you think I am?" I shot back.

"Well," he huffed, rising from his chair and pacing. "I know you're not a wolf, bear, or vampire. You're definitely not an elf. They haven't been seen since the Hell Wars. Same with a lion. Nor a faerie," he said pointedly. Brooks stopped his pacing, staring straight at me. "Perhaps you're a dragon?"

My insides quivered. I forced myself to keep a straight and passive face. I felt myself crumbling. Crossing my arms over my chest, I cocked my hip out.

"That's an interesting theory," I replied nonchalantly.

Brooks strode up to me, the smug grin widening on his face. I backed up to the bookcase, magic swirling in my hands to make a quick getaway. I glanced down at my feet, ready to whip my hands around, cast, and skedaddle to Aiolos.

He towered over me, lifting my chin to meet his eyes. "It's not a theory, sweetie."

"So, what's your plan?" I stuttered.

He shrugged. "To keep you."

Bringing my hands around, I pushed him away. Brooks flew back across the room, smacking into the door and hitting the frame with his head. The other two sprinted toward me. I brought my magic close to my body, forming a tight ball. I put all my fury into it until I felt it crackling against the constraints. I chucked the magic at them, grinning as it exploded in front of them, launching the two vampires backward. Korbin crashed into Brooks while the other one went straight through the wall, skidding across the marble floor.

Bringing the magic around, I compressed it into a tight ball, forming a triangle in the middle. I thought of the old historic bookstore I went to when I passed through on my way to Nukpana. Brooks got to his feet, shaking his head clear.

"Hadley," he called out, his voice cracking.

"Fuck off," I snarled, casting the magic and stepping through.

Twenty-Three

Brooks

S peeding over to her, I crossed through her portal
before it had the chance to fully close. Tall bookcases
surrounded me. The musty smell of leather and paper
made my nose crinkle. I craned my neck back, seeing
old wood beam ceilings where single yellow bulbs dangled from to cast an ambient cozy glow. Wall sconces on
the old brick walls afforded more soft light to maneuver
through the stacks, piles, and shelves of books.

I followed Hadley stealthily as she perused the
books. Other vampires from my coven read in a nook
in the dark corner of the bookstore. A vermillion eyed

dragon puffed on a long pipe, sending the smoke out through his nostrils in a perfect ring to filter up toward the ceiling. My brow puckered, keeping a wary eye on him.

Turning a corner, I peered out the window into the night beyond. Rain softly pelted the led framed glass. Old gas-lit streetlamps flickered light out on the cobblestone streets. Old styled carved signs bounced in the wind.

Aiolos, I thought, rolling my eyes. *Of course she picks here.* It was the only place in Quivleren that still looked old and untouched by modern things.

Hadley's red hair and quick movement caught my attention. Already, she was purposefully striding toward a different section, perusing the labeled bookcases. I followed her from a distance, watching her fingers lightly brush against the leather spines. Finding one she liked, she plucked it from the shelf and whipped it open.

"Hold it right there, *witch*," the male dragon librarian huffed from behind the counter. His vermillion eyes narrowed on Hadley, scales already bristling across his skin.

Fuck, I mumbled under my breath.

"I'm just looking at it," Hadley sweetly replied.

"I know," he snarled. "That's the problem. You're gonna just *read* a snippet then not buy it."

Hadley groaned, shoving the book in place. "Have a good day," she flippantly answered.

I smirked, watching her go toward the door. I stopped at the book she was looking at, tilting my head to the side to read the spine. *Fundamentals of Spirit Magic.* My eyes narrowed, wondering why she would need that book. Isn't all magic the same for a witch?

The door to the bookstore rattled open. Hadley yelped as the wind whipped her hair around. I grabbed the book, slapping it on the counter.

"How much?" I asked, grabbing my wallet.

"Two gold pieces," the librarian demanded, tapping a wrinkled finger on the cover.

I tossed the money on the counter. The dragon grumbled, his vermillion eyes closing in on me. Smoke wisped out of his nostrils. He cracked his neck to the side, flashing me his bright green scales as a warning. I yawned, displaying my fangs. The guy slowly scraped the money off the counter while sliding the book toward me.

"Good luck," he nodded toward the door and sniggered.

I tucked the book under my arm, going toward the door. Hadley walked under the covered awnings of the buildings, heading steadily north. She hugged herself against the building to avoid the tempest outside, shoulders hunched, and arms crossed.

"Hadley," I called.

Her body rigidly stopped. "Please," her voice begged, "just leave me alone."

The orange magic in her hands fizzled like the dying of a pathetic fire. She leaned against the cold brick building as her attempt at magic faded. Dark circles lined her eyes, made more prominent by the yellow glow of streetlamps and the building lights lining the sidewalk.

"Not until you tell me what you are."

"What does it even matter?" she asked exasperated.

She put a hand to her forehead, giving a breathing laugh that turned into more tears. I heavily sighed, fed up with the tears. At every turn, she cried; though I noticed she never cried for herself, more for others or for her situation. Still, tears solved nothing.

She wiped her face, folding her arms further over herself. She moved closer against the building to avoid the rain. Hadley quivered under the awning. The short-sleeved dress and knee-high length of it did nothing to give her warmth. Even the backpack offered her nothing. I handed her the book and began taking off my dress shirt. The rain pelted my bare skin, but I didn't notice. Hadley scowled at my proffered shirt, then deepened the look at me.

"Keres promised me Toan Castle," I offered.

A slow smile split her face. A rumble of laughter erupted out of her. "*Oh. My. Goddess.* I was wrong in calling you a dumbass—"

"Thank you," I smugly interrupted.

Hadley kept chortling. "You're a word beyond a dumbass. In fact, it's like you're a super duper one. A gigantic dumbass!"

I crossed my arms over my chest, still holding out my shirt to her with a finger. Hadley scoffed, taking a step back from me. I took several steps toward her, closing the distance between us where our noses were almost touching. She let the book fall as magic swirled vibrant orange in her hands, holding me where I was.

"I will kill you," she breathed.

"You're not strong enough to."

"But I am."

I leaned down, my lips hovering just above her ear. "Then what's stopping you?"

She swallowed. Her heart rate fluttered wildly. I smiled, leaning back from her. While her eyes were locked on mine, I grasped her right wrist. Hadley attempted to wrench it away, but I held her fast.

"You've never killed a thing before, have you?"

"Leave me alone," she whispered.

The brokenness of her plea caught me off guard. Even now, after all the hassle of attempting to escape, she didn't want to use her power. She didn't want to fight. She was demure even in her words, there was a feisty zing to her that eventually fizzled out. Every interaction we've had, she refused to speak, refused to use her power. Back at the underground hovel, she didn't want to hurt me. She only wanted to escape.

I glanced down at her thin arm. My hand easily wrapped itself around her right wrist. Her entire body was lithe, save for the voluminousness of her hair. Her bright blue eyes stared into mine, silently pleading with me to let her go. I wouldn't. She was intriguing to me. Every witch I had previously encountered, including Senna, loved the chance to flaunt their magic, their special capabilities. This witch wanted me to kill her, didn't want me to know what she was or of her capabilities. It made me curious about her and part of me was irked by it solely because of what she was.

"You never answered my question," I finally said, bending over and picking up the book. I tucked the item behind me, shoving it down my back and halfway into my pants so my hands would be free.

She huffed lethargically. "Which one?"

"How were you able to be caught so easily?"

She stamped her foot impatiently. Her open gaze turned into a simmering glower. "There are spells for protection against all paranormals in Quivleren. I didn't have the one I needed against vampires. And since my mother negotiated terms between our species, I never thought twice about it."

"Look who's the dumbass now."

"Oh no, you still have me beat," she quipped.

I peeked over her head. Several wolves ahead watched our interaction. A tall, dark-haired male took several steps in our direction. I grabbed hold of her wrist again; keeping a firm grip, I twirled her around to be on my left. I tucked her arm inside mine and began leading us up the sidewalk where Hadley was originally going. Unfortunately, it would lead past the mutts.

"What are you–"

"Just walk with me," I whispered, holding onto her arm. "The mutts are watching you."

She leaned on me. Her legs wobbled with each step. I kept my pace at a slow shuffle, enough for her to keep in stride. I wrapped my other arm around her torso, holding her close to me. The thrum of her body sent tendrils of warmth through me.

"They're a much better option compared to my current company."

"They'd take you directly to Keres."

"As will you," she shot back.

"I will not," I said firmly. "I give you my word."

Hadley venomously giggled, wrenching out of my grapes completely. "Your word means *nothing* to me."

I sighed, ranking a hand through my hair, and pushing it back. A strand of hair caught on my signet ring. Realizing my bargaining chip, I wriggled the ring off my finger. Turning slightly, I kept her back with the wolves and their green-eyed stare, so I could keep an eye on them. Two of the three had dispersed while one nonchalantly waited on a bench seat outside of a hostel.

"Here," I said, handing the ring to her. "This will give you protection from vampires."

I held out my hand, waiting for her to take it. She didn't twitch a muscle. Mumbling under my breath about her stubbornness, I took her right hand and slid it onto her pointer finger.

"And what is *this* supposed to do?"

"The ring of my blood kin has been passed down for generations. It is a well-known object, as each true blood family has a certain ring. Only true bloods are given a signet ring. So," I paused, putting my hands in my pockets, "if you are in trouble or in need of protection, you may go to any coven, and it will be given without question."

"Where's the caveat?"

"Help me get Toan Castle from Keres."

"And I get to keep your ring forever?"

"Yes."

"And you won't eat me?"

"No one will eat you so long as you wear the ring. You'll have infinite protection."

Hadley nodded, gently using her casted left hand to shove the ring further on her finger. "Why are you being so amiable? Why now?"

I shrugged. "I find you interesting. Plus, I would rather fry Keres's ass as opposed to giving her what she wants. I never cared for her. I only cared for what she promised me." I finished, holding out my shirt.

She shrugged off her backpack and took the shirt, wriggling it on. The dress shirt, what minimal warmth it truly offered, dwarfed her body. She pulled her hair out of the back of the shirt then held her hand up by her head. The little mouse climbed in her hand. Hadley stuck it in my dress shirt pocket.

"Tell it not to pee in there," I said disgustedly, throwing her backpack over my shoulder.

Hadley shrugged. "I told her to take a big shit."

I yanked the book out of my jeans, handing it to her. She took it slowly, arching a brow at me, then at the book.

"Come with me back to the mansion," I said, offering her my hand.

"Why?"

"Well, for starters, there's food, warmth, a bath, bed, and I'll get you warmer clothes," I paused, watching her frizzy hair soak up the rain. "And a hairbrush."

"Then what?"

I shrugged. "I dunno, sleep, eat, then help me plan."

She crossed her arms, taking several steps back from me. Hadley peered down at the mouse poking its tiny head out of the pocket of my shirt. The mouse squeaked at her, its beady black eyes glaring at her before it shot back into the dress pocket, angrily tittering.

"She's mad at you," I breathily chortled.

She pushed wet hair off her face. "It's because I'm full of terrible decisions."

"Oh?"

"Taking my chances with you instead of the wolves, for starters."

"I'm safer."

"No, you're not. You've proven that tenfold already. Only a coward hurts a species weaker than them."

I winced at her jab. "Then why are you coming?"

"You've ruined my house, so there's no way I can go home; not until I have everything I need to replace all the spells and barriers. I have nowhere else to go, no other witch to turn to. And you were truthful when you said you didn't care for Keres. If Keres used you to get to me, there's no telling what else she's done. So, for now, you're the slightly better option."

"Then let's go," I stated, my tone hardening.

I held out my hand, waiting for her to take it. She did so apprehensively, holding her fingers above the palm of my hand. The mistrustful glare in her eyes could almost burn a hole through me. Using what little magic I had, I teleported us both back to the mansion, standing on the landing of the stairs to go up. The house was devoid of anyone. Nothing but clouded moonlight and rain made itself known.

"Do you remember the way to your room?"

"I'll manage," she replied, ire lacing her tone.

She wrenched her backpack off my shoulder and slapped it over hers; the force knocked her forward. I caught her in my arms and steadied her, then carefully backed away. The bags under her eyes became more prominent in the moonlight.

I nodded, turning on my heel to go back to my office. I turned my head slightly, watching her doggedly make her way up the stairs. The chattering of her mouse brought a smile to my lips. Whatever telepathic conversation they were having, I was certain it was a heated one. Hadley turned to the left once she reached the top of the stairs. Her narrowed eyes shot daggers at me. She straightened her spine, tilting her chin up defiantly.

I continued the path to my office. "Go to sleep, little witch," I called up to her.

Her upper lip curled at me, giving her this cute, angry, fluffy cat look with the way her hair frizzed. She turned on her heel, storming away. I breathily laughed. Rounding the corner, I opened my office door.

Having her here was certainly a bargaining chip against Keres; one I would fully exploit. I promised she'd be safe against vampires, not anyone else. The thought of turning her over to anyone else didn't sit well with me.

Dragging my feet, I strode to my desk, took a seat, and kicked my feet up on the polished wood desktop.

"What the fuck?" I groaned, sinking into the chair.

How one woman could get under my skin by her pathetically cute defiance, her basic uncommunicative quips, was beyond me. Part of me wanted to fully eat her while the other wanted to get to know her to see what made her brain tick. I wanted to see how I could use her to my advantage, if I could at all. I wanted to know what kind of powers she had, what she could do that made her so afraid of herself, yet desired by everyone else.

I huffed a laugh, thinking of the multiple times she could have overpowered me but chose to run away. She was correct in saying she was terrified of what she knew she could do. That part was horrifically clear. But she constantly hesitated in following through. She only did something just enough to get away. I rubbed my chin, itching at the scruffy stubble coming in. *She must be part dragon*, I surmised. *It's the only logical explanation to why she's constantly running.*

"Why is that witch back here and wearing your ring?" Eckard asked, striding up to my desk and plopping himself in the chair on the left. "I saw her in the hallway, trying to find her way back to her room."

My head snapped up from thinking about her origin. "We came to an accord. And she's wearing my ring because I told her it would protect her."

Eckard laughed. "You like her."

"Did she find her room?" I asked, ignoring him.

"Yeah. I took her there, then came straight here."

Korbin strode in, directing the humans he brought to start repairs on what was broken.

"What's the accord?" Eckard broached.

"She gets to live so long as she helps us get Toan Castle."

Korbin took the other seat in front of my desk. "Then afterward?"

I shrugged. "Depends on how helpful she is."

Korbin shook his head, leaning back into the seat. "Senna ruined you."

Swiping a hand over my face, I leaned further back in my seat. Senna didn't ruin me. She taught me that no witch could be trusted. She purred promises in my ear while stabbing a knife in my back. She painted pictures of a wonderful life that included us and a family, then destroyed everything. *I want love. I want a content life. You promised me the world and lied, so Rezon gave me what you never could,* Senna seethed at me the night I proposed. I closed my eyes, clenching my hands at the memory. Senna didn't ruin me. She just made me realize that no woman, witch or not, is worth the headache or heartache of trying to build anything with.

"She made you angrier," Korbin added.

I snorted, shaking my head. "Stop," I growled, getting up from my desk. "Have the Elders decided yet?"

"You've never been like this, even to other prisoners," Korbin pressed, leaning forward in his seat. "You dispatched everyone else without playing around like a cat does to a mouse, but not with Hadley. Why is she so different?"

"She's a witch, so it's different," I grit out, hardening my tone.

"No, it's not," Korbin boomed, striding out of the room.

Ignoring him, I looked directly at Eckard.

"No, they're currently in a meeting," Eckard offered, tentatively glancing between us.

I nodded, leaving the comfort of my office for the deplorable insipid meeting.

Twenty-Four

Hadley

*W*hy *don't you just climb down a wolf's throat next time,* Aysel seethed. *We finally got away, only to come right back! What the fuck, Hadley!*

I angrily paced in front of the bed. I flexed my hands, drawing what minimal magic I had and forcing it to dissipate. Exhaustion begged me to climb into the sheets and sleep, but I refused. I was just as furious with myself as Aysel was. However, there was nowhere I could run to, not without being found and not without certain items for setting barriers and protection. Dammit all, it took me two months to finally find a dead virgin that wasn't decayed beyond use.

Plus, I couldn't go back to my house. The barriers were more than likely destroyed thanks to Brooks and his minions. And if I went back home, I had a feeling the local mutt pack would be on my scent before I even had a chance to set one barrier. No witch would dare help me and risk the wrath of Keres. And if that nasty old toad killed the Supreme of Willow Coven, then they wouldn't help me either as Keres would be merging covens. I was stuck, ultimately and devastatingly stuck.

Flopping myself down on the bed, I stared at the ceiling, counting the individual tiles. My mother's words replayed in my head like annoying static, reminding me to dry my tears and to stand. I had been standing, albeit not very well. I never cared for violence. I never desired to harm anyone or anything. I didn't want someone else's blood on my hands. Ending a life out of anger or hate didn't appeal to me. And I didn't want the being's soul to be stuck to mine. If I ever was to kill someone, my compassionate nature would be super glue to the person I slaughtered, leaving me stuck with their soul until I passed. The thought made me shiver. *Screw that.* Dealing with myself was enough. I didn't care to be trapped with another's soul.

I rubbed my hands over my face, trying to clear my eyes and thoughts of how hopelessly stupid I could be. I didn't feel entirely dumb. I couldn't stop myself from getting captured at the Kadia Ruins or tortured by Brooks. I was overpowered and outnumbered in every situation. But coming back definitely felt illogical even though my reasoning was sound. It still made me feel dumb.

Brooks is a safer bet for right now, I reiterated for the sixth time.

He tried to kill you. And he ate you twice!

I touched the bandage on the side of my neck. Shivers ran up my spine. The way his hot breath brushed against my skin, how his fangs penetrated my flesh, and his lips clamped over it all, made me feel disgusted. I felt violated by the way he held me firmly where I couldn't even get away. The way he gently tilted my head and held me when I became too weak to stand. Not even my magic could get him to stop. Every slurp of blood made me feel lethargic until I finally crumbled.

I crossed my arms over my chest. *I know... I just don't know what else to do. If the wolves are hunting me, it's only a matter of time before others do too. Keres will keep increasing the price on my head until she has me. But since I secured myself with the vampires, that's one fewer species to worry about. Plus, I don't have any spells of protection against vampires. Keres has those. So, for now, unfortunately, he is the safer bet. I'm too drained to teleport away. I need a place to safely recoup and regroup.*

I know. I'm tired and drained too. It's just, she paused, brushing her whiskers. *I'm just scared Hadley,* Aysel sat on her haunches and pouted. *I'm scared of losing you. And you're right. We can't go home, and we can't really run anywhere.*

You won't lose me. I sat up on the bed, craning my neck side to side until it popped. *I'm going to head to his office. Care to come with me?*

Aysel nodded, standing up on her hind legs. *Yes. Don't you ever leave me alone again.*

I smiled, picking her up and setting her on my head. *I promise.*

Thank you, she sniffed. *Why are you going to his office?*

Research on Toan Castle. If I'm to help him claim it, then I need information. Plus, the more I know, the more I can exploit.

I like the way you think.

Oh, now you do, I quipped, heading out the door.

The first rays of dawn were blooming, slowly forcing the black to turn to light gray. I carefully poked my head out the door, glancing both ways before I took the wary step outside the minimal safety of my room. The world beyond my four walls had yet to begin breathing. Nothing stirred.

Cautiously, I tip-toed barefoot down the hallway. Between escaping hours ago till now, I'd yet to acquire shoes, though it didn't bother me. I disliked shoes anyway. I snuck down the carpeted steps, turning to the right.

The doors above my head snapped open, omitting various heated voices. I paused at the bottom of the landing, spying several male vampires exit and turn immediately right. A pair of them lingered on the landing, one making a move to descend. The raucous yelling overtook the mansion until the doors slammed shut. Before they could spot me, I kept moving toward Brooks's office.

"What are you doing?"

My head snapped in the direction of the voice. I deflated a little when I saw Korbin. I crossed my arms over my body, flaunting the ring on my right hand. "Heading to Brook's office to read," I replied, continuing my path to his office.

Korbin nodded, following me. I moved away from him when he got close enough to brush my arm. I hugged the wall, turning the corner to make a beeline to his office. Workers hovered in and outside the office repairing the wall I sent a vampire through. Korbin dashed ahead of me, getting the door before I had the chance to get there.

"What book are you looking for?" Korbin broached.

"What happened to Toan after the Hell War and possibly a book about it prior to?"

"There really isn't a book about it. But I can tell you."

I walked to the back of the office space, keeping an ample distance from Korbin and everyone else. My eyes were riveted to the right side of the bookcase.

"Any information is helpful," I replied, reaching for a book about the area of Scirwode Forest.

Korbin came up beside me, getting the book down. "Toan Castle is on the very eastern cusp of Scirwode."

I nodded, stepping away from him. A small, polished worktable hugged the wall several steps behind me. A legal pad of paper and pen rested on top. Taking the book from Korbin, I went to the table and took a seat at the end.

"Are you hungry?"

"Why are you being kind?" I finally snapped.

Part of me felt terrible about not keeping the irritation from my voice. Korbin had always been amiable out of all of them. Even if he hurt me too, there was remorse in his voice that Brooks didn't have. Korbin sighed, taking a seat across from me. Ignoring him, I opened the book and quickly scanned the table of contents for anything useful.

"I'll bring you back something," he said, rising from his seat.

I wearily eyed him. "Thank you."

He nodded, hanging his head. His dark brown hair hung in his grayish-silver eyes. "I'm sorry," he whispered, heading out the door.

I watched him leave to ensure I would be left alone. The workers' impact drills and low mumbled responses to each other were the only noise I cared to listen to. Going back to my book, I opened to where a map was neatly folded in the middle. Carefully, I unfolded it. The beautiful script handwriting and delicate care to note the forest surroundings with the rare flora and fauna brought a smile to my face.

Snails Tooth, Aysel said, crawling out of my hair and down my arm. *We need to go there to collect it.*

I agree. It would be good to have it. Snails Tooth is perfect to imbue a protection spell against wolves.

It's also good against vampires, she giddily added, rising on her haunches.

Look over here, I said, pointing to an area on the map. *The note on the side says this area has Brain Bark along with Screaming Roots down in the holler. Brain Bark is an excellent plant against vampires.*

Oh, it is, she agreed. *We must figure out how to get there.*

I watched her small black eyes scan every bit of the map, committing it to memory. Aysel was much more proficient at remembering maps and places than I was. Setting the map to the side, I continued reading about how Toan's exterior was set up. The castle had ramparts going all the way around the exterior, while four postern walls housed a small corner building with arrow slits. This place was built to fortify and protect. If Keres utilized this to her advantage, it would be difficult to get inside. I quickly scanned the next few pages, searching for another entry point into the castle. If I could find it, then I could give this information to Brooks and go on about my life without being on the hook to him.

"After the Hell War," Korbin said, retaking his previous seat and setting down a tray.

He pushed a plate of pancakes, eggs, and bacon in front of me. Korbin set a small dish of diced carrots and strawberries down for Aysel to the side of the map. A steaming teapot sat on the tray with various options like cream, sugar, and honey.

I glanced up at him, arching a speculative brow. It took everything in me not to be cruel. I was angry and hurt; and just all-around fucking pissed. Now that I had a ring on my finger promising me protection, it was like their nice button had been turned on.

"After the Hell War," he continued, ignoring my look, "alpha Evander Akselsen used Toan Castle as a pack house, putting all wolves under one roof. One solitary pack was the first of its kind in centuries. Prior to, it was the Moon Walkers as one pack versus the smaller outlying packs. But one pack simply cannot last. A couple of decades ago, the pack split. Evander remained at Toan until a few years ago, when he took the wolves loyal to him and went east beyond the Chay Forest, previously housing faeries. The rest formed their sub packs like the ones who captured you."

"Interesting," I replied, finishing my eggs.

"Before we could infiltrate Toan and finish off the remaining wolves, we were met with witches and their dragon allies," Brooks added, pulling up a chair on my left.

Bristling, I stayed where I was. Unfortunately for me, I was now stuck between the two of them. I tucked into the rest of my food, side-eye glaring at Brooks. He leaned back in the chair, giving me his stupid smirk. I rolled my eyes.

Brooks leaned toward me. "We were overrun before we ever got started."

"What took you so long to start?" I shot back.

"It takes seven out of nine coven leaders to come to a major decision on anything like whether or not to attack a wolf pack, or how to train our small military."

I nodded, finishing my food. Aysel laid down on the table, her legs kicked out at the sides. I smiled warmly, stroking her soft fur. Out of all the chaos, I was thrilled to have her alive and by my side.

"Hot tea?" Korbin asked.

"Please."

"She looks content," Brooks said, pointing to her.

I only nodded. I didn't care to speak with him. His presence irked me. The way he smiled, thinking he was all cute, made my entire body flare in irritation. He was a cruel, arrogant ass. There was torture for the sake of it being torture, where it did not deviate from being cruel. Then there was what Brooks did. His emotional, manipulative abuse, physical, mental, all of it, was torture in its most hateful form. He took sadistic pleasure in seeing me crumble. This nasty bloodsucker was cruel and hateful, yet he was still the better option than Keres. *I think that's what vexes me the most,* I decided.

Brooks leaned forward, elbows on his knees, and hands clasped. "Any questions?"

"When are you leaving?"

"This is my office."

"You can still leave."

"I kinda like it here."

"I've had quite enough of you."

Korbin fixed my tea, adding a touch of cream and sugar. I never had it prepared that way, usually opting for honey if I added anything at all.

"Thank you."

"Well," Brooks said, rising from his seat. "I'll be over here, *not* leaving, working at my desk."

I snorted derisively, shaking my head. I went back to my book, rereading a section about the foundation of the castle. So far, I discovered the stone foundation was several feet thick with no breaks in the floor for underground passage. The southwestern side of the castle housed a garden area with a tall metal fence spelled to keep animals and others out. The discovery made me grin.

I reread the section, noting the spells used. Out of seven distinct spells, there was one I had not heard of. I reached over my teacup for the pen and paper, quickly drawing out the garden area the book described.

"What are you doing?" Korbin asked.

"One second, please," I whispered.

I noted the points where the spells were said to have been cast. "Interesting," I whispered. "Each spell had been cast three times. Each spell was then linked to the other three times."

What did you find? Aysel said, clambering on top of my hand.

I think I found a loophole. But I definitely found something suspicious.

I kept reading, noting the two protection spells, three healing spells, and one strong warding against evil spell; all done in three, but the seventh one threw me off. I've never heard of the Demilune Trifecta spell. With a demilune being a crescent shape, a half a moon which also has two points, and a trifecta being the power of three, then combined equaling the power of five.

I scowled at the paper. *If the demilune trifecta equals five, plus the seven spells, that makes eleven. But what does eleven mean?*

Divine, Aysel answered.

Divine?

Divine, Aysel stated absolutely. *You know, divine,* she said, making her voice go up and down like human kids do about spooky ghosts. *Like the Goddess.*

"Like the Goddess!" I shouted.

"What does three mean?" Korbin whispered, pointing to my scribbling.

I glanced at him and screamed, not having seen Brooks standing beside Korbin. Brooks leaned against the wall, crossing one leg over the other. His chocolate hair was now slicked back off his head. His attire changed from his previous black suit to a navy blue. Korbin pushed his mop of dark brown hair off his head and held it there, staring intently at me.

"I believe I may have found your way inside Toan Castle," I replied, turning the book around so he could see the garden area. "To answer your question, three is a powerful number for a witch."

"Why?" Brooks asked. "It's just a number."

I shook my head. "It's not *just* a number. Did Senna not tell you anything?"

Brooks blanched at the mention of her name. "How do you know her?" he snarled.

"Easy bat boy."

"I prefer bat man."

"*Pfft,* yeah," I giggled condescendingly. "Anyway, most witches use the power of three or three-fold law. Whatever energy is put out, whether negative or positive, it is thus returned to the witch in three-fold strength. Although, to reap the benefits of this, one must do whatever they're doing with sincerity of heart, otherwise, it will backfire."

I paused, waiting to see if they were following. Korbin nodded, his eyes wide. Brooks continued to scowl at me, crossing his arms over his chest.

Brooks leaned over, pointing to my drawing. "I don't understand how you found a way inside using a damn number."

"I don't understand–"

The door to his office opened. The other asshole of the group stepped inside, gently shutting the door behind him. Aysel scurried up my arm, embedding herself into my hair. I got up from the table, snatching the book, map, and drawing.

"Lord Zygrath," he addressed.

"What is it?" Brooks snapped.

"Keres is here."

I gasped, finding it hard to breathe. Tears stung my eyes, falling down my cheeks on their own accord. My heart thundered in my chest. Anger roiled through me.

All his promises of being safe and protected were nothing but a damned lie. I tucked the book and pad of paper under my arm.

"What the fuck," I yelled, magic jolting in my hands.

I cast it, holding him in place. I lifted him into the air, squeezing my right hand tight to hold him while my left hand was free to manipulate his body.

Brooks struggled, kicking his feet. "Hadley," he choked. "Stop. I didn't know. I swear–"

"Bullshit," I seethed, clenching my left hand to close around his throat.

"Tell Keres it will be a moment," Korbin shouted over his shoulder. "Hadley, he didn't know. He was in a meeting since he brought you back."

"Fucking bullshit!" I cry-snarled, tightening my hold on Brooks. Releasing my clenched left hand, I used my magic to force his left hand out to his side. "You all keep *fucking* with me because you think I'm weak or stupid, or easily manipulated."

I forced his left hand to snap backward. Brooks winced; mouth agape as he tried to breathe. Bringing my left hand up, I pushed the magic outward, forcing his elbow backward until it cracked.

"I swear... I didn't know she was coming," Brooks yelped. He gasped, sucking in a lungful of air. Compressing my magic together with my hands, I forced the air out of his lungs. "Hadley," he choked. "I'll take you somewhere safe."

"We'll protect you," Korbin said, striding toward me with his hands out. "I promise. You're wearing the ring. We *will* protect you from her. Brooks didn't know she was coming. He was in a meeting all night. I swear."

I threw him against the bookcase across the room and released my magic. Brooks dropped to the ground, sputtering for breath. I strode up to him, kicking him square in the chest as hard as I could.

"Now we're even, *bat boy.*"

Brooks coughed. "I deserved that."

He rolled to his knees, slowly coming to stand. I diverted my eyes from looking at his mangled left arm and the odd shape it twisted. I went back to the table I was at, gathering up the items I dropped when I held Brooks with magic.

"Come with me," he choked out, pulling at the collar of his shirt. Brooks staggered to his feet, tottering forward toward his desk. "Come on," he breathed.

Tentatively, I followed.

Twenty-Five

Brooks

For being a slight little thing, she packed a damn punch; just as she had back at her home nestled in Nukpana. My hand rubbed my chest where she kicked me. I honestly didn't think she had it in her to go as far as she did.

Peeking over at Hadley, her scowl deepened. Orange magic crackled in her hands. She blinked her shining cornflower blue eyes, hardening her glare with each flutter of her long black lashes. Her mouse poked out of her hair, glaring at me and twitching her nose.

Going to my desk, I pressed a button on the inside of the upper right drawer. The bookcase behind me sunk in, sliding to the left. A cold draft wafted out of the tunnel. Automatic lights flickered on, omitting a bleak yellow glow leading to an escape area.

"Come," I rasped.

Hadley tilted her chin up defiantly. "You first."

Shrugging, I strode into the dark secluded hall, being careful not to move my left arm. Automatic lights popped on at my approach, leading the way around the corner to the left and twisting down several sets of stairs.

"Where are we going?" she demanded.

"To an escape area," I stated, clearing my throat. "It will take us down to a large holding room. From there, if you choose the south tunnel, it will put you out into a field going toward Scirwode. If you choose the west tunnel, it will bring you to an abandoned city. However," I paused, clearing my throat again, "if you leave, I cannot protect you."

"Are you suggesting I completely trust you after all you've done to me?" Hadley spat.

Her glowering blue eyes were bright in the shadowed darkness. Her hair, left in the style Korbin did earlier, frizzed out to halo her face. She bit her bottom lip, chin wobbling. Bruises peppered her arms and legs, making them appear darker and more painful in the minimal light. The cast on her left hand needed to be redone. Hadley snorted, shaking her head at me as she delicately crossed her arms over herself.

Wincing, I took my jacket off, handing it to her. "No," I finally said. "What I did wouldn't be so easily forgivable."

"At least you're aware," she scowled, shoving her arms through the jacket, and shrugging it on.

The way her lip pouted as her brows scrunched was cute. I breathily laughed. Having no rebuttal, I continued on, leading her down the stone steps until it opened to a wide room. Several dark leather couches and rugs occupied the corners while the middle of the room was left open for transportation to go through the tunnels. I went toward one corner, housing an enclosed shelving unit. I pulled out a space heater and a few blankets, setting them on the nearest couch.

"I'll come get you when Keres leaves."

"What makes you think I'll stay?"

"By all means, leave," I said nonchalantly. "But don't come crying to me when you're captured by someone else and turned over to that awful bitch." I moved past her to go back up the stairs. "Now, if you'll excuse me. I gotta get that disgusting woman off my property."

"Lord Zygrath," Korbin whispered, pointing to my left arm.

I nodded, almost having forgotten about it. Being immortal came with some perks. Broken bones healed within the hour, whether set or not. Glancing down at my elbow, it had yet to go back to normal. I held out my arm, allowing Korbin to take it. He held it out straight to my side. With a quick push and a crack, he set my elbow back into place.

"Oh shit," Hadley dry heaved behind me.

Glancing over my shoulder, her face had paled significantly. "You okay?"

"No," she sputtered, sucking in a breath.

I went back to the enclosed cabinet, pulling out a blue barf bag for her. Hadley continued dry heaving, sucking in deep breaths intermittently to calm herself. It didn't last long. I handed the bag to her right when she lost her breakfast.

I gathered her falling hair in my hands, holding it out of the way. "You're not like other witches, are you?"

"How did you ever," she paused, trying to hold back the flow, "come to that conclusion?"

"Let's call it a hunch."

She breathed out raggedly and smirked.

"Here," I said, handing her the kerchief I had in my pocket.

"Thank you." She closed her eyes and wiped her mouth.

"Are you going to be alright?"

She nodded. "I'll stay here. Just *promise* to get rid of her."

"I promise."

She took a seat on the couch, pressing the kerchief to her mouth. I unfolded a blanket, draping it over her shoulders. I then took the barf bag from her, tossing it in the trash on my way back up the stairs. Korbin strode ahead of me. I dared a final glance over my shoulder at her, seeing her curled up on the couch with her pale face hardly poking above the blanket.

I jogged up the stairs, stepping on the light by the door. The door beeped. The automatic lights shut off behind me. I stepped out of the way as the door slid closed, going back to its previous position, and locking Hadley safely inside.

I went to my bottom left desk drawer, whipping out an extra shirt I had tucked inside and changed into it. Peering up, workers continued repairing the wall Hadley had put Eckard through.

"Lord Zygrath," Eckard said from the main doorway.

"Go ahead."

He opened it, stepping to the side. Keres strode in, grinning triumphantly like a kid winning a sports trophy. She tottered in, taking a seat directly in front of my desk. Her make-up plastered face did little to help her look appealing. Orange eyeshadow creased her eyelids while bright green eyeliner framed it all in. Her usual black goopy mascara brought the hideous look together. Whatever was on the rest of her face was cracking, leaving gnarled lines like tree bark across her face. She had cut her black hair shorter and curled it, giving her a mushroom head. It took everything in me not to puke.

"Have you found Hadley?" Keres finally broached.

I closed my eyes, ignoring her grotesque smile. Her teeth looked like she was the champion of eating apples through a chain-link fence.

My lip curled on its own. "No, I have not."

Keres laughed delicately, leaning back in her seat. "So, what of this wolf pack I heard you destroyed?"

"You of all people know we've been feuding with wolves for the past several centuries."

"But I heard it was over Hadley."

"You've been misinformed."

"Lydon says you have her."

"He's mistaken."

"*Hmmm*," she purred, strumming her pointed finger-nails on the arm of the chair. "On the first day of August, three weeks from today *exactly*, there will be a full moon. Have her soul to me no later, *then* you shall reap the benefits of my benevolence," she stopped, leaning forward in her chair. "Unless, of course, you wish to marry one of my daughters like Lydon does?" she finished, motioning to the door.

A petite, raven haired woman strode through the door, standing just behind her mother. Her long hair was swept up in unmanageable curls on top of her head. Amethyst eyes shone bright under the thick hood of her dark brows.

"Lord Zygrath," she stated, dipping her head.

"I'll have Hadley's soul to you by the allotted time," I stated, getting up from my desk.

"Are you refusing my daughter?" Keres huffed.

"Yes." I rounded the corner of my desk, motioning to the door. "After having dated two witches–"

"Third time's the charm," Keres smirked, motioning her daughter forward.

"Nope."

"Senna was always a flighty one, but I'm not," the daughter's dulcet voice stated as she took a step toward me.

Keres leaned back in her seat. "Do you want to know *why* Senna didn't blood-rite with you?" she maliciously purred. "It's because you have *no* power. I can give you power."

I bristled at her comment. "I have power, Keres. You, however, have none; not over yourself or coven," I snarled. "Why else would you want Hadley's soul if you already have power?"

Keres snapped to her feet. "By the first of August, *Lord Zygrath*," she hissed, spinning on her heel.

I watched her pass through the open door, marching hurriedly to the left to head out of the mansion. I motioned for Korbin to follow her, ensuring she leaves.

"Fucking bitch," I growled under my breath, retaking the seat at my desk.

"You know that wasn't her daughter, right?" Eckard said, taking a seat at my desk.

"I figured. She's been trying to get me to blood-rite with one of her witches since Halvor appointed me his successor."

"I wonder why you and not Lydon," Eckard stated, his face scrunching. "It makes me wonder further if Lydon will not inherit the eldership since Halvor officially made you lord. And Halvor gave the army to Elder Indrek."

I snorted, shaking my head. "*Small* army," I chuckled. "Comprising of our lower security team. It's like fifteen people."

Eckard chortled, leaning back in the seat.

"If you're both done giggling, I have a bigger problem," Nyura grumbled, slamming the door shut.

Korbin entered behind her, grumbling at my sister while giving her a distasteful look. My sister and I haven't ever been the closest. She's the apple of our mother's eye, never doing a single thing wrong. Being the only daughter, she's the automatic golden child of the family. I muttered under my breath as Nyura glided over to my desk, taking a seat in the only empty chair.

"When are you going to speak to Father about me?" she pouted.

"When I have a moment."

"You have one now," she countered, crossing her arms.

"Just because I look like I have a moment doesn't mean I do. I have matters to attend to."

"Like what? Your little red-headed witch that you can't figure out whether to eat or fuck?"

Eckard snickered.

Shooting him a silencing glare, I turned my stare back at my sister. "She's helping us with something huge for our coven."

Nyura dismissed me with a wave of her hand and rose to her feet. "I ask you for one thing, and you can't even help me."

"I will help you. But you have to give me a moment to do so."

Nyura grumbled, shaking her head. "Fine," she barked, storming out of my office.

Once the door slammed shut, as per her usual every-day tantrum, I laughed. She was so used to getting her way, so easily and quickly, that being told to wait was like telling her to step into sunlight.

"So, what's your other matters?" Korbin asked, taking the seat my sister vacated. "And Keres left, not without grumbling and mumbling gibberish under her breath."

I rolled my eyes. "Hadley is helping us with getting into and overtaking Toan Castle ourselves."

"If we can get into Toan, we can move all nine covens into it," Korbin added, leaning forward in his seat.

"Then what? We still have to deal with nine people who can't decide on what brand of toilet paper to buy," Eckard quipped. "If we overtake the castle, then we move what covens we are direct allies with into it."

"We can cross that bridge when we get there. First, we need to *successfully* get into it and take it over," I said, rising from my seat. "Hadley was working on a plan before we got interrupted."

"I'll go get her," Korbin said, rising from his seat.

I nodded, reaching under my desk drawer for the button to unlock the secret door. Upon pushing it, I went around my desk, heading out of my office to where my father would most likely be.

Out of all the things I wanted to do today, speaking to him about my sister wasn't one of them. I took the stairs up to the meeting room and yanked open the door. My father sat at the far right of the table with Elder Indrek going over a map.

I took a seat to my father's left and stared at the map in front of them. It took every ounce of control not to groan. Again, they were whispering where best to attack the wolves; how best to conceal and where to attack from. Even though they both just voted to wait to get their people trained and ready, they were plotting a secret attack.

"I'm glad you're here," my father's droll voice stated. "Was your last bounty successful?"

"Yes, sire," I replied, leaning back in my seat.

"Then why is she still alive? Nyura informed me you adamantly refuse to finish the girl off."

I scoffed. "Sire—"

"Then why does she live?" Elder Indrek added.

"She's useful. She's found a way to regain Toan Castle."

The two men stared incredulously at me; eyebrows practically meeting their hairline. They glanced at each other, then stared at me for a moment. The map fell from my father's hands, sliding across the table.

"Certainly, you jest?" Halvor asked, pointing to Toan on the map. "Toan Castle?"

"I do not. Therefore, the witch breathes," I replied, leaving my seat. "Thus, I came to ask to postpone Nyura's impending blood-rite to Ulric."

Indrek bristled. A snarl pulled at the edges of his lips. "On what grounds?!"

Placatingly, I held up my hands. "What better way to tie our covens than to have the blood-rite take place inside our sacred home where we're secure and with the spells of a witch more powerful than Keres herself?"

Indrek guffawed, shaking his head as if what I asked was the most absurd request he ever heard. "No. Absolutely not. I do not mind postponing the blood-rite on reasonable grounds. This is not reasonable. This is a foolish fantasy. Regain Toan Castle," he growled, pointing a crooked finger at me. "I take serious offense to this."

"I meant none," I stated, trying to salvage the conversation. "I was attempting to make the moment more special for my beloved sister."

My father clapped me on the shoulder, beaming at me. "I wish you had a daughter, Indrek. My son would make any woman a most thoughtful husband. While I agree it would be special, the blood-rite will continue without delay."

Outwardly, I forced a smile. It took everything in me not to combust into laughter from this entire ordeal. My father would kiss a skunk's ass if it meant gaining any of the elders' favor. It was also a fucking blessing Indrek did not have a daughter. She'd probably be good-looking, however just as dimwitted as her brother, which, I can understand why my sister didn't want to blood-rite with the man.

I bowed my head, thanked them for their time, and promptly left. I couldn't get away fast enough. I seriously needed to laugh. I shut the door behind me and slapped a hand over my face to lessen my laughter.

"Seriously?!" she seethed.

"Hello sister," I greeted, feeling my sister's presence as the door clicked shut.

"I hate you!"

"He's not a bad guy, sis," I placated. "Slow in speaking and responding, but an all-around good guy. You could do worse."

"I want to blood-rite with Damion! Now I can't, thanks to you! Dammit, Brooks, you fucked up my entire life!"

Her dramatic antics of tossing her hair and hand waving gestures made me chuckle. She looked like an inflated balloon person on the side of a highway meant to draw customers to car dealerships. Coupled with her dark purple eye makeup, she looked more like a flailing deranged racoon.

Crossing my arms, I kicked back on my heel, watching her panic and pace. "Wait, Damion? Elder Yulene's son?"

Nyura nodded, sniffling; tears welling at the edges of her lashes. "Yeah! Who else would be hot enough to be with me?!"

I barked a laugh. "He's an absolute prick. You'd be miserable. I understand Ulric isn't as attractive, but Ulric is kind and simple. He'd be good to you."

"NO!" Nyura pouted, turning the waterworks on full blast.

"You fucking asked father if you could blood-rite to Ulric, dipshit, or have you forgotten?"

Nyura stamped her foot, screamed, then sprinted off somewhere. I groaned, rolling my eyes at her petulant behavior. I pinched the bridge of my nose, shaking my head. *Stupid brat*, I chuckled to myself.

Rapidly, I took the stairs back down. Rounding the corner, I closed my eyes and clenched my hands. Senna's swaying back side opened the door to my office and went inside. *Fucking hell.* Before she fully closed the door, she was flying across the room.

Twenty-Six

Hadley

The smug smile Senna cast at me when she entered the office immediately made me pissed. The way her eyes lit up and crooned, "Oh, my," was all the confirmation I needed. Senna would tell Keres where I was. Senna would ensure my downfall.

Bringing my magic up quick, I blasted her out the door. I sprinted out of Brooks's office, grabbing Senna by the throat with my magic. I lifted her off the ground, squeezing with all my might. Her cold gray eyes bore into mine as a cunning smile split her face. My body chilled. Vampires had gathered around me, muttering amongst themselves. Brooks stood off to my left, holding out his hand while softly calling my name. Ignoring him, I lifted Senna further off the ground, bringing up my other hand. Using my power, I forced Senna's right hand to hover above her heart. She fought against me. Gritting my teeth, I forced her nails to sink into her flesh. Senna cried out, kicking her feet wildly.

"Keres," Senna grunted, struggling for breath. "Will kill you." She thrashed her head. "She'll kill you!" her voice screeched, echoing throughout the entire mansion.

"No," I answered, "she won't."

"What is the meaning of this?!" the moldy avocado man yelled, making a beeline straight for me. "Put my mate down, *witch*!"

Brooks intercepted him, getting in between us. "Fuck off, Rezon," he yelled over his shoulder. "Hadley, put her down," Brooks said calmly.

"No. She'll tell Keres about me," I barely whispered.

"No, she won't. I promise you. Just like I promised you Keres would leave." He motioned for me to put her down. "Hadley."

The way he whispered my name sent shivers crawling up my arms. It was so soft for his baritone voice. I slowly lowered Senna to the ground, keeping my hold on her person. I allowed her arm to fall to her side.

"Let me go, *sister*!" Senna snarled at me.

I held her there, not wanting to release her, not wanting to make myself vulnerable again.

"Come," Brooks said softly, reaching out a hand toward me.

I took a step back. His gray-silver eyes pleaded with me. His outstretched hand was wide, calluses puffed before letting his fingers extend out to me. A lone clump of hair fell in his eyes, covering a scar that ran from his forehead in diagonal to his left brow. The afternoon sun waning cast a shadow on his jawline, accentuating the shadow of stubble peppering his face. In all my attempts to get away, I never paid close attention to how he looked. If he wasn't such a prick, he was quite handsome.

"Brooks," the sordid vampire snarled, "get your bitch to release my mate or I will deem this an act of war on you and your coven!"

Brooks closed his eyes, his fingers tensed enough to turn into claws. He wheeled around, masking his ire. "You couldn't fight me let alone your way out of a wet paper bag to even start a war, *fucking rat.*"

"Brooks," another man similar to Brooks in looks and build yelled.

I clenched my magic around Senna, bringing her toward me. The damn bitch struggled, making me smile. She even attempted to use her own pathetic power to no avail. Reigning in my magic, I released my hold around her throat, opting instead for her body.

Senna giggled, "You lose."

"I'm playing the long game," I snapped back, sending her flying toward the old man.

They collided, skidding across the ground. I raised my hand up, about to lift them both and launch them through the window, but Brooks grabbed my hand, lacing his fingers in with mine. My eyes snapped up at him. I was confused at why he did that when he could've just grabbed my arm or my hand. Fingers still laced, he tugged me along, leading me through the crowd toward his office.

The man who looked like Brooks called for him to eat me, to kill me and regain honor for the coven. Brooks gently tugged me in front of him, pushing me through the door first.

"I'll handle it!" Brooks yelled over his shoulder, slamming the door shut.

I strode over to the cushy seats in front of his desk, taking a seat and curling my feet up underneath me. My body tingled. I leaned back in the chair, sighing deeply. After that, I was drained. Since being on the run until now, my body hasn't had the chance to recover. I was tired, exhausted, and just wanted a moment to myself.

"Do you have a fucking death wish or something?" Brooks asked, draping a blanket over my shoulders. "Seriously, how fucking stupid can you be?" he fumed, pacing the side of his desk. "Elder Rezon has sway over most of the elders. His coven is huge, and that *fucking woman* is his mate! Dammit it all, Hadley! You put me in such a fucking mess."

"Senna is my half-sister," I said nonchalantly, leaning my head on the back of the chair.

"What?!"

"She's my half-sister. She's older. I can't stand the bitch."

"You're related?!"

"Yeah... We share the same mother. Senna's father is as big of a joke as she is."

"Why did Senna leave the coven?"

I shrugged. "I dunno. I left before she did. But Senna must be scared of Keres too," my head lolled to the right. "How did you two meet?"

Brooks ran a hand over his face. "I went to a coffee shop to find a contract since I bounty hunt for the covens. That's how we met." He sighed, waving his hands. "That's beside the point. You put me in such a fucking mess!"

"How?"

"How? Really? You just about killed an Elder's mate then launched her into said Elder!"

I giggled, recalling the look on her face when I flicked my wrist and set her free. She didn't even bother to bring her hands up to stop or catch herself. She plowed right into that old man with a sharp yelp and a tangle of limbs everywhere.

"Were you and Senna close?" I finally asked.

Brooks growled, clenching and releasing his hands. He stood in front of me, leaning against the desk. He pulled on the dress shirt around his neck, loosening it.

"Stop changing the subject."

"How about you answer me for once?" I shot back. "You loved her and are mad at me because I hurt her. I knew there was something between you when you tried to block my view in the atrium."

"I'm not mad you hurt her."

"Then what's with the look on your face?"

"What look?"

"That me wanting to kill her just about destroyed you."

Brooks groaned, leaning his head back. His hands clenched the side of the desk until they turned white. "Ya know what? How about we just drop this entire thing and go back to the task at hand? Have you found a way into Toan Castle?"

"You're an idiot," I giggled, staring up at him. "You loved her, and she rejected you. Didn't she? She's power hungry like Keres and while you have power, it wasn't enough."

"I fucking hate you witches," he shoved his desk back, making it screech across the marble floor.

"You just dislike when someone has figured you out."

"How about you figure yourself out, *hmmm*? You're afraid of your own shadow."

"I'm not as scared as I once was. I have a new fear now thanks to you."

"And what's that?"

"Being caged."

His silver eyes bore into the very soul of me. His face fell, jaw loosening as it wriggled back and forth. Even his posture deflated. Brooks straightened his desk, finally taking a seat behind it, and ignored me for his paperwork.

I curled up in the chair, watching him scribble across papers and re-stack them into different piles.

I wriggled in my seat, listening to the groaning of the material and earning myself an ireful glance from Brooks. I stuck out my tongue at him as I tried to figure him out. His eyes never truly matched his actions. I found the observation puzzling. Ever since we met, his eyes were hard at times and soft at others, like he tried to convince himself to be cruel. And he was cruel, intensely so; though now, ever since I dished him back what he did to me, it's like we came to a mutual understanding. If he ever hurt me again, or attempted to, he would be my first ever kill.

Movement in my hair caught my attention. *Aysel, you okay?* I finally asked. *I feel bad I haven't checked on you during all this chaos.*

Yeah, she sighed, crawling out of my hair. *Between you kicking Brooks's ass, barfing your brains out and near-ly killing your sister, I'm whooped from trying to survive in your hair.*

I grinned, curling up in the chair. *I'm whooped too.*

Do you have a plan to get to Scirwode? I think we may find all we need in there to reestablish barriers and protection spells for the house.

I don't. Not yet anyway. I still want to try to find the Mother's Amulet, I said adamantly. *And my vision about Keres also scares me. If she found the amulet and wants to unleash her, then we're all fucked.*

Do you think she will? Aysel squeaked, crawling down my arm.

I wouldn't put it past her. Few know about Diomedes and Elohi's sister, Māceklis. But the old books detail the Mother Goddess locked her away, deep under the Ruinous Mountains, in the cave of Aizmirsts Miris is where Mācek-lis is said to slumber until awakened by the destruction of the Mother's Amulet. But those places are no longer known in Quivleren, even in the old books.

Aysel's beady, black eyes widened. *Then why the hell do you want it for?*

Because the Mother's Amulet protects the wearer from all harm, using the power it's sucking off Māceklis. Once the amulet is destroyed, not even hell itself could stop her.

Aysel swiped her paws over her face. *By the Goddess...*

Yup. Which is why I'm determined to find it. I'm sure Keres only wants my power for the time being until she can find it too.

Aysel squeaked, plopping down on my blanket and rolling to her back. *How do you get yourself involved in this shit?! Honestly... I don't even get it. You keep to yourself then* bam. *It's like you're a walking beacon for bullshit.*

I laughed, stroking her soft fur. *I don't know.*

"What're you giggling about?" Brooks asked, arching a speculative dark brow.

"Keres and how to get into Toan," I coolly answered.

"The sooner, the better," Brooks grumbled, scribbling on his papers.

"No kidding. I'm tired of this too."

Scooping Aysel in my hands and plopping her on top of my head, I got up from my seat to head to the door. I ached for a long hot bath and to cast my runes. If I was going into the lion's den, I wanted to know or have an idea about how fucky things could get.

"Oh, no you don't," Brooks replied, sprinting up to me.

"What the hell now?" I shot back, hand on the knob.

"Where're you going?"

"My room. To take a bath."

"I'll escort you."

I arched a brow. "Why?"

"Well, since you put the both of us in a shit situation with the Elders, I don't want you to get eaten."

I wriggled the ring on my hand. "So, this means nothing?"

Brooks deflated. "It means something, it does. Elder Rezon doesn't play by the laws or even coven etiquette. Since you hurt Senna, he'd take *any* opportunity to hurt you back and no one would bat an eye."

"Fine, escort me," I grumbled.

"We'll head to my room. Once you're safely inside, then I'll go get your backpack."

"What?!"

"You heard me. It's the only way to keep you safe."

I crossed my arms over myself. "The only way my left butt cheek."

"It will be your whole butt if Elder Rezon gets ahold of you," he replied, getting the door. "Trust me."

"I love how you keep stating I should trust you," I smarmily answered, giving him a side-eye.

"Good. I'll say it more," he smirked, taking my left arm and tucking it inside of his. "Does it hurt? Your cast has seen better days. Let's get it redone."

"I'm fine. I'll use magic and fix it."

"Witches can do that?"

"I can."

Brooks led me up the flight of stairs and to the right. Immediately, I tensed. This wasn't the way I was used to coming and going. This was the way to the dungeon.

"Easy," he said, patting my arm.

"I'm not a dog," I seethed under my breath.

"That's not what I meant," he huffed. "We are headed to my room the back way because Elder Rezon and Senna live to the left, whereas the coven resides to the right."

"So why did you have me stay to the left? Korbin said it was to keep an eye on me."

He nodded, striding down the hallway and opening a random door on his right. A long hallway stretched before us, devoid of any other doors. Evenly spaced portraits in gilded wooden frames adorned the walls. One portrait of an older woman with a hard stare sent shivers down my spine. We strode down to the end, turning left and ascending a narrow staircase.

"You stayed on the left because your room was directly below mine, so I was monitoring you. I'll get your backpack for you too," he finished, cresting the stairs, and turning to the left again.

"How were you monitoring me?" I ventured.

Brooks didn't answer. The hallway unfurled into a wide, square room. A dark wood chair rail, the same color and stain as the wood floor, split the walls. The wall above the chair rail was cream colored, complete with old-fashioned black metal wall sconces and some potted plants hanging from metal hooks in between. The bottom half was dark green, giving way to the polished dark wood floor. Two doors were ahead of me and to my left. To my right only had a singular set of double doors.

Brooks pointed to my right, "That chamber there is where my father, Elder Halvor Zygrath and my mother, Phyrena, reside. The first door on the left is Korbin's. The one following is my older brother, Lydon's. Mine is the first one ahead of you and to the right of that is my older sister Nyura's."

I nodded. "Are you and Korbin related?"

"He's my cousin and my bestie."

I cracked a smile at the word he used. "That must be nice."

"Do you not have a bestie?"

"Aysel is my bestie."

Brooks gave me a weird look as he led me to his bedroom door. "But a person?"

I shrugged, "No. Not since I left the coven."

"What about the witches in Nukpana?"

"I always wore a disguise."

Brooks opened the door, ushering me inside. "You'll be safe here," he stated matter of fact, heading to the bathroom.

He hurriedly gathered all his clothes laying everywhere, shoving them into the closet. I peered around his spacious bedroom, not believing he would be the type of man who liked color, especially a rich eggplant purple. Gray curtains covered the windows. A plaid comforter matched his room, complete with decorative pillows, graced his large bed in the middle of the room. Hardwood floors bare of a rug reached until the bathroom where they transitioned into a light-colored tile.

"Half expecting a coffin?" he teased, taking another enormous pile of clothes to his closet.

"Kinda," I answered, taking a seat on his bed. "Why don't you do your laundry instead of letting it pile up?"

He shrugged, taking a third pile to the closet. "I do my laundry."

"Once a month?"

He snorted, ignoring me while heading to the bathroom. He came back out, laden with an armful of towels.

Brooks stopped in front of me, his goofy smirk already parting his lips. "More like twice."

"You're not bad when you're amiable," I said, crossing my arms.

Knocking made the bedroom door rattle. "Hey Brooks," a male voice called on the other end.

"One sec, Lydon," Brooks called back. He turned to me after shutting the closet doors. "Stay in here, but help yourself to whatever you want. Pull this chord twice," he said, going to a cream-colored tassel by the door, "to get food. Someone will bring it up and knock when it's outside the door. I'll be back."

"What about my backpack?"

"Brooks, we gotta go now!" Lydon hollered. "Sire is summoning us."

"I'll have Korbin bring it up and set it on the bed," he said, going out the door. "Stay here."

The door slammed shut behind him. Brooks's deep voice grumbled while the higher octave of his brother shot back. I left the bed, heading to the bathroom. A large cream claw-foot tub butted up to a window that over-looked a garden. Landscapers moved from plant to plant, trimming and shaping the ornamental bushes. Plants graced the bathroom countertop at either end.

"I did not expect him to have such taste," I comment-ed aloud.

You and I both. I wonder if Senna did this, and he didn't change it back. Aysel answered from my hair.

Could very well be. At least he's being amicable.

Aysel snorted disgustedly. *Don't let him fool you. He's probably just planning when to eat you again.*

True. The sooner I hold up my end of the bargain, the quicker we make a new home in Scirwode Forest.

Why there?

Why not? There are plenty of plants for spells. According to the book, everything we need is in there. Plus, Scirwode is considered an old forest. If the amulet happens to be there, then we can scope it out while we get plants.

Aysel crawled to my forehead and dropped in front of my face. *Scirwode it is.*

"Hey Hadley," Korbin called from the bedroom.

"Yeah?"

"Your backpack's on the bed. See ya later."

The door slammed shut. Warily, I went into the bed-room. My backpack was on the edge of the bed. Black jeans and a shirt lay beside it, complete with a sports bra and undies. I rummaged through my backpack, pulling out my own undergarments, my runes and blessed salt.

Ready? I asked Aysel, loading the items into my arms and going back to the bathroom.

Yup.

Twenty-Seven

Brooks

The dim light of the meeting room made my eyes twitch. Or perhaps it was the fact I was stuck inside with all the elders, their next in command, and Senna. All the open seats were taken, leaving roughly eight people standing on the back wall behind me. I leaned back in my seat, arms crossed as Elder Indrek grumbled to the others about the importance of attacking the wolves post haste. Lydon sat to my left, muttering sarcastic, idiotic responses under his breath to whatever anyone said. I rolled my eyes.

A large map projecting on the wall in front of me outlined the covens, and the known wolf packs in Quivleren. Large purple circles with 'W' in the middle of them labeled the wolf packs. The wolf pack my brethren and I took out to get Hadley had a giant red 'X' through it. Nine triangles dotted the map, labeling each spaced-out vampire coven. The nearest wolf pack to our coven was outside of Aiolos to the east.

Elder Nefen interrupted Indrek for the third time to droll on regarding the importance of attacking the outlying packs first before proceeding to the largest. Nefen paced in front of the projector, describing in much unneeded detail what everyone should wear, utilize; even how, when, and where to attack down to the second.

I pinched the bridge of my nose, becoming more incensed by the passing moment with his jabbering. Not that I disagreed on what to utilize or how to attack, moreover war never followed a calculated plan; shit always went sideways, and nothing ever went according to plan down to the second. Furthermore, at least half of the covens, mine included, were not prepared for war. We needed time to prepare and to train in hopes of being remotely effective.

"We need to attack here," Elder Nefen said, slapping his pointing stick on the wall to a much larger wolf pack than the one at Aiolos.

I kept my eyes either on the map or focused on the buttons on my dress shirt. Senna's eyes darted toward me more than a dozen times. I wasn't about to fully look at her or acknowledge her. Knowing how she worked, if I acknowledged her, it would give her a reason to constantly seek me out and speak to me.

I moved my neck side to side, hearing a large crack at the motion. Feeling satisfied, I stared at my fingernails while I listened to Indrek blather about the need to attack, while my mind wandered to how I felt about Senna now. It'd been at least four months since she left me. I peeked over at her, finally deciding that I wasn't upset or hurt anymore. She made her choice and while, for a time it nearly destroyed me, I now was just done with her.

"She's staring at you again," Lydon muttered, digging for something in his pants pocket.

"Let her," I replied, leaning back in my seat. "I no longer give a fuck."

I huffed a laugh. There was a time where I cared immensely, where I warred with myself about begging her to come back and letting her go. The latter won out; while at the time, I thought it would kill me, it forced me to realize Senna never loved me in the way I loved her.

It began with the little things. I would bring her flowers or take her somewhere I thought she would like, restaurants, dates, shopping, but there was always a problem. She never truly loved something, truly cherished it. She would love the flowers but hate the color. So, I'd find the same flowers in a different color, but she'd hate those too; then complain that flowers just die. Finally, I had stopped getting her things, and she complained about that. There was no winning.

I wonder what Hadley would do if I got her flowers, I mused. I snorted, shaking my head. *Fuck nope*, I chastised myself. *Not another witch, not her. She's too...* I paused, grumbling at myself. *Fuck... She's cute.* The map changed view, offering an aerial look of the wolf pack near Aiolos, and garnering my attention.

Indrek's brusque voice thundered over the meeting room, silencing Nefen again. "We need to attack here. At the stronghold. If we overtake the strong hold, infiltrate it, then we can secure our reign, then go after the outlying packs."

"No," Nefen countered, his voice gaining in angst. "If we attack the stronghold, it will give the mangy dogs time to regroup for a large offensive move against us. We need to start small, rally our forces, then attack the main pack."

Elder Ghiza stood and banged her hand on the table. The motion rattled the wig on her head, causing it to bounce around. "Cease!" Her high-pitched voice screeched. Ghiza banged her tiny, balled fist on the table several more times. Her hand slipped, sending her body flying forward and the wig tumbling on the table. I promptly got up from my seat and turned to face the wall, trying in vain to contain my chuckles.

"Lydon!" Korbin hissed.

I turned around, finding Lydon toppled over in his chair, wildly kicking his feet; both hands clamped tightly over his mouth.

"It shot off her head!" he whisper-snorted.

"Shut up," I snapped, trying to suppress my giggles.

Several people coughed, trying to politely hide the snickers of others. Ghiza stood, hands holding the edge of the table for stability. She picked her wig up, setting it back on her head while casting a wicked glare around the room. "We attack the stronghold and succeed. It's more defensible to have a fortress to protect us instead of scattered mansion homes."

"It's time to vote. Already we've been too idle," Weldon cried, taking a stand. "We are all in agreement to attack. Let's vote on *where* to attack. All in favor of attacking the outlying packs?"

"We are not in agreement, Weldon," Yulene's soft voice interjected. "We need time to prepare. We need time to ensure our people have sufficient supplies to begin this tedious act of war."

"We can configure that along the way, Yulene," Weldon shot back.

"Yulene is correct," Nefen interjected, effectively taking the opportunity to go on a tangent regarding the importance of organizing for warfare.

I rolled my eyes. Why I was summoned here by my sire, I will never know. It was ultimately the most point-less meeting. If a decision was *ever* made, notification would be sent out by the elder in charge of the coven anyway. So far, this two-hour meeting dragged on re-lentlessly. Everyone else in the room looked bored out of their minds.

Lydon inhaled deep, finally rolling to his side, and sitting upright. "That's the highlight of the century," he whispered.

"Then we allow time to prepare," Yulene shouted. "This war must be effective. We need to take a moment and utilize all resources available to us."

My head snapped in the direction of her voice. The normally calm and collected elder hardly ever raised her voice. The slender woman rose from her seat, pushing her short bob-style black hair behind her ear.

"Give our people at least two weeks before we set out for the main pack," Yulene firmly stated.

"I agree," Nefen added.

Rezon slowly stood, leaning over the table, and glar-ing at Yulene.

"Be quiet, Rezon," Elder Janae snarled before he could open his mouth. "Of all the brethren in this room, *you* concern me the most." Janae stood, pushing her long blonde hair off her shoulder. "I vote for two weeks to prepare, then attack the main pack."

"All in favor of preparing for two weeks then attack-ing, please stand," Elder Weldon boomed.

Chairs screeching back echoed in the cramped room.

"Ghiza," Janae snarled, "are you standing or sitting?"

Ghiza harrumphed, fixing her horrific wig, and standing straight. "I'm *clearly* standing."

"*Clearly*," Janae shot back.

Per usual, Elder's Ubel and Rezon remained seated. I nodded, heading toward the door. Now that whatever the hell this was finally ended, I could prepare my coven and hopefully get Hadley to find a way into our ancestral home. Whatever number scheme she was planning, I hoped it would be beneficial.

Hand on the knob, I pushed open the door. "Finally," I hissed under my breath.

"Brooks," my father's voice boomed.

I sighed, spinning on my heel. "Yes, sire?"

"You owe Rezon an apology."

I chortled, continuing my path to my room.

"Brooks," Elder Halvor's voice boomed through the mansion.

I spied Hadley's fire red hair out of my peripheral. She rounded the corner to my office, then paused. I turned to fully catch her staring. Her shrewd blue eyes peered up at me. I winked at her, eliciting a glare and a roll of her eyes. It made me grin.

"Yes, sire?" I finally replied.

"You heard me," Halvor growled. "Elder Rezon deserves an apology regarding earlier today."

Several of the Elders shook their heads, maneuvering around my father. Their murmured voices about leaving and planning made me envious to do the same. Ubel glared at me over Rezon's shoulder. Eckard came up beside me, whispering in my ear about swallowing my pride. I nudged him in the stomach.

"Sire," Lydon interjected, "let's make this a private matter."

"It was not private when that *witch* nearly killed my mate," Rezon snapped.

"Agreed," Halvor nodded.

Rezon smirked, hands behind his back as he expectantly waited for an apology that would never be forthcoming. Senna smarmily grinned beside him, clinging onto his arm and whispering in his ear.

My father took several steps toward me. "Brooks," he hissed. "Apologize."

I felt Hadley's presence beside me before I dared to glance at her. She put her hand on my right arm, straightening her spine as she sidled up alongside me.

"Be gone, witch," Halvor snarled.

"Forgive my intrusion," Hadley calmly began, eyes locked on her kin. "Senna, dear sister, how are you faring?"

Senna's face dropped, her body bristling. "Why, *sister*, you have quite the audacity to show your face after what you've done."

"As do you for trying to seduce Brooks while being mated to someone else. I was merely protecting your treasured marriage. I know how dearly you treasure your mate."

Senna flipped her hair, gaping between her and Rezon while stuttering for a response to Rezon's surprised face. Halvor's eyes darted between me and Hadley.

"I humbly apologize for the chaos earlier," Hadley said, bowing low at the waist. "Take care, dear Senna. And congratulations on your nuptials," Hadley smiled sweetly. "I wish you much happiness with your mate. *Brooks and I* are headed to his office to discuss an important matter." She finished wrapping her arm in with mine and laying her head on my shoulder.

Hadley tugged me toward the stairs. I felt her body quake beside me. I tucked her arm further into my hold while making a side-eye motion at Korbin to follow closely.

"That was unexpected," I whispered.

"Yeah," she breathed out, putting a shaking hand to her head. "Definitely not planned."

"What possessed you to intervene as you did? You were safe in my room."

"I wanted to read the book more. Plus, I disliked what they asked of you," she stated, taking the stairs down and holding onto the rail. "*Apologizing to Senna*," she spat, sticking out her tongue. "How disgusting."

I chuckled. "I was dealing with the situation."

"You were doing *so* well," she quipped.

"Aren't you the little heroine," I grinned, leading the way toward my office. I held the door open for her, noticing she plated her hair in two braids going down her head. "Thank you... And your hair,"

"Yeah?" she paused, staring up at me with those large blue orbs.

"It looks really pretty."

"Thank you," she replied, shooting me a confused glance.

My heart stammered for a moment, bewildering me. She looked so beautiful with her hair out of her face, making her eyes appear larger and more vivid. The freckles splashing across her cheeks and nose were faint and... cute. However, the mistrusting bafflement on her face at my comment made me regret saying anything out loud. Her soft footfalls padded over to the desk at the far side of my office. I hung my head, shutting the door behind me.

"Dammit, Brooks," Lydon said, sticking his arm inside the door. "Lemme in."

I opened the door, permitting my brother. "What do you want?"

"You there, *witch*," Lydon called, pointing a wobbling finger at her.

"*Male vampire*," she snarked back, mimicking the same pointing action.

I chuckled, going to my desk, and taking a seat. "What do you want, Lydon?"

"I'm here for her," Lydon said.

"The fuck you are," I said, rising to my feet.

Lydon waved me off. "I'm not here for her like that. Witch," he said, turning around to face Hadley. "I heard you can access Toan Castle?"

"Vampire, I'm in the process of figuring that out," Hadley replied, moving away from Lydon.

"Well, how long until you've figured it out? I demand to know," Lydon asked, striding closer toward the table.

"It's going to take me a while," Hadley said, putting a chair in between herself and Lydon.

I strode over to Hadley, standing on her left. She took a seat closest to the wall. Aysel scurried down her arm, sitting on top of the notepad and pen. I took a seat beside her, scooting what she was working on earlier to her while simultaneously blocking Lydon from her.

"Witch," Lydon sighed, taking a seat across from us.

"Her name is Hadley," I replied. "Show some fucking courtesy."

"Aren't you one to talk?" Lydon snapped. "I need a spell."

"I'm the wrong witch for that."

"What can you do, exactly?"

"Divination and potions."

"Then you *are* the witch I need. I need a love potion," Lydon exclaimed, slapping a hand down on the table.

I groaned. "No, you don't."

"I want her to love me. So, I want to give her a love potion."

"I have a potion for that. It's in my backpack," Hadley smiled sweetly.

I arched a brow. "There are really love potions?"

"Absolutely. One moment."

Hadley summoned magic to her hands, compressing the ball of flames into a circle. She closed her eyes, muttering incoherent words under her breath while the magic twisted into an elongated diamond. I tried to slow down her words in my head to make sense of them. It only sounded like I was underwater. In a blink, the magic erupted, shooting out of her hands up toward the ceiling.

"Here," she said, holding out two lime green shimmering vials to Lydon. "Follow the instructions on the bottle. Stay in the same room with her for it to take effect."

"Thank you, witch," Lydon beamed, rising from his seat.

"How did you get that so fast?"

"It was in my backpack. I simply did not want to teleport to go get it, so I asked the potions to come to me," she answered, going back to the book.

"See you later," Lydon grinned triumphantly, scurrying out the door.

Once the door to my office slammed with Lydon's departure, I moved back to my desk, giving Hadley some space. She wriggled in her seat, flipping through the pages of the book. The clothes I found for her hugged her petite frame and accentuated her long torso. The only speck of color on her person was the hot pink lace undershirt poking out from the bottom. She looked studious in the seat, flipping through the book and jotting down notes.

I rubbed the back of my neck. "Hey Hadley?" I nonchalantly asked. Desiring to look busy, I picked up a contract Elder Yulene wanted me to handle, skimming it over. "I thought love potions were a farce."

"They are," she replied.

"Then what did you give Lydon?"

She shrugged, grinning from ear to ear. "Let's just say they're going to feel really cleaned out."

I glowered over my paper. "What do you mean?"

"The laws of magic do not bend for love. They never have nor will. That potion will make them feel invigorated; happy, euphoric like they are absolutely in love and will detox their body. Then it will give them both massive shits," she giggled. "They're gonna feel sooo good."

Watching the mirth light up her face made me start chuckling. "That's awful!"

Her shoulders scrunched, her cheeks becoming pink from giggling. "Are you going to stop them?"

"Abso-fuckin-lutely not," I grinned at her.

She focused back on her book, fiddling with the ends of her hair as she read. I watched her for a moment, her lips pursing side to side; the way her eyes squinted at something she found interesting before she wrote it down. I caught myself smiling at her, then quickly turned back to my work. I raked my fingers through my hair, giving it a small tug, and reread the same sentence for the third time.

"Fuck," I grumbled under my breath, rising from my seat. "I'll send you food," I called over my shoulder as I went out the door.

Twenty-Eight

Hadley

I scowled, watching him leave. I had no clue what his deal was, but he seemed more emotionally turbulent than I was on my period. Throughout our entire exchanges, his eyes betrayed his words. His actions were cruel and malicious, but only in front of others watching. *He's a fucking weirdo*, I decided, shaking my head clear of him and his mood swings; I went back to the book.

My eyes scanned the pages again, looking specifically for how the spells were performed and what was used to perform them, whether utilizing animal sacrifices or plants. I couldn't find a damn thing so far and the book was almost done. I huffed, flipping through another page detailing where the spell was placed.

How do you think these spells were performed, Aysel?

The little mouse lay sprawled out on my notepad. *I don't think the old witches used sacrifices. I think they were just powerful.*

True, I nodded. *Magic has changed even before the Hell War. Everyone used to mate with whomever then somewhere along the way, everything became segregated.*

Exactly.

Which makes me want to contact a dragon and ask. Their memory goes back a long way. I bet you they even have a book on it.

I'm sure they do, but asking them is out of the question. Aysel sat up, squinting her beady eyes at me.

Yeah, I know. Just sucks. They would take one whiff of me, then burn me where I stood. I sighed, flipping through another page. There were only a few pages left until the book was over. If I couldn't deduce how the spells were performed, then I guess I would have an idea when I got there. The funny thing with magic, at least for witches, is I could tell who did what. It's like every witch leaves a signature of who they are behind after a spell is cast, like a scent for a werewolf.

When are you wanting to leave for Scirwode?

I shrugged. *Hopefully, in the next day or two. I want to get an idea of the castle layout and the landscape before I take off anywhere with Brooks. If anything happens, I want to know of a way to escape.*

Definitely a good idea.

Yeah, I replied, tapping my pen on the notepad. *Wish my divination from earlier could've told me something a little more useful.*

I think you're a bit too exhausted. I think a good night's sleep will be your cure to try again tomorrow.

I nodded, rereading a paragraph about the Demilune Trifecta spell. It was cast on the northwestern most edge of the garden area on the southwestern side of the castle. I rubbed my chin while I stared intently at the words. The location of this spell made my insides jumble. I was excited at having found a way inside.

The northwestern most point at the moonset would be the ideal place to get inside. I drew a quick map of the gardenscape based on what the book detailed along with the points where the spells were determined to be cast. I grinned, happily stamping my feet. In a few days, my turmoil with this asshat would be over, and I could live peacefully for the rest of my days with the protection of these bloodsuckers.

"Hey," Korbin said, opening the door. "Brooks said you were hungry."

My head snapped toward the door. "He just said he would be sending me food."

Korbin nodded, pushing a silver cart inside the office. "I've brought a smorgasbord. I wasn't sure what you liked."

Are you hungry? I asked Aysel.

Starving! Did he bring any berries or seeds?

I strode to the cart. Silver domes covered numerous plates the cart was laden with. On the tier below, cups and a pot labeled coffee were offered. My mouth salivated.

"Do you have any berries or seeds?"

"Yep," Korbin said, handing me a small bowl of blackberries. "Brooks asked the kitchen what mice like best."

"Brooks or you?"

Korbin held up his hands. "Brooks. I've been dealing with getting our coven ready to head to Toan Castle."

I arched a skeptical brow. "Thank you."

"He's not as terrible as he makes himself seem," Korbin offered, pulling the dome off a couple of items.

Brisket, baked potatoes, and more were set on individual serving plates. My stomach hungrily roared. It'd been so long since I'd eaten anything and I'd just contented myself to the fact that even though I was now a "welcomed" person, I was still an outsider who probably wouldn't be offered much.

Korbin handed me a fork. "Take and eat what you want."

I grabbed an individual helping of brisket, mac'n'cheese and mashed potatoes, balancing it all on my arm as I strode back to the table. Aysel struggled to push the book back.

"I got it," I softly said.

My little mouse stopped, huffing, as she waited for me to set down her fare.

"What do you want to drink?" Korbin asked, holding out a cup.

"Coffee is fine."

"It says coffee, but it's tea."

"That works. Thank you."

"Does Aysel want water?"

I nodded, regaining my seat at the table. I pushed the bowl of blackberries toward Aysel before helping myself to my own food. Korbin served me the drinks, then took a seat across from me, staring at his plate while looking over my notes. He sighed, raking his fingers through his tousled mess of brown hair.

The door to the office opened, omitting Brooks, and slammed it shut just after he passed through. The ass strode to his desk, yanked the drawer completely out, sending papers flying everywhere. I rolled my eyes. *Yup, worse than a woman on her period. Good Goddess Above,* I thought, snorting derisively.

"Fuck," Korbin said, screeching his chair back.

He needs some hormone regulation, Aysel shared, glaring intently at him.

I burst out laughing. I couldn't agree more. Brooks growled, flinging out another drawer. He dropped to the ground, trying to find something. Korbin joined him in the search.

I wonder what they're looking for, Aysel squeaked.

I do too.

I mulled a piece of brisket in my mouth, savoring the zesty flavor. Brooks snatched a piece of paper, rocking back on his haunches until his butt hit the floor. His suit pants ripped, creating a large gash from his inner thigh then straight through his crotch. Having a full view of his large commando front, I quickly looked away, feeling my cheeks heat.

"I'm decent," Brooks hollered at me.

My cheeks heated further until I thought my entire head was on fire. "Thanks."

Brooks laughed. Ignoring him, I went back to my meal, scarfing down everything in front of me before I went back for seconds. I moved the notepad back in front of me, staring at the self-made map and scribbled notes regarding the spells and their locations.

The general spells around the garden area were for healing, protection and warding against evil, or malicious intent. There was no way I could affect the healing spells. From what I gathered, it was to heal the area, the plants and promote general well-being. It was a benevolent spell.

The one for warding against evil may prove the most troublesome for me to get by. If Brooks or whomever was near me while I tried to break through, it could prove fatal depending on how the spell was done and if there was a booby trap within the spell.

I tapped my fork on the pile of mac'n'cheese. How to get around the spells was stumping me. Mainly, it was the Demilune Trifecta. Since demilune meant crescent, was this trifecta spell completed during the waning or the waxing crescent moon? And if either of them, then I needed to get my ass in gear and figure out how to access the gardenscape and start plotting a way around the spell to get inside.

"What day is it today?" I asked out loud.

"July 17th why?" Brooks hollered.

"When was the last quarter moon?"

Brooks swept his hair off his face, scowling at the computer. He clucked his tongue as he clicked away on the computer screen. "The 10th and 11th. The New Moon is today."

I nodded, delving back into the book. I scoured the last several pages, hoping to find when the trifecta was completed. I kept reading and rereading parts, making sure I didn't miss a thing.

"If you stare any closer, ink may get in your eyes," Brooks teased.

"Rather stare at ink than you," I snarled back.

Brooks chuckled. "Take a break and walk with me outside. The fresh air will do you both good."

I muttered under my breath.

"You know I'm right," he teased.

I nodded, getting up from the table, when my eye caught what I've been searching for. "Whoohoo!" I grabbed the pen and paper, jotting down what I'd been searching for.

"What?"

"The Demilune Trifecta was performed during a waxing crescent moon. So that puts us at July 22nd, give or take a day. It will give us time to prepare."

"How does the moon affect how a spell is done?" Korbin asked.

"Certain spells are performed on certain days for them to have a longer and more powerful effect on whatever a witch is casting the spell on."

Brooks leaned on his desk. "So, because this spell was cast on a waxing crescent moon, does this mean you can undo it?"

"Possibly. It gives me a date and a time frame to attempt to undo it. I must be more powerful than the witch who cast this spell to fully break it."

"Ready to walk with me?" Brooks asked, pushing off his desk and striding toward me. "The sun is going to set in an hour."

I nodded, gathering Aysel in my hands. She scampered up my arm and nestled on top of my head. Brooks took my arm, leading me out and to the left. I hardly began to look around when I spied Senna outside through the window, and walking with the ugly avocado corpse. I stiffened. They were headed to the same door we were.

Brooks turned to the right, going further down the hall that led to the atrium I recalled going to. He gently patted my hand, leading me to a different door where we made our escape to. He opened it for me, holding on to my hand.

Once I stepped out, he retook my hand, folding it back into the crook of his arm. The fresh, warm summer air hit my lungs; I felt my insides melt. It was so refreshing to breathe the outside air instead of being cooped inside for days on end. I grinned, closing my eyes to feel the breeze on my face. A single tear slipped down my cheek. How long had it been since I enjoyed any semblance nature had to offer?

Opening my eyes, I took in the garden before me. Stone pathways led through numerous gardenscapes. One path to the right led through manicured trees, while the one before us led through an evergreen maze of sorts where the hedgerows came up to my chest.

"Watch your step," Brooks said softly.

I took the several steps down to level ground before I closed them again to take in the breeze, the smells of summer flowers, and wheat fields. I filled my lungs with deep breaths, ensuring to soak up the tranquil aromas. The summer sun warmed my entire body, and I turned my face toward the sunlight. Brooks gently led me to the left. I opened my eyes to absorb where we were headed and found myself smiling at all the delightful flowers.

"Do you like flowers?" he asked.

I nodded. "I do. I love them."

"I figured you did based on your home. You had them everywhere."

"*Pfft*. I wouldn't say everywhere. It was organized. Do you like flowers?"

Brooks shrugged, giving me a soft grin. "I think they're pretty. I don't understand a lot about them or the varieties."

"I love them. My favorite is a calla lily. They are very toxic, but if used properly, you can use them to dress wounds."

"How are they toxic?" he asked, leading me through rows of herbs and medicinal flowers.

Off at the very end of the pathway stood a small cottage home; smaller than mine back in Nukpana. The dark cedar shake house, framed in white trim, was breathtaking against the backdrop of manicured flower beds and fruit trees.

I stopped, picking up a stem of rosemary and smelling it. "If you eat it, it will cause swelling and burning of the mouth and tongue. Same with if you get it in your eyes."

"So," he paused, picking a beautiful white clustered flower. He let go of my arm, looking at the flower, then at me. Brooks pulled at the skin on the back of his neck. "For you."

"Thank you."

I twirled the flower in my fingers as I kept an eye on Brooks out of my peripheral. His gaze softened on me. He shoved his hands in his pockets, his whole-body relaxing. It made me leery. Ever since I've met him, he was such an asshole. Then earlier, Korbin told me Brooks wasn't as terrible as he made himself seem; however, until today, I truly had known no other side to him. Just recently, he'd been decent, and I didn't trust it.

I took two steps back, peering up at him. The sun had shifted, casting an amber glow on his white skin. His silver eyes had a richness to them, giving off varying shades of grayish silver flecked with amber. It was quite pretty. Brooks raked his calloused fingers through his hair while widening his stance and thrusting a hip out.

"I've no idea what that flower's called," Brooks offered.

"It's a valerian flower."

He nodded. "What's it used for?"

"It has many uses. Though, most commonly for insomnia, anxiety, and nervous restlessness."

"What do you use it for?"

I shrugged. "Depending on what the customer needs, I use to help induce peaceful sleep with a vivid dream to prompt the opening of the third eye for them to understand the path they are seeking. For myself, I make tea so I can sleep."

"Do you struggle to sleep?"

My eyes narrowed on him. "What's with all the questions?"

"I'm trying to understand you. I find you interesting and want to get to know you."

"I find you alarming."

Brooks blew his breath out, rubbing the back of his neck. "I understand."

"Do you, though?"

"I do. I hurt you in more ways than one. I don't like what I did to you."

I took several steps back, sticking the rosemary and valerian flower in my hair. I didn't trust him at all. I didn't trust he was being sincere. Even though he looked it, even though his eyes gave way to what he was feeling, the same eyes I saw numerous times before he did something, I didn't trust it at all.

"Why the sudden change of heart?" I demanded. "What game are you playing at?"

"Because I was wrong. Can a man not admit when he's wrong?"

I blew my lips. Was he trying to get me to be complacent? Compliant? Get my guard down so he could feed on me again? Part of me was absolutely terrified of whatever he was trying to play at. The other part felt the sincerity of his words reflect in his eyes and it all warred with me.

"I'm not blowing smoke out my ass," he grumbled. "I truly am remorseful for what I've done."

I couldn't find the words to reply.

"You're going to have to trust me at some point."

I crossed my arms over myself. "Actually, I don't. This is a transaction between us both. You want my help to get inside Toan Castle. I want your coven's protection. We don't have to be anything other than cordial."

Brooks turned around, huffing, and pulling at his hair again. He spun back around, hands on his hips. "I'm holding up my end of the bargain."

"How?"

"This house is for you," he stated, striding toward it.

We walked through the row of flowers, then turned east. A small retaining wall with a staircase leading down to level ground gave way to gorgeous cobblestone surrounding the outside of the home. Potted plants in black glazed stone containers lined the perimeter equidistantly. Dark brown cedar shakes covered the house, giving off a granny's cottage vibe out of a storybook. White trim around the windows was the only contrast. Two beautiful purple clematis grow on a black iron trellis on either side of the purple front door.

Brooks opened the front door, standing off to the side while the door creaked on unused hinges. "I've had some of my coven go to your house to collect items since I figured going back there would scare you. You'll find most of your things inside."

I gave him an incredulous look, passing through the threshold of the door.

Twenty-Nine

Brooks

I watched her tentatively walk in the house, her body on edge, and prepared for the worst. Her skin prickled at the change in temperature. I flicked on the light. Hadley nearly jumped out of her skin.

"The kitchen is in the back," I softly offered.

She breathed out raggedly, hand on her chest as she turned around to go inspect where I instructed. I huffed, raking my fingers through my hair again. The terrified dubious look on her face when I apologized made me realize just how awfully I had treated her. While part of me struggled with what I've done, the other part felt it was just part of my job, what I've always done. I was at war with myself. I kept trying to justify my actions, yet I struggled to even do that. The way I treated Hadley differed greatly from any other bounty I had treated prior. I blew my lips, tabling the war in my head for later.

Hadley came back out, rounding the corner and heading up the steps to the immediate right. The home was small, just enough space for Senna and me. Since that phase of my life was long gone, I had no use for this home or all the damn plants surrounding it.

Right off the front door was the living room, small enough to entertain less than ten people. Beyond the living room to the left was a small office or guest bedroom. I strode to the back, passing through the small hallway separating the living room and the kitchen.

The kitchen was quaint and cozy, lining three of the four walls. The refrigerator hummed. I yanked it open, pulling out a bottle of the six-pack of beer I had stashed inside when I was working on the house.

Going back out toward the living room, I paused in the middle of the hallway and gently opened the door to the bathroom. I checked the faucet on the sink and the tub to ensure the water was still on. Having verified the water worked, I went back out and took a seat on the couch.

"Why are you giving this to me?" Hadley asked, coming down the stairs.

"You need a place to live, don't you?"

"I guess I just don't understand why you're being so kind all of a sudden."

I knocked back the beer, setting the emptied contents on the table in front of me. "I was wrong about how I've treated you and what I've done. There's no apology I could give to even remotely make it right. Plus, as you've said back in Aiolos, I've ruined your house and you've nowhere to go. I also promised you infinite protection, so what better way than on the outskirts of the mansion's garden?"

Hadley took a seat on the gray loveseat across from me. She leaned forward, fiddling with the hem of her shirt while she chewed on her lip. She looked lost, a little worried yet dejected, a look I hadn't seen on her since our bargain. Aysel clambered down from her hair, plopping to her shoulder before sliding down her arm to the couch.

"Want a beer?" I asked, getting up from the couch.

"Please."

I went back to the fridge, grabbed two bottles, and strode back. Hadley deflated against the couch, leaning her head back as she stared at the ceiling. I popped the caps off the bottles and set one in her hands.

"Thank you," she whispered.

I retook my seat. "You're welcome."

"I'm trying to understand you," she murmured, her voice sounding strained.

I didn't reply, not knowing what response would be appropriate. Her hushed words were so pitiful, like it ached for her to say them. She swiped at the lone tear tracking down to her chin.

"The only time you were ever intentionally cruel was in front of others. Why?"

"You won't like the answer," I quietly replied.

She leaned forward, taking a sip of beer while her blue eyes, tear rimmed, stared right back at me. "An answer I don't like is still better than none at all."

I polished off the second beer, setting it down on the wood-stained coffee table. The condensation from the bottle dribbled down, creating a ring on the table. I stared at it, trying to find a way to answer her. Nothing I offered as a response would be fabulous.

I heaved a sigh, leaning back on the couch. "As a display of power. I am the sole heir to this coven. I must appear strong, resolute, and in control. I was taught, when the coven is watching, there should be no question in their eyes as to how powerful I am." I swiped a hand over my face. "No one was supposed to be up on the roof that day."

Peering up, I met her doleful eyes. Her expression was a perplexed mess between pity, anger, and hopelessness. I stared at my hands, not wanting to see her pretty face morph into hatred, though I rightfully deserved it.

She sighed raggedly. "Thank you for your honesty."

I nodded, clearing my throat. "I'm sorry."

"I don't think sorry will be able to cut it for me."

"I know." I got up from the couch, going back to the fridge to snag the entire six-pack.

Coming back out, her head lolled to the side as she stared out the window. The sun was setting, casting an amber glow across the flower garden. I went to the windows and closed the curtains.

"You'll be safe here," I stated.

"You keep saying that," she mumbled, sitting up. She polished off her beer, grabbing another out of the cardboard case. "And just because cruelty is expected of you as a leader, doesn't mean you ought to do it," she paused, cracking it open and drinking half of it. "A great leader isn't someone who flaunts their power or their greatness. It's a leader who knows they have it, and decides to *be* better, to *do* better."

"You're right," I said, taking a seat beside her.

"I hope the next witch you hunt you will treat differently."

"There won't be a *next* witch. I can't," I paused, shaking my head. "I can't."

Her blue eyes shot up, staring into mine. The incredulity on her face took my breath away. Even now, her holding onto so much animosity toward me, she was a stunning woman.

I got up, clearing my throat and paced around the living room. "Once the sun sets, I'll leave."

"Why not teleport? I thought vampires could at least do that."

I nodded. "We can. Our magic is limited to short bursts. I can teleport, shape shift from a bat to a wolf, or to a raven. All vampires can at least take one different animal form from a bat. More powerful ones can do three or four."

"What about mind control?" she asked almost angrily.

"Works on humans. It can work on witches if the witch allows us."

She stared at me, her eyes pinching together so tightly, I couldn't tell if she was angry or thinking. Hadley knocked back the rest of her beer, setting the empty bottle back inside the cardboard pocket.

"And feeding on people?"

"What about it?" I asked, taking a seat across from her again.

"I've heard if you feed on someone three times, they'll change into a vampire. You've already fed on me twice."

"Yeah," I said, leaning back on the couch. "That's partly true. If the *same* vampire feeds on someone three times, then the being will become a vampire. If someone feeds on the being twice then a different vampire feeds on that same being, then they won't. It must be three consecutive times before the next full moon. Otherwise, it won't take effect. Or, if the being wants to be a vampire and mated, then it can be done by a blood-rite."

She nodded, tears welling into her eyes. Shivers racked her body as the tears freely rolled down her cheeks. "Please... don't turn me," she cried.

"I promise I won't."

"Thank you," she whispered, patting her cheeks dry. "You've kept two of your promises to me so far, and I'm grateful."

"I don't say what I don't mean."

"You've said a lot of things I could list, but if you're saying, from our point of comradery forward, then yes, I would agree with your statement."

Hadley leaned hard to the right, her head crashing onto the pillow as she curled up. I chuckled at how she just keeled over to the side. I walked over to the nightstand to the right of the couch where I was and got a blanket for her. I used the opportunity to peer outside. The sun was still in the process of setting completely.

"Damn," I mumbled to myself.

Turning back around, Hadley stared blankly at the wall, her left hand tucked underneath her cheek. I stared at her for a moment, just now realizing her cast was off. I draped the velvety eggplant colored blanket over her. Aysel clambered out of somewhere and rested on top of the blanket too.

"Aysel says thank you," Hadley mumbled.

"You're welcome little mouse," I replied. "And I am sorry for the way I treated you too."

The mouse picked its head up and squeaked at me.

Eyes closed, she murmured, "She says she accepts your apology."

"Thank you."

I turned away from her, swiping a hand over my face. I walked through the house, double checking the window locks and the overall security of the house. Ensuring everything was battened down tight, I slipped out the back door. I planned on having Korbin get someone to watch over the cottage, just in case Keres or anyone else got an idea to hurt her. After all, I did promise to protect her while on my lands.

I trudged my way back to the mansion, picking a haphazard path back as I didn't care when I got there. More than likely, I would pass the night away in my office, coming up with a training plan for my coven and another plan to collect the needed resources for this impending war. I thought it was stupid to solely go after the werewolves when we should also keep an eye on the witches too. Hadley mentioned Keres was more than likely plotting something against me. I believed her. The problem would be getting the coven to back me on it.

Movement caught my attention. I stopped in my tracks, peering to the right. Senna picked her way down the path toward the house I had Hadley in. I craned my neck side to side until I heard it pop.

"Fuck," I grumbled, spinning on my heel to follow.

Senna flitted to the left, going past the gardenscape to an outcropping of fruit trees. I paused a couple hundred feet behind her, not wanting to be seen. My eyes slowly adjusted to the oncoming darkness. The sky faded slowly from the vivid orange red of sunset to a deep blue gray. The bitch paused, whipping her hair up on top of her head.

"What the hell is she doing?" I mumbled to myself.

Senna's faint blue magic swirled in her hands. She picked up a stick, transferring the blue light to the stick and proceeded down the path. I narrowed in on her, wondering what the hell she was doing amongst the fruit trees. The path went to the river. Beyond the river was unworked ground our coven leased to the local werewolves.

I carefully followed, picking a meticulous way to not be seen or heard. The trickle of the river became ever louder with each step I took toward her. Senna paused on the water's edge, looking both ways before levitating to go across it.

I took the moment to shift into a small bat, one of my other forms besides the large, humanoid one I could do. I quickly flapped from tree to tree, hiding behind the thick base of the trunk. The only downside would be when I had to cross the river, as I would be completely exposed for a moment.

The light from Senna's torch slowly faded from sight as she dipped down the hill. Grunting, I dashed to the other side of the river. I lurked behind the trees long enough to ensure my concealment before flying to the next tree. The fruit trees toward the back of the cluster were not as large as I imagined.

Grumbling, I dropped to the ground, scurrying my way to the end of the tree line. Senna's light became fainter, but I dared not shift into my other two forms. My wolf was the exact size of the real animal; still too large to not be seen. And the raven, though larger than the bat, would also be too noticeable.

Taking a chance, I took to the sky and flapped a wide berth around Senna's faint light. I made for the tall tree on the outskirts of the clearing she was in and waited.

Thirty

Hadley

Crunching of rocks outside woke me from my sleep. Mumbling, I rubbed my eyes and listened. I tilted my head to the side, turning my ear to the window. A light breeze caused something to tap the window. Groggily, I pushed the blanket off and went to the window, yanking back the curtain. The culprit was a potted tree's leaves being tousled in the summer breeze.

Ugh, I groaned, wiping my face. I never recalled falling asleep. I didn't recall having a blanket draped over me either. I just remembered staring at the wall as I tried to process what Brooks had told me about turning someone into a vampire and the truth behind why he was so cruel to me; how his silver eyes couldn't meet mine and when they finally did, held the deep depths of his remorse. But why now? And all of a sudden? Unless he felt it all along and he was doing what he did to me out of coven obligation?

Maybe I'm reading too much into this, I thought.

Go to sleep, Aysel grumbled.

Sorry, I didn't realize I was projecting my thoughts to you.

Well, you have been, she yawned, wiping her eyes and whiskers. *I think he's remorseful. I sensed it. Still wouldn't trust him fully yet.*

I nodded, heading to the bathroom. *I agree with you. I'm scared to trust him.*

Padding back out to the living room, the moon glowed through the skylights. Scooping Aysel up in my left hand and the blanket with the other, I went up into the loft of the cottage home.

A king-sized bed lay centered in the room. Fluffy burned orange bedding called to me to crawl inside. I laid the velvety blanket on the bed, setting Aysel inside the circular shape. I then face planted on the bed with a groan.

Feel better, Aysel asked.

A-huh, I stretched, rolling to my back. *I feel comfortable here.*

This could be a great home.

I think so too; especially if I have the protection of the coven. I would still want to check out Scirwode Forest for the rare plant life and see if I could cultivate my own.

A spark of light blue magic caught my attention out of the east window. The light shot into the air, going straight up to kiss the clouds, then fizzled out like a firework. I rubbed my eyes, trying to ensure what I saw was some kind of joke. My entire body quaked like I had been dipped in a glacier.

Did you see what I think I saw? I asked Aysel.

I tried not to look to be honest.

We gotta go!

I scrambled off the bed and sprinted down the stairs. My backpack lay against the backside of the couch, along with a small tote. I yanked open the tote lid, finding some of my clothes inside. I rummaged through, finding a pair of black jeans, a shirt, and a sweater. I chucked what I had on, quickly getting dressed in my own clothes.

Picking up my backpack, I threw it on and dashed up the stairs. Aysel lay curled up on her side in a folded crease of the blanket. Her neck stretched out and her mouth was agape. The first time I saw her lying like that, I immediately began crying because I thought she had died. Little did I know, she just sleeps weird.

Do you need to use the restroom? I asked Aysel.

Her body jolted. *Yeah*, she grumbled, rolling to her side. *So much for one damn peaceful night.*

I know. I'm sorry. Keres is here.

That light could be anything.

No. It's her. We need to go.

Okay. Take me outside.

I scooped her up and dashed down the stairs. The handle to the front door jiggled. I skidded to a stop, almost toppling over. My breath caught in my throat. I quietly dashed back to the bathroom, locking the door.

The front door burst open. Heavy boot-steps thundered into the home. I held my breath, slowly backing into the corner by the claw-foot tub. Deep, muffled male voices vibrated through the door. One set of steps dashed up the stairs. I stuck Aysel on my shoulder. Her little paws danced across my shoulder as she nestled herself on the back of my neck and tucked herself in my sweater.

I summoned magic to my hands, forming a perfect triangle. In the middle of the triangle, I pictured Brook's office. The bathroom door handle rattled as I cast the magic and stepped through.

Breathing out in relief, I stood in the middle of the dark room and watched the magic fizzle out behind me. Turning around, I went to the door and flicked the light on. Brooks's office was just how he left it, save for more papers piled on his desk.

Nothing like waiting until the last minute, Aysel squeaked.

I didn't reply to her comment. I went to Brooks's desk, searching for anything noteworthy. In the middle of the pile, the map of Quivleren caught my attention. It was the same map I recalled seeing when I snuck in here before. I swung the backpack to the front and opened it.

I'm stealing this map, I told Aysel, rolling the map up and stashing it in my pack. I dashed to the side table I was at and grabbed the notepad and book too. *Can't forget this either.*

And what is this map supposed to tell us? She grouchily responded.

Where the wolf packs and the vampires are. It can help us avoid them.

Are we ditching Brooks?

The office door lock turned. The slow groan of the deadbolt grinding against the polished wood sent a chill up my arm. My heart leaped in my throat. I shot magic toward the door and flicked the light off. I dropped to the floor, crawling under the desk. I pressed my back against the far-right side, nestling the backpack in between my feet.

"Where's Hadley," Keres barked.

Brooks sighed, stomping his way toward me. "She's not here. You just saw where I had her staying, and she's not there."

"Who tipped her off?" Keres yelled. "We struck a bargain, *vampire*. And so far, you haven't held up your end."

I quietly clamped a hand over my mouth to stifle any noise. My gut roiled, forcing bile up in my throat. I swallowed it down. Panicking wouldn't help me here. My mother's words resonated in my head. I couldn't run anymore. At the same time, I felt I had to.

Aysel quaked against the back of my neck. *That winged rat is going to sell us out!*

I had no response. I felt the same. Only the past day or so Brooks had become amiable toward me. It put me on edge. Now, I understood why. I held my breath until I felt my lungs would burst.

Keres's nails strummed against the tabletop. "Where is she?"

Brooks said nothing.

"Where is she!"

Brooks groaned, rising from his seat. His right hand moved toward a button underneath the desk. "Why don't we check my mansion together?"

The other chair screeched back. "I've a better idea."

A dark purple smoke enveloped the entire area. Howls came behind the door. Screams echoed throughout the entire mansion. I summoned magic to my hands and closed my eyes, forcing the magic to form a cube. The magic hissed at the compression.

"Fuck," Brooks mumbled, moving back from the desk.

Keres purred, "Oh Hadley." The desk rattled, screeching back on the floor. Keres laughed patronizingly. "Come out from under the desk."

I licked my lips. Aysel quaked against my neck, moving around to hide herself in my bra. I held the cube still and closed my eyes.

Universe, Keeper of what disappears,

hear me now, open your divine ears.
What is lost, I now wish to find,
please help me to stop being blind.
Direct me now to what I seek,
by Fire, Air, Earth, and Sea.

I repeated the chant three times, each repetition becoming more forceful and desperate than the last. I felt the protective barrier of the desk move away from me. The bright light of the office combined with the hazy purple magic of Keres swirled around me, yet it was like I was immune to it all. My eyes were completely transfixed on my magic. The cube bounced in my hands, rattling against the constraints I bound it in, until I thought it would burst and blow my hands off.

"Hadley," Brooks called.

At some point, he had moved in front of me. He continued to call my name; his voice sounding so distant and deep. I glanced up, seeing his silver eyes widening as he took several steps back. I forced my eyes back to the magic. The orange mist bounced on the cube walls. I repeated the spell three more times, hoping this spell would give me what I so desperately sought.

I got to my feet, outstretching my hands. The air inside the office became too humid to breathe. Keres took several steps back from me, her dark eyes widening. I repeated the spell three more times, putting more emphasis on the words. If I could not get the Mother's Amulet with this, then it didn't exist at all.

"Hadley!" Brooks yelled. "Stop!"

The cube cracked, orange magic seeping out like water from a jug. My magic overtook whatever smoky bullshit Keres was trying to pull. The cube cracked further, omitting light that shot out like a gun.

"Hadley, stop!" Brooks growled, moving closer to me.

"You stop!" I snapped. "Get back!"

The cube tripled in size. I breathed out, forcing the cube to compress as I tried to contain it. I failed. The cube burst, sending me flying backwards against the wall.

Warm hands grabbed my arm. "What the fuck Hadley!" Brooks growled.

"Get her!" Keres yelled.

I cracked my eyes open, seeing a sea of movement. Keres rocked back and forth like a boat. I shook my head, realizing I was the boat. My hands felt heavy, my left one hurting the most.

"Move!" Brooks said, yanking me.

I barely got my feet underneath me when Brooks threw me over his shoulder. He sprinted past Keres, out the door to the open mansion. Wolves sprinted all over the mansion grounds. Vampires, in their beastly forms, fought back against the dogs but were losing. The inside wall crumbled, exposed completely to the night air and stars.

"Hadley!" Brooks called again, jostling me on his shoulder.

"What?" I groaned.

"What's in your left hand?"

I glanced down. A dark blue stone encased in silver dangled from a silver chain. The oval stone was probably three inches in diameter. I held it up closer, completely entranced by the beauty of the stone.

"I did it," I whispered. "Holy shit, I really did it."

"Take a holy shit later. We gotta split!"

The stone heated in my hands. Flipping it over, in silver, was an outline of a mountain range. In the middle of the fourth mountain was a squiggly arch, what I deduced to be a cave or something. Underneath the mountains, carved into the stone, was a face.

Brooks stopped running, setting me down on the ground. "What is that?"

I shook my head. "I think it's the Mother's Amulet."

I rubbed a thumb over the stone, feeling the power vibrate through my body. I brought magic to my right hand, shining it over the amulet. Whomever engraved this stone, elegantly carved the face of a beautiful woman with closed eyes and full lips. Her soft features made me envious of her beauty. The carver very delicately crafted curls in her hair, going as far as noting the soft crow's feet by the eyes. I moved the stone over in my hand and squinted. Māceklis was etched onto the back.

Howls came from all around us. Blasts of bright magic gave me an idea of where the rest of the Black Ash coven happened to be. Peering skyward, dark clouds whipped overhead, hiding the moon and stars. I quickly donned the amulet.

"Where are we?" I whispered to Brooks.

"Back at your house. Stay here, I'll be right back. I need to get my family."

I latched onto his arm. "We should stay together."

Brooks sighed, raking his fingers through his hair. "Okay. Let's go."

Thirty-One

Hadley

I latched onto his hand as we crept our way back to the mansion. Brooks led me through a maze of shrubs that came up to my chest. The glass doors leading from the mansion out to the garden area were smashed. Smoke billowed from the north side. Wolves prowled the perimeter, their snarling, snapping jaws waiting to get ahold of anything.

I spied the small frame of Keres barking orders to the wolves to the west of me. She held her arms out at her sides while purple magic swirling in twisting pillars in her hands. A person kneeled before her on the ground, hands clasped together. Keres took a step back from the person, her magic swirling at least several feet over her head. The deranged witch blasted the person in the chest, sending them rocketing into the mansion wall. The stone crumbled, landing on top of them.

"Oh shit," I mumbled under my breath, trembling uncontrollably.

Brooks squeezed my hand. "Stick close," he said, pulling me along.

Peeking over the last bush concealing us, Brooks looked every which way. Tugging on my hand, we dashed from the safety of the garden toward the smashed glass doors leading inside the burning building. Brooks set his hand on the small of my back.

"I want you to stick close to me," he whispered in my ear, lacing his fingers in with mine. "It will be easier for me to protect you."

The heat of his breath sent a shiver up my spine despite the suffocating heat of the smoke and consuming fire on the north side of the building. We carefully picked our way to his office. Smoke slithered out from under the door. He tucked me behind him, using his left arm to shield me. Brooks kicked the door open; flames came bursting out.

"Fuck," he grumbled, retaking my hand as we dashed for the stairs. "Follow me." Brooks shoved me ahead of him. "Go to where I first brought you. At the end of the hall, push the white button."

"Why can't we just teleport there?"

"The dungeon has layers of concrete, steel, and iron. There's no getting down there except for physically going."

I went to rebuttal then stopped. Four wolves had their eyes fixed on Brooks. I stood there, torn between helping him and fleeing for my life. Brooks transformed into his beastly bat form, his wings spreading wide until the smoldering ashes licked his right wing.

"Go!" Brooks snarled at me.

I whipped magic to my hands. The power of the amulet vibrated through my body. The magic came quicker, the orange color even brighter.

Let's go, Hadley, Aysel cried from my bra.

I stood my ground on the stairs. Wispy smoke danced all around me, leaking out in the cracks of the building. Brooks tangled with two wolves while the other two stalked toward me. I blasted one in the chest with an orb. He shot back, skidding across the marble floor to strike against the stone wall. I quickly called another orb to my hand, putting more magic and force behind it. The dark wolf in front of me wriggled on readied paws.

"Hadley, go!" Brooks yelled.

I shot the orb toward Brooks, getting one wolf he battled in the side. The wolf whimpered, shifting into his human form. I pressed a hand to my mouth. The man lay on his side, sizzling from the magic I shot him with. Black, charred skin went from his face down to his hips. Brooks used the distraction to snap the neck of the other wolf while the fourth fled.

"Hadley!" Brooks growled, taking my hand. "What the hell were you thinking?"

I gagged, vomiting on the carpeted stairs. "I don't want to be alone."

Brooks didn't say a word. He stayed in his shifted form, putting a hand on the small of my back and guiding me up the stairs.

"You're helpless," he grumbled.

"I burned a wolf for you," I snapped back.

The image of the charred wolf flitted across my mind, and I gagged again.

"That you did, but you're still helpless."

I rolled my eyes, having no rebuttal. At the top of the stairs, he grabbed my hand. We dashed to the right, going around the corner.

"Where would your family be?" I asked.

"The dungeon," he replied, staying at the edge of the hallway.

The smoke thickened down the hallway. Brooks grabbed a doorknob, immediately wincing and pulling a way.

"Fuck," he yelled. "Stand back,"

He kicked the door open. Flames and smoke barreled out, leaving little room to see anything else. A door down the hall burst open, flames licking at the door frame, crawling out to demolish the end of the hallway. The largest wolf I've ever seen emerged from the burning room in his human form, carrying the severed head of some grizzled old lady. His fierce green eyes paralyzed me. He tossed the head to the side, splattering what remained against the wall.

I ducked behind Brooks, dry heaving and choking on the smoke.

"Hand over the witch," the wolf snarled.

Brooks backed up, cocooning me behind him. He kicked open the hallway door and peered inside. This hallway wasn't fully engulfed though smoke wisped out of the cracks of the baseboards.

"I know it's scary, but go through this door, run down the hall, turn right, and go through there. You'll come to two doors, take the left one then take the elevator down. You'll be safe down there," Brooks softly said, just turning his head slightly toward me. "Go Hadley."

I faltered; torn between leaving him to fend for himself and saving myself. And if I saved myself, doing as he bid, then that left me to the devices of his family, who, I was pretty sure would turn me into an appetizing midnight snack.

Standing my ground, I summoned magic to my hands. I compressed it tightly into a ball, infusing it with enough power to turn this wolf into jerky. I stepped in front of Brooks, shooting the ball at the wolf. The mutt dodged. The magic exploded behind him, crumbling the wall, and incinerating the rest of it. The flames from the mansion combined, bursting into the rest of the building and rattling the foundation. The wood under the wolf groaned.

"Fuck," I choked, moving back behind Brooks.

Brooks tossed me over his shoulder, sprinting back down the stairs. The wolf shifted, giving chase. My mouth dropped open. The fucker was huge! Brooks leaped the last few steps, going to the right and back out the way we came.

"He's gaining on us," I shouted.

Brooks spontaneously stopped. The motion launched me backward off his shoulder. He caught me in his arms.

Keres, at least a dozen witches, and even more wolves blocked our path. Wolves quickly closed in around us. I detached my arm from around Brooks's neck and wriggled my feet. He set me down, folding his leathery wings back to his body. The loud sound, like someone running a nail over a stack of cardstock, made goose-bumps appear on my arms.

"I hope you and Senna weren't close," Keres began, taking several steps toward me.

Without even realizing it, magic swirled to my fingertips. "I hope you and the Goddess are."

Keres laughed. Her sickly purple magic wafted in her hands like ocean waves. "Dear girl, come home to us, bind yourself to the coven, and all will be forgiven."

I bristled, shooting an orb at her. She caught it with her left hand. My orange magic dissolved into her body like cotton candy in water.

My mouth dropped. "What the fuck?"

Windows burst out behind us, unable to take the heat from the encroaching flames. Peering to my left, the smoke bellowed out of the building, giving fresh air to fuel the fire and making it harder to breathe. The heat from the flames made my skin crawl. The building cracked from the blazing fire behind us.

Keres waved her hand dismissively, her magic shooting beyond me to stall the fire. My insides jittered. If she was powerful enough to stop a fire from spreading, then how many souls has she collected?

What's the plan, Hadley? Aysel quaked from my bra.

I swallowed. *Stay alive.*

Then what?

I'm gonna try to stay alive long enough for you to get somewhere safe. Then I want you to sever our bond.

NO!

You must. I don't think I can survive this one.

"Come home, Hadley," Keres purred, her magic wisping in her hands.

I turned my body to the side, taking a readied stance as my father taught me. Closing my eyes, I envisioned the other half of me; the half that made the dragons want to slaughter me and the witches envious. I'd only taken this form with strict instruction from my father, but he wasn't here to help me this time; nor was he here to save me from myself. I let out a deep breath, picturing myself from how I remembered I looked when I took this form years ago.

Hadley?

Go Aysel, I commanded. *Run.*

Hadley no!

I sighed, staring down at my chest. *It's the only way. I'm sorry. For so long, I've been terrified of what I was, what I know I could do, but there's no outrunning it this time.*

I love you, she squeaked.

Aysel popped out of my bra, shimmying over my arm, and sprinting down my body. Out of my peripheral, Brooks picked her up, cupping his hand and cradling her against him.

I love you too.

Growling, I rolled my shoulders, allowing the shift to continue. The scales crawled over my arms, sending uncomfortable pin pricks all over my body. I rolled my neck, not liking the feel of the orange scales or the bright cornflower blue horns coming out of my forehead. Spikes went down my back, stopping just past my shoulder blades. My hands elongated into claws, tipped in blue. My mouth painfully stretched, allowing my teeth to come through. I wriggled my jaw back and forth, sliding my forked tongue over my now pointed teeth.

"Holy shit," Brooks said, taking a step back.

"Not even the holiest of shits can help you," I quipped, using his line against him.

Keres gasped, a slow malicious smile forming to her wrinkled dark face. "Oriel always said you were unique."

"My mother always thought you were a toad," I growled, smoke pluming out of my nostrils.

"Even so, she's not here to save you," she finished, snapping her fingers.

"I don't need saving," I snapped, charging at her.

The wolves surrounding me shifted, blocking my path. Witches summoned magic to their hands, rolling their wrists over themselves to create an orb to cast. I stole a quick glance at Brooks. Bringing my magic up, I formed a perfect triangle and shot it at him.

"Stay safe," I whispered as they disappeared through the portal.

I whipped my right hand around, casting an orb at Keres and her minions behind her. I was nowhere near the prowess of a wolf, but being a half breed had to count for something. One wolf lunged. I caught it by the chest, throwing it back into its pack. Three witches cast their magic at me, yet somehow it bounced off my scales like it was nothing.

I roared, flames billowing out of my mouth. A wolf, too stupid to move, jumped too late. I knocked him to the side, making a beeline for the witches. I didn't like killing my own kind. I didn't like the fact I knew most of them; where we spent summers by the stream, swimming and catching tadpoles as we debated which one might be prince charming; riding bikes and chasing the ice cream truck. But heck, if it came down to it, I chose my life over theirs. Damn the memories, they chose against what was right.

My hand latched around the throat of a witch I had long thought was a friend and snapped it. I launched her dead body into a charging wolf to grab another witch. Keres, wide eyed, made for the back of her little entourage. Furious, I roared, sending my clawed hand through the chest of a witch and ripped her heart out, squishing it in my hands. I thirsted for the blood of those who wronged me. I thirsted for vengeance for my mother and myself. My body shook with hunger. I ate the heart of the witch, devouring it in two bites.

Spinning on my heel, I went straight for the nearest wolf. I dove on the pup, landing on its back when it tried to run. The wolf yipped. I sunk my teeth into the back of his neck and spat out hair. Taking another bite, I ripped into the side of his neck. Sinking my clawed fingers in, the feel of bloody tissue brought a smile to my face. I licked its blood, my body shuddering gleefully from the taste. Sticking both hands in, I severed his head from his body. The wolf's howl died on its lips.

The wolf's pathetic little friend charged. I snatched it by the throat, pinning it down on the ground. The painful anguish of his cry made me giddy. I laughed, shoving both hands into his bloody neck and peeling out tissue. The wolf went limp, falling to his side and whimpering for help. Freeing my right hand, I clamped it down over his mouth while I fed.

My mind went blank as the dragon in me completely took over everything in my body. It felt like I lost my grip on my identity, yet I didn't care. This was who I am now, who I was made to be. Spinning on the horde of wolves, I charged into the fray as the shield Keres had on the building failed.

Thirty-Two

Brooks

I landed on my ass in the house I had let her stay in. Aysel bounced out of my hands and rolled to her paws. Hadley's orange magic fizzled out behind me. The house was eerily silent; not even the droning hum of the refrigerator reverberated from the kitchen. I glanced between the mouse and the door.

I sat there for a moment, completely stunned. Out of all the things I had thought Hadley to do, saving us wasn't among the list. She was so gentle, seemingly weak, as she hid behind me and couldn't decide to save herself; yet when she shifted into the half human, half dragon form, it gave me profound clarity on why Keres wanted her so badly. She was more than just a half breed. She was the direct descendent of the old line. No other half breed I had encountered was as strong as Hadley. Hell, that woman had more magic in her pinky finger than Keres had in her whole disgusting body.

Scrambling to my feet, I went to the door, yanking it open. I climbed the small hill to get a better view of what was left of my home. The mansion, now fully engulfed, crumbled in a rolling wave. My jaw dropped. The flames and dust burst into the air before the roaring crash of it all falling reached my ears. Wolves and witches scattered, lingering on the edge of the area where it was safe. I intensified my gaze, looking for Hadley. I couldn't see her orange form, but I found something slumped over the back of a male.

"Fuck," I whispered. Turning back around, I went to the cottage. My eyes scanned the room for the mouse. I found her perched on the couch. Even in the moonlight, Aysel's beady black eyes portrayed so much profound grief.

"Stay here. Stay safe," I said to the mouse. "I'm going to bring her back."

Shifting back to my human form, I sprinted out the door, making a straight line for where I saw the wolf. I leaped over a bush, shifting while in the air. My wings unfurled, sounding like cotton sheets whipping off a bed. I pummeled into the large male from earlier, taking him and Hadley to the ground. Hadley, knocked out cold, rolled to her stomach. In the quick glance I got of her, blood poured from a gash in her left side and a nasty head wound.

The wolf shifted, snarling. I lunged for it. The wolf ducked, plowing into my body, and taking me to the dirt. The beast's teeth sank into my left bicep. I went to rip him off, but he dodged, thrashing his head side to side, and taking me with it. I snarled, gaining my feet with him hanging on the backside of my body. Grabbing his head, I sank my clawed fingers into his skull and ripped him off; his body flying over the top of mine while I held onto his head.

Hadley groaned, rising from the ground. The amulet dangled from her neck. I turned my attention back to the wolf. The large male lunged at me, knocking me to the ground. I kicked him off, sending him reeling into a tree.

"Hadley run!" I yelled, sprinting for the wolf.

Before the mutt gained his feet, I picked him up by the back of the neck and took up into the sky. Peering down, Hadley wasn't even steady on her feet yet. Her body twinkled between her human form and whatever the half dragon form was. Several wolves swarmed around her, knocking her back to the ground. The wolf in my clutches thrashed against my grip. I squeezed tighter, soaring higher, then dropped him. I dove after him, kicking him with such force, he smashed to the ground, making a crater in the concrete.

Landing, I folded my wings and sprinted toward Hadley. Her dragon form rippled over her skin, looking like kinetic sand sliding down a kid toy. She shook her head, roaring so violently I was forced to cover my ears.

"Hadley," I yelled.

She rounded on me. Her blue eyes glazed over. The animal in her destroyed any semblance of the cowardly witch I came to know. The amulet dangling from her neck cracked. White magic wisped out, going to the heavens in a jagged line. I took a step back from her, holding my hands up. Her forked tongue slithered out of her mouth. She tilted her chin up, then spun away from me.

"Fuck," I mumbled.

A wolf charged her from the right. I dashed, catching it by the head before it struck her. Movement to my left caught my attention. Keres strode forward with a dozen other witches, casting a magical soft pink dome over us. I let my grip on the wolf go, making a grab for Hadley instead. The petite witch whirled on me. She slashed her clawed fingers at my chest, catching me over my heart.

"Hadley!" I yelled, grabbing onto her wrist. "Stop!"

The blank look on her face made me nervous. I wasn't sure if she heard me, recognized me, or anything. Her blue eyes flickered between the dragon consuming her and the soft expression of the woman I came to know.

"Hadley," I said, shifting. "We gotta go."

She shook her head. The scales over her eyes pinched. She tilted her head, staring at me. The lizard-like slits receded from her eyes, going back to the gorgeous cornflower blue I adore. The horns on her head slowly sunk back under her skin.

Peering beyond her, wolves closed in as did the dome over us. The amulet on Hadley's neck cracked further. Keres lifted the pink veil like a sheer curtain, stopping feet from Hadley and I.

Keres laughed, *tsking* her tongue at us; arms straight out at her sides, brought her palms and magic up together until it was over her head. Purple magic swirled into a ball. White streaks, like lightning, bounced off the inside of the orb. I shifted back, wings out to shield Hadley. I stole a peek over my shoulder. Hadley battled with her shift, trying to come back to herself.

Keres blasted her orb at me. I took it full in the chest, unable to move to protect her and unable to fully block it with what limited magic I did have. I crash landed on my back, trying to stay shifted as the magic rippled through me.

My breath hitched. "Hadley," I croaked out, "run!" My body convulsed without my consent.

Hadley leaped over me, diving headlong for Keres. The old witch brought up her hand to shield herself. Hadley slashed through the witch's barrier with a swipe of her clawed hand, using the other to latch around Keres's throat. Hadley growled, her forked tongue flicking out. Her scaly lips pulled back, revealing sharp curved teeth. I fought against another wave of magic coursing through me and rolled to my knees. Air finally hit my lungs, suffocatingly hot and smoky. I shifted back, folding my wings behind me.

A power struggle raged between Hadley and Keres. Hadley had her hand wrapped around Keres's throat, while the Supreme had magic wrapping around Hadley's. The amulet on Hadley's neck rattled, the chain breaking off. The blue stone shimmered, hovering in between the two witches.

Keres gasped, her magic dropping. "The Mother's Amulet," she whispered.

The shimmering pink dome around us dropped. All witches stared at the blue rock floating in front of Keres. The Supreme snatched the stone, pulling it close to her body and caressing it like a child. Hadley wobbled, collapsing to the ground. Her dragon form slowly receded from her body completely. The horns along her spine and on her head, pulled back under her skin like a beetle disappearing under sand.

I dashed forward, grabbing Hadley by her wrist and teleporting us back to the house. I laid on the floor beside her, breathing raggedly.

Soft pattering across the hardwood floor made me smile. "I got her," I said to the mouse.

Turning my head to the side, Aysel climbed up Hadley's right arm, settling herself on the witch's chest. Groaning, I sat up, taking a long look at her.

I nudged her arm. "Hey sleepy head."

Her arm rocked back and forth, flopping over with her palm face up. Hadley's face was pale, her chest not rising with breath.

"Hey," I said, nudging her again. "Fuck."

I slid over to her, picking up her wrist and feeling for a pulse. Nothing. Leaning over her, I started chest compressions. The mouse sat on her head, rising on her haunches, and squeaked profusely at me.

"Come on, you little wicked witch," I teased. "Wakey-wakey." I kept the chest compressions going to the tune of the human rhyme row your boat. "Come on, Hadley."

Aysel closed her beady black eyes, leaning down on Hadley's head where her whiskers kissed the witch's skin. Hadley sputtered, finally inhaling sharp and deep. I sat back on my heels, relieved she was alive. The witch rolled to her side, panting for breath.

"Glad you're back," I said, scooting to her side.

Hadley nodded, slowly sitting up; bringing her knees to her chest and leaning over them. "Me too," she huffed. "The amulet," Hadley said, frantically grabbing at her chest. "Does Keres have it?"

I nodded. "Yeah."

Tears streamed down her face. "Fuck!" She screamed, hanging her head while tears splattered in her lap.

"What's so important about that?"

She wiped her face, laying back down on the floor. "The Mother's Amulet gives the wearer an insurmountable amount of power. Now, Keres can do whatever she wants. However, if the amulet breaks, it will unleash a force more powerful, more terrifyingly heinous than Diomedes."

"Who's worse than that prick?"

"Māceklis."

"Maz-ee-kliss?"

She nodded. "Yeah... *her*."

I shook my head, getting up to peer through the curtained window. Nothing outside stirred. Smoke continued to plume off the mansion. Grimacing, I turned back to Hadley.

I groaned, sitting back down. "I'm not following. How is she worse?"

"In the old times, there was the mother Goddess, Oluina. She wanted children so badly, she created Elohi, the god of all that is light and wonderful. But what is light without the darkness? Olunia then had a most beautiful daughter, Māceklis. The three of them created a most wondrous world, full of beings and—"

"Enough," I said, waving my hand. "Get to the point of this bedtime story."

"I was about to if you'd shut the fuck up, rude person!"

I sputtered, "Okay, I'm sorry. Continue."

"Māceklis grew jealous of how close Elohi and their mother were. Becoming incensed by their bond, she destroyed everything; every being, every animal, anything with a soul. In despair of how wretched her daughter had become, Oluina sacrificed herself to undo what Māceklis had done. Oluina locked her daughter deep under the Ruinous Mountains, in the cave of Aizmirsts Miris to slumber for eternity. However, not realizing how powerful her daughter was, Oluina created the Mother's Amulet. The stone carefully crafted into the face of her beautiful daughter. The amulet would siphon off her power and give life to the area the amulet resided in, unless destroyed. Now that Keres has the amulet, if she destroys it, it will awaken Māceklis. Then we're all fucked."

"So how powerful is she?"

Hadley shrugged. "How would I know?"

"How was Diomedes created then?"

Hadley sighed, leaning back on her hands. "If memory serves me correctly, after Oluina sacrificed herself to undo what Māceklis had done, it left Elohi all alone. In

Elohi's loneliness, he created Diomedes to be his friend. But that shit backfired and Elohi locked Diomedes in hell with a key. And, well," she paused, moving hair off her face. "Alpha Evander and Zuri took care of *that* issue 60 years ago."

I nodded. "So how do we know when Keres–" Rumbling vibrated the entire house. Hadley bolted up, ramrod straight. "Please tell me you farted."

"Really," she seethed. "That's where your mind goes?"

"I was trying to be funny," I said, gaining my feet.

I helped Hadley to hers, wrapping an arm around her waist. She didn't object, so I left my hand idle there. Her warmth seeped through my body, crawling up my hand in tingles. I smiled, never having felt that before with anyone. Her hair still smelled of summer wheat fields. A small smile crept to my lips as I caught myself staring at her side profile. Her bright eyes shone under the moonlight. Pink full lips pressed together in a thin line.

I coughed, breaking the stillness of the room. "I think we should leave," I whispered.

Hadley nodded. "Yup, definitely time to go. Just need my backpack."

I blew my lips. "You haul that thing everywhere, but I never see you use it."

"You'll see me use it," Hadley quipped, going up the stairs.

The front door boomingly rattled. The glass in the windows imploded. I zoomed to Hadley as the front door flew off its hinges, rocketing back toward the kitchen. I shoved Hadley up the stairs. The witch scrambled to the top, grabbing her backpack out of the corner of the loft bedroom.

"Can you teleport?" I asked her.

She put the pack on the front of her chest. "Where are we going?"

"Anywhere."

She took a wide stance, summoning magic to her hands. The house rumbled, shaking the entirety, and rocking the foundation. A high-pitched scream, like someone being stabbed, rent the night air. My head whipped in the direction. I turned, wrapping my hands around Hadley's ears as the scream rolled over like thunder.

Hadley's face paled. "Māceklis."

"Oh Hadley," Keres purred from the doorway.

The witch paled, shaking to the very core.

I cupped Hadley's cheeks "Let's go, okay? I'll protect you. Let's just go."

She nodded, wielding her orange magic. The orb formed in her hands, slowly fizzling out. Tears peppered her long, dark auburn lashes.

She shook her head. "I can't. I'm too tired."

Internally, I groaned, having used much of my magic already. Aysel crawled down her hair, resting on the top part of her backpack.

"All of us together then."

I put my hand on Hadley's shoulder, willing what little magic I possessed to pass to her. The little mouse dipped her head down, touching Hadley's forearm with her whiskered nose. The scream crashed through the house, ripping the roof completely off. The witch's magic flickered to her hand like a weak halogen light. She forced the orb into a triangle and cast it.

Thirty-Three

Hadley

I fell to my ass; my body being tossed backward by the force of the landing and into something squishy. I looked behind me, finding Brooks staring at me. My back was pressed up against his chest, his hands around my waist.

"Hi," he whispered.

"Hi."

I checked my body for Aysel, finding her sprawled out on my pant leg. Cupping her in my hands, I stuck her on my head before I got off Brooks. I carefully rose to my feet and set my backpack down. Everything in me was super sore and tense. I walked stiff legged to the front door, locking it, and setting a minor spell over the door. I flicked on the light switch. The lamp by my recliner turned on, offering a soft glow of my home.

"Home sweet home," I said, turning back around.

Brooks sat up, groaning and holding his head. "Do you have any beer?"

I went to the fridge, getting out the six-pack of hard apple cider. I wasn't much of a beer or hard cider person, but sometimes one hit the spot. I popped the top on two of them and went to where Brooks still sat on the floor. I handed him one, kicking my feet out in front of me and to the side.

We sat in silence, sipping our drinks. I stared off at my home, noting all the overturned items, askew pictures on the walls and anything of note. The picture of Mahak and me was missing. Tears welled in my eyes, but I pushed them down. I would cry later.

"You okay?" Brooks asked.

I pointed to the picture. "My picture is missing."

Brooks nodded. "I took it. I'm sorry."

My head slowly turned in his direction, uncertain if I heard an apology or not. From my understanding, vampires weren't ones to issue apologies, yet I've received several in the last few days.

"I took it to compare your features to your lock of hair."

I blanched. "Lock of hair?"

Brooks nodded, polishing off his drink and getting up. He went to the fridge, helping himself to another. "Yeah," he said, popping the top. "Keres gave me a lock of your hair to help me find you." He came back, sitting in front of me and kicking his legs out too. His booted feet touched mine, while a perplexed look flitted across his features. Brooks raised his brown head, swooping the hair off his face with a calloused hand. "How did Keres even get your hair?"

I hung my head, willing the tears to suck back up into my eyes. I had given my mother a small lock of hair as a present when I was six, not really understanding the importance or the significance of it. I just wanted her to carry me with her since she was constantly going places, leaving me with dad, or when after he died, with stepdad. I sniffed, thinking of the memory of when I gave her the small trinket; how my mother's face lit up with happiness but also a hint of sadness that I couldn't quite discern even years later. Now, I believe I understood.

"It was a gift to my mother when I was six. She kept my hair in a locket she wore. So, when Keres killed her, she took it."

"What's the significance, anyway?"

"Some believe it holds a witch's essence to their power. Some believe it's a connection to the Mother Goddess Olunia and a symbolic link to nature, while others just use it in their craft to make whatever they're doing more powerful with their intentions. Whatever the belief, giving hair is the ultimate gift, the biggest display of love."

Brooks nodded, sipping his beer. He took the cap out of his hand, poured a little in the lid, and set it on the hardwood floor.

"You could use some too," he said to Aysel. "Fuckin' hell, we need it."

I smiled, appreciating his thoughtfulness for Aysel. My mouse took a sip and squeaked. I laughed at her sound. Brooks polished off the hard cider, setting his bottle beside the other. I leaned back, observing him. The scar running from his forehead in diagonal to his left brow was faint in the light. He turned his head to the right, staring at my wall and the pictures on it. His strong, square jaw clenched and released, making the muscles in his cheek tick. An afternoon shadow caressed his face, where he looked even more handsome. His silver eyes captivated me the most. The silver held a hint of dark gray and hazel. It mesmerized me. He was a fantastic looking man. He stared thoughtfully at my wall, then finally he looked away. I shook my head, snapping myself out of it. He'd been kind to me all of two days.

"You're the first witch I've ever known to smile in their portrait," he said, reaching into his pocket. He unfolded something, wincing when the firm paper cracked. "I scanned this into my computer. Once we get somewhere, I'll get another one made for you."

"This is just fine," I said, my voice cracking.

"I take it the owl meant something to you?"

I nodded. "Mahak was my first familiar," I sniffed. "Excuse me for a moment."

I got up, rubbing my hands over my bare arms as the coolness of the house made my skin pebble. My home no longer had the cozy feel it used to have. It felt numb, so empty and devoid of all I made it to be.

I went to the bathroom, checking on my plants. The beautiful purple clematis wilted, no longer stretching toward the open window. Even the aroma was different. The jasmine, fern and clematis didn't smell like they used to. Instead, the scent of over wet soil made my nose wrinkle.

Heading out, I checked the thermostat on the wall between my cauldron room and bathroom, seeing it at 57. I turned on the central air for ten degrees warmer. I strode lethargically to the bedroom, seeing it was still intact. I kept walking past, going back to the kitchen.

"Are you hungry?" I asked, opening the fridge.

"Starving."

"I don't have any blood."

"*Pfft*. I need to feed like that about once a week. If I can't get an animal, then I have artificial blood."

I scowled. "So, you can eat real food?"

"All the time."

I scowled further. "I thought vampires couldn't eat."

"I might be dead, but I got taste buds. I need blood to keep myself going, but I still need food."

I got out the whole milk, checking the date. Seeing it was still good, I got it out along with some eggs. I turned on the oven to 350 degrees, then got out my large baking dish.

"What are you making?" Brooks asked.

"A fluffy pancake."

He nodded, getting off the ground and taking a seat at my two-person dining room table. Small pattering flitted across the floor. Brooks picked Aysel up and set her on the table beside him. Peeking outside, I noted the sun was getting ready to make an appearance.

"Shit," I left my mixing bowl full of flour and egg to pull the curtains closed. "You might want to head to my cauldron room. It's darker there."

Brooks nodded, heading toward the room. "I'll just stay by the wall, so I can still talk to you."

I whipped in the milk, vanilla, and pinch of salt until the mixture was creamy. "What do you want to talk about?"

The oven beeped three times, announcing it reached temp. The warmth of the oven coupled with the air blowing out the vent at my feet felt like I was at the lake on a humid summer day.

"Whatever you're making. It smells good."

I laughed. "I haven't even finished it yet."

"Still smells good."

"I think your brain got a little fried by the fire. Or maybe your nose hairs."

"HA!" He chortled. His rich baritone voice made a shiver crawl up my arms. "So, you're part dragon of the old blood, huh? That's why Keres wants you so badly."

I nodded. "Yes. My father, Alger, is of the old dragon blood, or so I was told. It's how I'm able to half shift."

I put butter in the bottom of the glass baking dish and poured in my mixture. The gray of the morning made everything a little brighter in my small cottage home. I put the fluffy pancake in the oven and set my timer for thirty minutes.

I walked out of the kitchen to where Brooks was in the hallway. The cottage was narrow, barely hosting his broad frame let alone mine. I turned sideways, scooting past him.

"Here's the bathroom. Feel free to take a shower. I keep the towels here," I said, going behind the door to the shelving unit I had hidden.

"I don't have any fresh clothes," his deep voice purred.

My cheeks heated. I kept my gaze focused on the light teal blue stack of towels in front of me. "I'm sure I can find you something."

"And how do you plan on doing that?"

His sultry voice made my knees wobble. I swallowed and continued staring at the towels. "Magic, obviously."

Brooks chuckled, turning around and strode out the door. I walked out behind him, relieved he was now ahead of me. To even more relief, he took his former hiding position. He leaned against the wall, sliding down to the floor. I sat across from him, staring between the kitchen window and him.

"When do you want to go look for your family?" I asked.

His head shot up, giving me a curious look. "You'd help me?"

"You've helped me."

He groaned, rubbing his eyes and face with the palms of his hands. "They're probably at another coven by now. The dungeon, where you wouldn't go, leads to a clearing in the east. From there, they probably teleported to the nearest coven."

I raised my brows, waiting for him to offer the name of the area.

"Maluhia," he finally said.

I cringed, "Why there?"

"Why not there?"

"The carnivorous, cannibalistic mermaids, constant rain and aren't there ogres?"

His soft chuckle brought a twinge of a smile to my lips. He leaned his head back against the wall, genuinely smiling at me. The bright sun finally crested the horizon, making me squint.

Brooks sighed, leaning in toward me. "Vampires rarely swim. We don't melt from the rain and yeah there are a few ogre colonies."

His attention made my cheeks flame. He raised one knee up and draped an arm over it; a smirk puckering at the edge of his lip. He was handsome, the kind that made him drool-worthy, but what he did played like a record in the back of my mind. I glanced at my feet, battling with myself over how I should feel.

"Will you come with me?" he softly asked.

The soft way he asked made my heart palpate. It sounded genuine, almost borderline begging. If anything, but only to keep myself alive, I nodded in agreement.

"Yes."

The oven beeped sonorously. I moaned as I got up. My entire body was stiff and sore. I hadn't shifted into that form in years, nor fought anything. I shook my head, unable to recall what I'd done in that shifted state.

I got the dish out of the oven and turned the appliance off. I set the glass bakeware on the cooling rack I had on the counter. The dishes in the cupboards rattled. My entire cottage groaned as the foundation lifted, sending everything pitching slightly left. The hot cookware screeched across the counter and shattered in the sink.

"Brooks?" I squeaked out, dashing to get Aysel off the table.

My little mouse scurried up my arm and into my hair. An enormous shadow blocked the sunlight. The deep, reverberating noise of whatever hovered over my house made my insides crawl anxiously. Bile rose in my throat. I swallowed it down, looking all around me. The glass windows in my home shattered as the entire cottage was lifted completely off the foundation.

"Brooks!"

"I'm here. I can't move until the sun rises."

I struggled to move to the backside of my kitchen island to at least have some protection from getting smashed. The cottage rolled like it was being put to sea. I latched both trembling hands onto either end of the kitchen island. The cottage creaked. Beams snapped like twigs somewhere under the house. Dust and pieces of the ceiling fell on my head.

A long howl rolled through my home like thunder. The sky instantly darkened to where I couldn't see my hand in front of my face. Lightning flashed across the heavens. The scream intensified, a mix between utter agony, heartbreak, and despair. My entire body trembled.

"Shit," Brooks yelped, colliding into the kitchen island.

I grabbed his hand, pulling him toward me. Suddenly, the movement stopped. The air was stagnant and still. I held my breath. My home dropped. I closed my eyes and screamed.

About E.A. Shanniak

E.A. (Ericka Ashlee) Shanniak is the author of several successful series – A Castre World Novel – Whitman Western Romances – Dangerous Ties. She's hobbit-sized, barely reaching over 5ft tall on a good day. When she wears her Ariat boots, not only does she gain an inch, she's then able to reach the kitchen cabinets to get all the snacks. When not in her fox den (writing cave), Ericka loves to spend time with her family – outside having firepits with wine, camping, fishing, or zooming in her jeep on another Midwest adventure. Ericka loves all the animals her kids bring home including numerous barn cats and their newfound duck named Delilah.

Ericka works in the Register of Deeds office residing in a small town in Comanche County with her supportive, wonderful husband, two amazingly compassionate kids, and all the animals (including those her husband knows nothing about yet). Follow her on her Kansas adventures with these social media platforms listed below.

- Facebook

- Facebook group: Shanniak Shenanigans

- Instagram

website: http://www.eashanniak.com/
email: erickashanniak@gmail.com

If have a moment, I would really appreciate a review. A review, whether you liked it or not, helps me know what aspects of the story you liked. Even a rating is helpful. Thank you so much for reading my work. I hope you have a fabulous day.

Also by: E.A. Shanniak

Alien Prince Reverse Harem – Ubsolvyn District:
Stalking Death - *prequel*
Securing Freedom
Saving Home

Bayonet Books Anthology:
Storming Area 51: *Stalking Death*
Slay Bells Ring: *Stocking Gryla*

Clean Fantasy Romance – Zerelon World Novella:
Aiding Azlyn
Killing Karlyn
Reviving Roslyn

Clean & Sweet Regency Romance – Bramley Hall:
Love At Last
Love That Lasts
Love Ever Lasting

Clean & Sweet Western Romance – Whitman Western Series:

To Find A Whitman
To Love A Thief
To Save A Life
To Lift A Darkness
To Veil A Fondness
To Bind A Heart
To Hide A Treasure
To Want A Change
To Form A Romance

Harlequin Fantasy Romance – Castre World Novel:
Piercing Jordie
Mitering Avalee
Forging Calida
Uplifting Irie
Braving Evan
Warring Devan
Hunting Megan
Shifting Aramoren – *short story*
Anchoring Nola – *short story*

Paullett Golden Anthology:
Hourglass Romance: *Love At Rescue*
Romantic Choices: *Love Flames Anew*

Slow Burn Enemies to Lovers Paranormal Romance – Dangerous Ties:
Opening Danger
Hunting Danger
Burning Danger

Slow Burn Enemies to Lovers Paranormal Romance – Wicked Ties:
Wicked Witch
Wicked Bonds
Wicked Ruin

Standalone Stories:
Winter Luna

Made in the USA
Columbia, SC
04 December 2024

47718160R00171